EMMA'S DREAM

A MORGAN'S RUN ROMANCE

M. LEE PRESCOTT

Emma's Dream
A Morgan's Run Romance
M. Lee Prescott

Published by Mt. Hope Press
Copyright 2015, M. Lee Prescott
Cover design by Ashley Lopez
Cover images from *stock.adobe.com/326503452*

For my family, always, with love.

CHAPTER 1

"This is a huge mistake," Ben Morgan muttered, his chest tightening as he steered the Range Rover near the Arizona mountain pass. "Maybe the biggest one I've made in five years."

Then he remembered it wasn't his decision. Doctor's orders propelled him eastward, away from his gorgeous new home in Santa Barbara and a rapidly expanding business, which needed his attention 24-7. The partners, his college roommates and dear friends, had assured him they could manage without him for a while, but the guilt was eating at him already. His stomach growled, but there was no place to stop in the desert that surrounded him. He would have to eat in town.

As the jeep climbed the Saguaro Canyon Pass, he thought back to the previous Thursday. On the Coast Highway, headed home for a swim in the ocean after a long day at work, he was still reeling from his last encounter with Miranda, his girlfriend of two years. Their official split had been several months earlier, when he moved out of their condo and into his new home, but unfinished business, mostly financial, had necessitated one more meeting, over lunch. The parting had not been pleasant, but they still needed to work together. Miranda's law firm handled all his company's legal work, and the partners wanted to keep her on.

As he exited the restaurant, the pain started. Chalking it up to indigestion, he had hopped in the car and endeavored to ignore it. Halfway home, the pain now excruciating, he almost blacked out but was able to pull over and call 911. He told the operator he was having a heart attack.

The young whippersnapper cardiologist smiled as she leaned over his gurney. "Fascinating diagnosis, Mr. Morgan, but totally incorrect. You've had a panic attack. I'm not sure what's going on in your life right now, but whatever it is, you'd better see that it stops now, or you'll be dead before your next birthday. Thirty-two is too young to die, don't you think?"

"So, I'm crazy? Is that what you're saying"

"No, what I'm saying is that something's going on that's triggering your physical symptoms. Are you under a lot of stress? Did anything unusual happen today?"

"Just work and the end of a romantic relationship."

She shook her head, regarding him as one might a two-year-old. "Two huge stressors. Do you have a cardiologist?"

"Why should I? I'm thirty-one, for Christ's sake."

"Right, okay. Well, then, let's pretend I'm your cardiologist. As your doctor, I am ordering you to take at least three to four months off work to decompress."

"Three to four months! Now you're the crazy one. I have a business to run and—"

"Which you won't be running for long if the stress and anxiety cause a massive heart attack. Either take time now to decompress, re-evaluate and learn ways to live your life differently, or we'll be spending a lot more time together. Do I make myself clear?"

Now, six days later, he was headed to his family's ranch in Arizona, Morgan's Run, and his enforced R & R. He laughed, wondering if returning home might actually increase his stress rather than the opposite. The Rover crested the peak, and he began his descent into the verdant valley that stretched out north and south as far as the eye could see. An orographic effect created this green, moist valley, surrounded by desert over the mountains to the east and west.

In the gorgeous valley, a largely undiscovered town existed, an oasis for its roughly three thousand year-round residents and an equal number of snowbirds, tourists and wealthy vacationers, who found their way through the passes in at various points in the year.

As Ben Junior made his way into town, he passed familiar sights, largely unchanged. Nothing changed much in Saguaro. The Town Garage had a fresh coat of white paint. "Whoop-de-doo," he said aloud, making a mental note to drop the Rover off for servicing soon.

As he turned right on Main and headed toward Gracie's Diner, a horn blared and the clunker in front of him screeched to a stop. Ben braked, but not in time to stop the Rover before it tapped the rear of the clunker. Ben swore under his breath and backed up, pulling over to park at the curb. As he did, the clunker's driver leaped from her car, screaming and waving her arms. He shook his head. Foolish woman had left her heap in the middle of the street. Tall and slender, she wore Jackie O. sunglasses, a baseball cap pulled low on her forehead, a faded cotton shirt over blue jeans, and cowboy boots, the uniform for nearly every female rancher in the valley.

"Geez, Toto," he muttered, patting the Rover's seat. "We're not in Kansas anymore."

As she approached the Rover, Ben noticed her jeans hugged every curve, full breasts not quite obscured by the baggy shirt. He couldn't see her face, but he had to admit the rest of the package was intriguing and also vaguely familiar. He approached as she bent to survey the clunker's bumper.

"What's the matter with you?" she screamed, walking in circles, arms still flailing. "Oh, my God, oh, my God, what am I going to do?"

Ben stared at her back, astounded at what was clearly a huge overreaction. The clunker was fine, hardly a scratch on it, although it would be hard to tell with all the other dings. Then, just as quickly as it started, the fire went out and she flopped down to sit on the curb, head between her legs, sobbing.

"Hey, hey, it's not that bad, is it? We hardly touched each other. No harm done." He sat beside her, wondering whether he should pat her on the shoulder. Immediately she quieted and looked up at him.

"Oh, my God. This just gets better and better. It figures."

Ben Morgan, the one person she expected never to see again, sitting beside her in the middle of Main Street. Could things get any worse? She leaned forward, hiding her face, wondering whether he'd go away if she sat there long enough.

"Maggie? Is that little Maggie Williams? After five years, I'm in town less than a minute and the first person I bump into is you."

Maggie groaned and buried her head deeper, praying this was all a bad dream. If she hadn't had to make a quick run to the bank, she'd be at work in the cool, dark stables. "Please just go. I'm fine."

She could feel his heat, his nearness rattling her to her core. A part of her longed to lean against him and draw comfort and strength from his warmth, but the wiser half screamed *danger*. She kept still, hoping he would disappear.

"You don't seem fine. Look, I'm sorry." Ben placed a hand on her shoulder. It sent shivers of warmth all the way to her toes. "And I'm not leaving until I'm sure you're okay."

Oh, no you don't. Maggie stood and shook herself, stepping away from his electric touch. She put on her sunglasses. Another second near him and she feared she might actually swoon. His soft chestnut eyes regarded her with obvious concern. Although he looked tired and thin, Ben Morgan was still drop-dead gorgeous, in faded jeans and sneakers, his broad shoulders straining the seams of a worn Stanford tee shirt.

"I'm fine, really. It's been a crazy day and you caught me at a bad time. I'm sorry I overreacted."

Ben watched her, wondering why a fender kiss had caused so much distress. "Can I give you a lift somewhere?"

"No, of course not! I mean, thanks, but I'm okay now. Got to get back to work."

"Where's that?"

"Sorry, I'm really late. Good to see you again. Take care."

She hopped into her car and drove away before he could utter another word.

What the hell was that? Ben thought back to his one memorable night with Maggie Williams. They had both left Saguaro shortly after that night, but a part of him always wondered if there was something more to explore with his brother Kyle's beautiful classmate. While he had pushed thoughts of her and their one night of passionate sex from his mind, as he watched her drive away, Ben realized that he had spent five years comparing every woman he met to Maggie Williams. His stomach growled, and he shook his head. *Enough, time to eat!* He left the Rover and walked the three blocks to Gracie's.

CHAPTER 2

Noon rush over, Gracie's was empty except for one booth occupied by a family of four savoring the last spoonfuls of a Gracie Gila Monster. The diner's signature sundae was made with Gracie's secret chocolate sauce, vanilla ice cream, and hot toffee sauce, topped with whipped cream, then sprinkled liberally with crumbled peanut butter cups. Ben was tempted to forgo lunch and go for a Gila but decided on a portabella burger instead. With a nod to the family, he sidled up and took a stool at the counter.

A young freckle-faced redhead, ponytail wagging, bounced up, flashing him a smile that lit up the room. "Hi, sir. Can I take your order?"

"Hi, yourself. I don't know you. Are you new in town?"

She regarded him quizzically with lots of eyelash batting. "No, but you are. I'd remember you. Been here three years. I'm a student at U of A, but summers I come up to Saguaro instead goin' home to Yuma. Too hot. My dad works down there. Just passing through?"

Ben gave her the hundred-watt smile that made most women swoon. She was no exception. "You could say that. Name's Ben."

"I'm Stacy. What can I get you, Ben?"

"Iced tea and a portabella burger, lettuce, tomato, and lots of Gracie's burger sauce."

"Comin' right up."

Ben watched her disappear into the kitchen, relieved that he had not yet met anyone he knew. He wanted to surprise his parents.

Well—he *had* met someone, he mused, remembering the curvaceous, lush-lipped Maggie Williams. It had been all he could do not to sweep her into his arms and kiss away those tears. Once again, he wondered at the subconscious torch he had been carrying for her. And what was with her behavior? *Who falls apart and sobs uncontrollably over a bumper tap?*

As he savored the last bite of his burger, Gracie emerged from the kitchen. "Still a vegetarian, I see. Crime in God's country."

Ben stood as she came around the counter to grab him in a bear hug. At six-four, he had her by a few inches, but Gracie was at least six feet herself, a towering figure in a grease-covered apron and frayed jeans, her wiry black hair streaked with gray, cut short, and sticking out at odd angles.

"How's my desert goddess? Have you missed me? You look younger than when I left."

"Tush." She waved her hand, clearly pleased at the compliment. "Always were the biggest liar from here to Albuquerque. Are you home to stay?"

"No, just a break from the rat race."

"Your folks must be thrilled. Can't believe they won't be angling for you to stay on, what with your dad slowing down and your brothers scattered hither and yon."

"Is Dad okay?"

Gracie gave him a measured look before answering. "Course he is. Strong as an ox, but he's not twenty-five anymore. Could use the help, I'm sure."

"Gracie, this is me. Has something happened to Dad?"

"He's fine, dearie. Had a minor dust-up last year, but from your expression, I guess he didn't tell you about it. Not my place. Let him or your mom fill you in."

He stared at her for a moment or two, knowing he would not get another word out of her. "If you could keep my arrival quiet till I see them, I'd be grateful, Gracie."

Ben went for his wallet, suddenly anxious to be home.

Gracie waved her hand. "Not on your life! Put that city money away and git up there and say howdy-do to your folks."

He leaned over and pecked her cheek. "Thanks, Gracie. Great to see you."

"Good to have you home where you belong," she said, gently nudging him toward the door. "Hope it's for good."

CHAPTER 3

Maggie drove through the main gate of Morgan's Run and pulled into her usual spot behind the stables. She killed the engine and drew out her cell phone. When her father answered, she breathed a sigh of relief.

"How's my angel?"

"Good as gold. What's the matter, sweetie? You sound upset."

"Nothing, just wanted to check in."

"She's napping. Should I phone when she wakes so you can say hello?"

"No, I'll see her in a few hours."

"Mags, what is it? What's happened?"

"Ben Morgan's back."

"Oh? Bump into each other, did you?"

"You could say that. We had a fender bender, right on Main Street."

"You okay?"

"Yes, just embarrassed. When it happened, I freaked out. Made a total fool of myself, crying and wailing over a minor bumper tap. Thank goodness no one else was around."

"Glad you're okay. You gonna tell him about Emma?"

A truck drove up beside her and Maggie spied Jeb, her assistant.

"Dad, I gotta go. See you tonight."

"Take care, honey."

Maggie waved to her assistant. "Hey, Jeb. You ready to tackle Tabasco?"

She referred to a spirited mustang they were training, the size of a small draft horse. Soon his rider, a Border Patrol agent, would join them to participate in the final weeks of training. Then horse and rider would return to Nogales as a team, ready to keep watch in the mountains along the border.

"Ready when you are. You okay, Boss? You look a little green around the gills."

"Fine, just tired."

"How's my little cutie pie doin'?"

"Full of it, curious, into everything, just like most four-year-olds. She keeps Dad busy."

"How's the therapy going?"

"Not much progress. She's just outgrown her third wheelchair."

"Wow, has it been that long?"

Maggie nodded. The sadness since the accident sometimes overwhelmed her, etching new lines across her brow and haunting her dreams. Afraid to be far from her phone, she watched the clock until it was time to head home. It wasn't that she disliked the work. Maggie loved training horses, assisting with the day-to-day running of Morgan Run's stables, but she worried continuously about Emma. Two years ago, the toddler had just learned to walk when her legs had been knocked out from under her, paralyzed when their car had been broadsided by a drunk driver.

Hands on hips, stared at Jeb, who seemed a million miles away. "Are you coming or not?"

"Sorry, Boss!"

He fell in step beside her as they headed for Tabasco's stall.

CHAPTER 4

Ben eased the Rover through the front gates, turned away from the house, and headed for the Lodge. At this time of day, he was pretty certain Ben Sr. would be in the lobby bar greeting guests, offering them a drink and a handshake. Ben Junior parked and hopped out of the Rover, pausing to gaze up at the massive log structure. Newly restored from a much smaller building, the renovated Lodge had been designed by his brother Sam, an architect who lived and worked in Flagstaff. Its new wings spread in either direction like the Lodge was a colossal condor ready to take flight.

Ben sprung up the steps and passed through the massive twelve-foot doors that stood open to the afternoon breezes. His eyes scanned the lobby until he caught sight of his dad. At six-foot-six, Ben Morgan was hard to miss. A thick shock of gray hair curled at his collar and deep blue eyes sparkled with warmth as he chatted with a group of guests.

As Ben approached, the elder Morgan spied him and paused midsentence. "S'cuse me, folks," he said, nodding as he extracted himself. He closed the gap to his son, arms open. "Well, look who's home."

After a hearty bear hug, Ben Sr. patted his progeny. "What're you tryin' to give this old man, a heart attack?"

"Hey, Dad."

"Has your mother seen you?"

"Not yet. Just got here. Wanted to see you first. See how things are."

"Great, couldn't be better. Especially now that you're home. How long you stayin'?"

"A month or two, maybe more. If it's okay?"

"Okay? You kidding? We'll take you as long as we can get you. Forever would be great."

"Thanks, Dad."

"Better get over to see your ma or she'll have my hide. I'll finish up the meet-and-greet and be over shortly."

"You look good, Dad," Ben said, and he meant it. His father hadn't aged a bit, his long, lean body in terrific shape, as always. Remembering Gracie's words, he hoped that whatever had befallen his beloved parent had been resolved.

"Pshaw. Go on, now, git. Be down in a few."

Ben started down the lane to the house but decided to take the long way around the stables. As he turned the corner, coming 'round the north side of the barn, there she was, standing beside the clunker, talking on her cell phone. She was bare-headed now, her sunglasses perched atop her head, holding back her long, thick chestnut mane, loose and falling around her shoulders. She was smiling, in animated conversation, a musical laugh punctuating her words. She was gorgeous, the gangly teenager all grown up, transformed into a voluptuous woman. Ben thought about Miranda. Stylish and chic, but oh, so skinny, a swizzle stick in comparison to this full-bodied, luscious creature. *Totally different species.*

Suddenly Maggie caught sight of him and the smile vanished. Her loose, open stance closed up, and she turned away.

"Emma, honey, gotta go. See you soon, Sweet Pea."

Turning back, Maggie watched Ben step from the Rover and steeled herself for another encounter. The man was magnificent, no doubt about that. To her annoyance, her treacherous body began to tingle from head to toe.

"Mr. Morgan, we meet again."

"What brings you to the ranch?"

"I work here."

"Oh?" Despite her defiant stance, he noticed that her lip trembled. *Don't know how I can change the dynamic between us, but she's sure worth a try.*

"I train horses, run the pony camps and lessons, and help organize most of the pack trips. Harley leads them, of course, and I do the day-to-day stuff." *You're babbling, Maggie Williams. Stop talking!*

"What happened to Princeton?"

"Dropped out."

"Why?"

"Look, it's been a long day. I've got to get going."

"Do you live here? On the ranch?"

"No. Still live in town with my dad."

"How's he doing?"

Ben racked his brain to think of conversation topics that might keep her talking. Gazing into those deep azure eyes, he discovered a warmth and stillness he had never experienced before. Had it been that way during the one night they'd spent together? He didn't remember those eyes, but he could still feel her soft skin, still smell her scent, a mix of citrus and jasmine.

"He's terrific. Same old, same old."

"Still wrangling and taking care of the valley livestock?"

"He retired a few years ago, but he keeps busy."

"Give him my best."

Gazing into his warm, dark eyes, Maggie felt herself going weak at the knees. And there was that treacherous tingle again. *Control yourself, woman.* "Will do. Gotta go."

"Would love to see your dad. How is he?" he called, but she was already gone. Ben watched her drive away and whistled softly. *They didn't make women like Maggie Williams in California.* He had forgotten what he had been missing.

CHAPTER 5

Ben pulled into the farm at the same time as one of the ranch trucks. His youngest sister, Ruthie, jumped out of the pick-up and screamed.

"Hey, Shortcake!" He opened his arms, she flew into them and lifted her, swinging her around as they had done all their lives.

"I'm twenty-two and a college graduate. Can't call me Shortcake anymore, you big lout."

He set her down. "Doesn't look like you've grown any since I left."

"You'd be surprised." She punched his gut affectionately, other hand on her hip.

"What happened to coming out to Santa Barbara after graduation?"

"Too busy. Was thinking of a trip in August, and now here you are. Does Mom know you're here?"

Ben shook his head.

"She's gonna have kittens when she sees you."

"I certainly hope not."

"She's been pining away for her favorite child, especially since last winter."

"What about last winter? Ruthie, what's up? Did something happen with Dad?"

Before his sister could reply, the screen door opened and Leonora Morgan emerged, hand shielding her eyes. "Oh, my Lord in heaven, is that you, Bennie?"

"Hey, Mom!" He waved, then crossed the distance between them and opened his arms as she launched herself from the bottom step of the porch.

"Why didn't you tell us you were coming?"

"He wanted to surprise you, of course."

"Ruthie, go call your father. He'll be over the moon."

"Just saw Dad."

Ben realized his mistake as soon as the words were out. Her face fell, knowing he had gone to his father first.

"As I drove in, I saw him headed into the Lodge, so I stopped," Ben lied.

"Never mind all that. Come on in. So good to see you, darling. We weren't planning anything fancy for supper, but I can send Carmela into town to pick up some groceries. What do you feel like?"

"Oh, Lord," Ruthie said, grabbing a knapsack from the truck. "The prodigal son has returned. Can't remember the last time Mom asked me or any of us what we felt like for dinner."

"Ruthie, stop chattering and go tell Carmela that Ben's home."

CHAPTER 6

"Carmela, thank you," Ben said, savoring the first forkful of sticky beans. "Oh, how I've missed these beans."

Carmela had planned skewered lamb, rice, and salad, but added skewers of vegetables and a bean dish she knew was one of Ben's favorites to the evening's menu. She beamed, nodded at him, then disappeared into the kitchen. Plump, but still a raven-haired beauty, Carmela never seemed to age. Her dark, flawless skin was as wrinkle-free as it had been in her twenties. Now in her early sixties, the talented, inventive chef had begun working for the Morgan family as a teenager. Over the years, she graduated from maid to housekeeper, then added cooking to her duties in her late twenties. She and her husband, Raoul, lived in one of the cottages behind the stables. Although they had longed for a family, they were never blessed with children and had thus adopted Ben and his five siblings as their own.

Raoul managed the livestock, except the horses. The ranch was home to several dozen rare varieties of chickens, a few pigs, and an assortment of goats, raised for their milk. They also raised four varieties of sheep—Columbia, Navaho-Churro, Dorset, and Royal Whites. The last were meat animals. The others were raised for their highly prized wool. At any one time, the herd ranged from three to five hundred head, and Raoul and his crew spent their days and nights tending to their safety.

Ruthie, Ben, and their parents shared Carmela's delicious dinner, with animated conversation throughout. Ruthie still lived at home. Their sister, Beth, three years younger than Ben, ran the organic farm, with Ruthie's assistance. She lived in Tucson with her longtime boyfriend, Bill, a biology professor at U of A.

"So, how long can you stay, honey?"

"I was thinking a couple of months, if you and Dad can stand having me around me that long."

"Already told him, forever would be okay with us." His father reached over to pat his wife's hand, eyes gazing at her with affection. After years of marriage, they were still high school sweethearts, more in love than when they began dating as twenty-olds.

"Not that you need one, but any special reason why you've come home now?"

His mother always saw right through him.

"Doctor's orders. Says I need to de-stress."

"Oh, honey! Well, you've come to the right place for that, hasn't he, dear?"

"You said it! We'll put him right to work! Doin' a nonstressful job, of course."

"We will do no such thing. He'll go right to bed, and Carmela and I will take care of him."

Ben cringed and gave Ruthie a look. "Mom, I'm tired, but I'm not dead. I'm ready to earn my keep. Whatever you need."

"We need a lot of help at the farm," Ruthie said. "Everything's coming in at once. Hard to keep up."

Leonora waved her fork in her daughter's direction. "Ruthie, don't be ridiculous. Your brother is not a farmhand."

"Ready to hop back in the saddle, son? I'm sure Harley, Maggie, and Jeb could use a hand. And Raoul is always looking for drovers."

His mother looked from husband to daughter. "Have you two lost your minds? If Ben works, he is management. I will not have Raoul, his sisters, or Harley Langdon ordering him around like a common laborer."

"I'm not proud, Mom. I'm here to help, and to tell the truth, I'd just as soon be the one taking orders rather than giving them."

Leonora Morgan threw up her hands. "That's it. My family's officially lost their marbles."

Ignoring her, Ben turned to his father. "I'm happy to help you at the Lodge if you need me, but I was thinking about the stables? Maybe leading pack trips again? I'm looking forward to riding."

"Glad to hear it." Ben Senior gave him a long look before replying, "Harley and Maggie can always use an extra pair of hands. I'll ring 'em in the morning."

Ben smiled at his father. When his horse, Loukas, came up lame and had to be euthanized, he swore he would never ride again. It was only a few weeks before he left his family and the ranch behind for life in California. "I was surprised to see Maggie. Seems a funny place to end up after getting into Princeton. What happened there, anyway?"

Three pairs of eyes looked at him quizzically. Finally Ruthie spoke up. "You have been gone a long time, brother, dear."

"Poor girl lasted less than two months in New Jersey," Leonora said. "Came home pregnant and moved back in with her father. Such a waste."

"Bite your tongue, woman. She's the best wrangler in a hundred miles, and she works for me."

"I still say it was a terrible waste of a promising future. She and your brother won every academic prize through high school. He's now in veterinary school and she's roping mustangs and cleaning stalls."

"What happened? Did she have the child?"

"Yup, a real cutie pie," Ruthie said. "Name's Emma. Her dad retired to take care of her while Maggie works."

Ben Senior shook his head. "Tragic, really. Drunk driver hit Maggie one night. Left the little one paralyzed."

Leonora stood, clearing their plates. "As I said, a terrible waste."

Ruthie rolled her eyes, giving her mother a disgusted look. "No, it's not. Maggie's crazy about Emma, and she's the apple of her grandpa's eye."

"Can we please change the subject?" Leonora asked. "Sad as it is, there are much more interesting topics than the travails of poor Maggie Williams. Tell your father and me about Santa Barbara and the new house. He promised to take me there this fall for a visit."

CHAPTER 7

Maggie parked, resting her head against the steering wheel to collect herself. When she greeted Emma and her dad she was determined to be present to them, not lost in the arms of Ben Morgan five years ago. She had thought of nothing else on the short ride home, his lips capturing hers so completely, strong arms enfolding her, drawing her to him until there was no him and her, but a pulsing, heated fusion of bodies joined as one, moving in perfect synchrony. Over and over, he had taken her and she him that hot August night. Impossible that daylight had come and heralded the rift that prompted them to part company. An excruciating separation, she realized now that the hurt had lain dormant, but not forgotten, in the deepest part of her. Now he was back. Shaken to the core with longing, she shook herself. *Get a grip, Maggie Williams. Do not let him break your heart again.*

She sat back, smoothed her hair, and pinched her cheeks to bring color back. Her dad, with his keen eyesight, would certainly notice her paleness. Finally she grabbed her backpack, alighted, and forced a smile as she went in. Fortunately, there was no need to force a smile when she spied them, hunched conspiratorially over a jigsaw puzzle. Emma's knitted brow matched her grandpa's, and each had chin in hand, intent on their task.

"Hey, buddies."

Maggie's heart ached as Emma looked up and smiled. Could she possibly love anyone more than she did her four-year-old angel, who had endured such pain with courage and fortitude?

"Mommy, hooray! You can help us now."

Ned winked at his daughter, his gaze full of concern. "Grandpa's not very good at puzzles, I'm 'fraid."

Maggie scooped up her daughter, twirling her in her arms, her fragile body like a feather. Emma ate like a horse, but she'd withered to almost nothing after the last surgery, and they were just now beginning to build her back up. "How was your day?"

"Super supreme!" Emma stroked Maggie's cheek, pushing hair from her face.

"How'd the therapy go?" Maggie looked to her dad as Emma went limp in her arms. "That bad, huh?"

"She was a trooper, as always, but they gave her some good yanks and pulls."

"It hurt, but I was brave, Mommy."

"I know you were, baby. I'm so proud of you. Let me take a quick shower to wash off the grit, then we'll tackle that puzzle, okay?" After dinner, bath, and story, Maggie sang to Emma, their favorite song, "Baby Beluga." She stroked the child's downy-soft chocolate curls, so like her daddy's. Emma had his eyes, Maggie mused, and his smile. Fortunately, only her dad and she had ever noticed, and Maggie intended to keep it that way.

"Night, Sweet Pea," she whispered, her toddler already half asleep.

Ned Williams sat on the couch, magazine in hand, observing as his daughter cruised the living room, picking up toys and empty glasses and cups. Still youthful and ruggedly handsome at fifty-six, he had his daughter's steel-blue eyes and a full head of curly salt-and-pepper locks that he kept short. Lean and fit, he still had the body of the wrangler he had been before Emma's birth. Despite the June heat, he was dressed in faded jeans and a flannel shirt. He could almost have passed as Maggie's older brother.

"Wanta talk about it?"

"Nope."

"Might help." "Doubt it."

"I'm a good listener, sweetie."

"Dad!" Maggie didn't bother to hide the exasperation in her voice.

"Okay, okay. How's it going with Tabasco? You bringing him along?"

"He's tough, but Jeb's been great with him. Much as I love him, his size scares me a little. I've never ridden anything that big."

"Reminds me of Junior, the Clydesdale they rescued out at Tyler's years ago."

Ned referred to the ranch where he had worked as trainer, wrangler, and quasi-vet for most of his adult life. Occasionally they still called him for births and minor surgeries. As a young man, Ned had gone east to Tufts Veterinary School on a full scholarship. A fish out of water, he had nonetheless dug in and completed nearly three years of training with distinction when the death of his father yanked him home to Saguaro. While he had never gone back to complete the degree, his training made him invaluable to ranchers in need of emergency vet care, especially on the remotest ranches.

"Be careful, sweetie. Keep your head in the game. No distractions with a horse like that."

"That's why Jeb's been doing most of the riding."

"Hooves on a beast that size are deadly. No daydreaming."

"Okay, Dad, go ahead. You might as well spit it out."

"All I know is you look like shit, and I'm guessing Ben Morgan does, too."

"Where did that come from? Besides, when I saw him, he looked cool as a cucumber so I think you can stop worrying about him.."

"Probably as good-looking as ever, too. Morgan boys have always been lookers."

Maggie sat down hard beside him, head in hands. "Dad, please. This is not helping."

"You gonna tell him about Emma?"

"Never!"

"He has a right to know, darlin'. Was one thing when he was gone, far away in California. But now? What if he settles here in Saguaro to help his folks runnin' that place? God knows they need it with Ben Senior ailing and their businesses growing every year. They're the second biggest organic farm in the state, and the sheep and—"

"Stop, please, Dad. I know what you're doing, and I appreciate your concern, but I don't care about the Morgans' millions, and they are nothing to me or Emma."

"That's not what I was sayin', but they might be willing to help with her care?"

"Never. Subject closed. I'm going to bed."

She leaned over to kiss her beloved father, the only parent she had known since her mom had left when Maggie was three.

"I don't know the story, sweetie, but the Ben Morgan I remember was a good guy. Any chance he might be still?"

"Good night, Dad. Thank you for all you do for us. Love you."

She patted his shoulder and headed for her room, glad for the time alone to gather her thoughts and process the tumultuous events of the past eight hours.

BEN TOSSED AND TURNED. Memories of life before his escape crashed back, along with a vivid image of one of his last nights. The wild, unexpected hours of unbridled passion he had shared with Maggie Williams had caught him completely off guard. Had his need to get away caused him to turn his back on the strong feelings he had for her that night? They had argued about why he was leaving, and then she was gone. He had turned his back on feelings for the beautiful young woman who had opened up and given herself fully to him. What a fool. Had he spent the last five years trying futilely to find another woman who made him feel like Maggie Williams had?

Maggie, too, slept fitfully, dreaming of Ben Morgan, and how she'd waited for his phone call, letter, email, some kind of message that would let her know it hadn't been just a roll in the hay for him.

Now he was back, completely unaware of his daughter, who shared his smile, his eyes, and so much of his strength and spirit. She knew it wasn't fair to father or daughter to keep their connection a secret, but telling Ben about Emma would break Maggie's heart all over again, bringing back the terrible loneliness and sense of abandonment she had felt five years earlier. Besides, the minute he heard about Emma, Ben Morgan would probably hop in that fancy SUV and vanish quicker than a jackrabbit.

Her dad was right, though. Ben had a right to know, and so did Emma. She would tear the bandage off quickly and tell him as soon as the moment presented itself. Then he could leave, and things would get back to normal. If he left, she would not say a word to Emma. If he stayed, well then, she could decide what to say when the time was right.

CHAPTER 8

Ben rose early, grabbed a quick breakfast before his mother could find him to fuss over, and was out the door by 6:45. His early morning routine in Santa Barbara involved a jog on the beach, but instead of running today, he headed to the stables, intending to take a ride. The barn was quiet, horses still nickering softly in their stalls. He went slowly from stall to stall, greeting each horse, getting acquainted or reacquainted. He decided to saddle Royal, his dad's horse, since he knew him well and he suspected his father didn't ride much anymore.

As Ben adjusted saddle and harness, Royal stood mostly patient, giving him the occasional nudge.

"Hey, boy, I'm a little rusty. Cut me some slack, will ya?"

As he led Royal out of the barn, Maggie drove up. She looked like a deer caught in the headlights.

"Morning!" He waved, then tipped his hat. "Gonna be a hot one."

"Hello." She didn't trust herself to say more. The man was twenty feet away and already her knees wobbled.

"Okay if I give Royal a run?"

She shrugged. "You own the place, not me."

"Technically, that's not accurate. My parents own all this. I'm just visiting."

Yeah, right. Maggie forced a smile. "I'm glad old Royal's getting some exercise. He's been a bit neglected the past few weeks. He's not out like he used to be, with your dad not riding."

There it was again, the business with his father and what no one was saying. Ben wrapped Royal's reins around the fence and approached, marveling at Maggie's creamy white skin, eyes as clear and bright as the ocean, their fathomless depths unreadable. He couldn't remember when he'd been this attracted to a woman. Just the sight of her and he grew hard, relieved that his shirttail was untucked.

"Can I ask you something?" he said.

"About?"

Alarms sounded, even as Maggie marveled at the man before her. He looked a bit tired and gaunt, but he was still drop-dead gorgeous. Nobody should look this good this early in the morning.

"I know I shouldn't be asking you this, but I can't seem to get it out of anyone else. Did something happen to my father this past year? Illness? An accident? Everyone keeps alluding to something, but no one will say what happened."

"Probably because they want to protect your dad's privacy. It's his story to tell."

"So, something did happen. Did it involve Royal?" Ben's jaw clenched as tension and fear shone bright in his dark brown eyes.

Torn between wanting to relieve his suffering and uncertainty about what her employer would want, Maggie's voice was soft when she answered. "He's okay now. That's what's important. We were asked not to say anything to anyone. Beth and Ruthie were here, so they could tell you more about it."

He stepped forward and gently grasped her arm. "Just tell me. I won't say where I heard it."

His clean, fresh scent and the heat of his touch almost undid her. A part of her wanted to reach toward him, inviting an embrace. His grip was magnetic, his beautiful eyes now inches from hers. How could she deny him when a huge part of her ached for the warmth of his arms, the touch of his lips, his body pressed against her, capturing her completely? *Get a grip, Maggie.*

Shaking herself, she took a step back. "He had a heart attack on a pack trip. The group was two days out, but they were able to get a chopper to him, thank goodness. He was on Royal when it happened. Hasn't ridden since."

Ben stared at her. His father was years too young for a heart attack, wasn't he? Maggie gazed up and spied tears rimming his eyes. Without thinking, she stepped forward and put her arms around him.

"It's okay. He's okay. I'm sure he's taking good care of himself."

Ben returned her embrace, holding on, marveling at her softness and the scent of lemon and jasmine he remembered so vividly.

"Oh, Maggie," he whispered, not sure if he spoke aloud or to himself. "What a fool I was to walk away from you."

Her body shifted, and he moved to cup her beautiful chin, bending down, his lips grazing hers. Her skin was silky, her eyes dark pools of fire as she gazed up at him. Regaining her senses, Maggie pulled back and brushed imaginary dust from her jeans, rummaging in her backpack to locate her sunglasses. *Don't do this. You cannot go through the months of mending a broken heart when he disappears again.*

"Ben, I'm sure he'll be fine. Talk to him. Ask Ruthie. You'll see. I bet he's healthier now that your mom's being careful with his diet and all."

As Ben observed her, every fiber of his being cried out to feel her warmth again. All business now, she had erected a wall behind sunglasses that hid half her lovely face. "Thanks for telling me. I promise I won't reveal my source. Don't suppose you have time for a ride before you start work?"

"Sorry, no. It's a beautiful morning. Enjoy yourself." With a wave, she turned and headed toward the barn. *Walk fast, Maggie, and don't look back!*

Ben watched her walk away, backpack slung over her shoulder, hips moving in perfect synchrony to his libido, which was now in overdrive. The feel and scent of her lingered, his body bereft and lonely without her pressed against him.

"See you," he called, hoping she would turn and flash one of her rare smiles. Instead, Maggie waved over her shoulder and disappeared into the barn.

Once in the tack room that doubled as an office, Maggie let out her breath and grasped the side of the desk to steady herself. *That can never happen again.* She continued to grip the desk, forcing breath after breath until she felt calmer. She was still leaning on the desk when Jeb popped his head in.

"Morning, Boss. Was that Ben Morgan I saw riding out on Royal?" Freckle-faced, his dark red hair rumpled, he stared at his boss. Jeb was what you'd call stacked, his body compact and all muscle. He wore jeans and a faded Morgan's Run tee shirt, the green almost gray now. Maggie suspected that Jeb turned more than a few women's heads in town, but if he had a girlfriend, he wasn't saying.

"Yup, that was him."

"So he's back?"

"Yup."

"For how long?"

"Haven't a clue."

"You okay?"

"Yup."

His boss was clearly not okay, but Jeb dropped the subject of Ben Morgan and began going over the chores for the day. Like everyone in Saguaro, he'd heard rumors of a fling between the Morgans' eldest and Maggie, but she'd never mentioned it or him. Jeb figured it was ancient history, but watching Maggie now, he wondered if that were true.

CHAPTER 9

Ben and Royal made their way past the corrals and alongside the woods toward open land, the ranch's spring colors in full glory. As they went on, he tried in vain, to shrug away thoughts of Maggie Williams's soft, full breasts pressing into his chest. "Steady boy." He spoke aloud, as much to himself as Royal. He didn't know how, but he intended to get reacquainted with his father's beautiful trainer.

Gazing eastward, he decided to ride up to the farm in hopes of finding Beth. Under his sister's management, the ranch's organic farm had grown to one of the top producers in the country. They shipped fruits, vegetables, and herbs all over the US and even overseas.

Ben had never been as close to Beth as he was to Ruthie. The elder sister's personality was more serious and taciturn than his or the rest of their siblings'. Beth seldom laughed at family jokes and stories. Relentless, Robbie and Kyle constantly teased and cajoled, but she refused to join in their pranks. While Ruthie rolled with the punches of life with four older brothers, Beth retreated to her own sphere of friends and activities. During her graduate work in biology at U of A, she met Bill, her boyfriend. While they would have been welcome to live in one of the ranch's cottages or guest houses, Beth chose to live in Tucson, where she and Bill jointly owned a condo.

As the woods gave way to open fields running north and south as far as the eye could see, the rambling series of farm structures came into view. The complex included four enormous barns, two for equipment and vehicle storage, two for processing and storage, as well as a number of outbuildings for tools and equipment. As he neared the barns, Ben spied Manny Ramirez, who had worked for his family for decades. A short, wiry man with the strength of an ox, Manny's skin was brown as leather. His work boots were held together with duct tape, and his jeans patched and mended in a number of spots. In his early forties, the man looked ten years older until one watched him lift a bale of hay or full crate of melons.

"Hey, Mr. B. How are you?"

"Hey, Manny. Doing great. How 'bout you and the family?"

"Can't complain. Manny Junior just graduated from Valley High School. He's goin' to U of A this fall."

The pride on Manny's face made Ben smile.

"That's terrific. Tell him I say congratulations."

"Will do."

"Hey, Man, is my sister around yet?"

"Which one?"

"Beth."

"Just got in. She's in one of the washing rooms. We're getting a shipment of spinach ready to go out this morning, and the pump's acting up."

"Thanks. I'll find her and see if I can help."

Manny laughed. "Good luck with that. You stayin' around a while?"

"A few months."

"Folks must be happy 'bout that. Here, lemme take ole Royal. I'll put 'im in the south paddock. Be happier there till you're through visiting."

Ben found his sister in the largest washing room, hunched over a pump, wrench in one hand, hammer in the other. She noted his presence but stayed focused on her task. "Heard you were back."

Of all the Morgans, Beth most closely resembled her older brother. She had Ben's angular jaw, chestnut hair, and lean, lanky build. Her eyes were the same dark chestnut, arresting if one was caught in their gaze. Bill was fond of saying that those eyes had stopped him in his tracks the first time he spied her in his Biology 101 class. Today, Beth's jeans were caked with mud and her flannel shirt soaked through. She swore as the wrench slipped from her grasp and clattered to the cement floor.

"Want some help?"

"Yeah, right."

"Sarcasm doesn't become you, sister of mine. You forget I have an engineering degree."

She straightened up, met her brother eye to eye, and held out the wrench and hammer. "Okay, Surfer Boy. Knock yourself out."

"No hug?"

"Let's see how the pump project works out first." Ben gave her a look and Beth laughed, extending her arms. "Oh, what the heck. A little incentive won't hurt."

As he folded her into his arms, Ben felt her stiffen. Touching was not Beth's thing.

"Good to have you home. Mom and Dad must have gone crazy when you walked in. You've always been their favorite, you know." She pulled up a stool. "This I gotta see."

Ben stooped to his task, quickly ascertaining the problem. As he worked, he asked Beth about the farm. Then, keeping his tone casual, he said, "Just came from the stables. How long's Maggie Williams been working here?"

"Let's see. About five years, I'd guess. Started not long after you left. She and Harley have turned the training program on its head, especially the mustang project with the Border Patrol. It's been really successful. Profitable, too."

"Regular horse whisperer, is she?"

"Actually, she sort of is. Her assistant Jeb's pretty good, too, and you know Harley. You interested in Maggie for some reason?"

He shrugged. "Just curious. Thought if I stay around, I might help down there, and I wanted to know the players."

"Players, huh? Oh, I see. Doesn't have anything to do with Maggie being beautiful and sexy, does it?"

"Is she? Hadn't noticed."

Beth laughed and nudged him with her boot toe. "Liar. Since when does Don Juan not notice a pretty lady?"

"She got a boyfriend?"

"Aha! So you are interested! How should I know? We're so busy down here I rarely see Maggie, Harley, and Jeb. If I had to guess, I'd say no, but I really don't know her. Maggie and Kyle were close in high school, I think. Not sure they keep up anymore now that Kyle's in Montana. Ruthie might know, if you're really curious."

He shrugged and turned back to the pump, tightening the last few fittings.

"She's not exactly a swinging single like you, brother dear. She has a young child. "

"I heard about that, and the accident. What a shame."

"Guy that hit them was a wealthy attorney from Phoenix, staying up at Westward Look for the weekend. Not sure why he left the spa and came to Saguaro, but too bad for Maggie and Emma that he did. Of course, he was so drunk, he walked away without a scratch. Bought his way out of it, I heard, but someone told me recently that the legal stuff is still ongoing. Must be a nightmare."

Ben wiped wet, muddy hands on his jeans and stood up. "There, that oughta do it."

Beth tested the pump and it turned over, humming, no leaks, no spray. "Thanks. You're hired. Got time for a cup of coffee?"

Brother and sister sat in creaky, unpainted rockers in the shade of the barn's crude porch, sipping strong, hot coffee.

"So, what's going on, oh long-lost brother?"

He swallowed, then turned to face her. "Had a sort of scary episode. Some kind of panic attack. Doctor ordered me to de-stress for a few months."

"Well, you've come to the right place, as long as you stay away from Mom."

"Fat chance. She's probably on the phone right now, activating the matchmaker hotline from Tucson to Flagstaff to find me a suitable lady. She seems convinced that lack of a wife is at the root of what ails me."

Beth snorted. "That's why Bill and I live in town. The meddling gets a bit much. I thought you had a girlfriend? Milly or someone?"

"Miranda. No, alas, the lovely Miranda and I have parted company."

"What happened? You were so perfect for each other."

Beth and Bill had stayed with Miranda and Ben the previous winter on a weekend trip to Santa Barbara. While the foursome had enjoyed themselves, it was clear that they came from different worlds.

"Well, looks can be deceiving. Who knows? We're done. That's all I know. Listen, Beth, what's the story with Dad and the heart attack?"

"Was scary, but he's okay. They found three blockages and put in stents. I guess that was the only option. He's been religious about exercising, and Mom's got him eating a more healthy diet, but you know Dad and his beef. He'd rather die than miss his steaks on the grill."

"Only once a week, I hope."

She smiled. "That we know about. We suspect he sneaks into town and gets Gracie to whip him up a T-bone whenever he can get away."

"Want me to talk to him?"

"Absolutely not. He's an adult and can make his own choices." She rose. "Sorry, brother dear. Would love to sit around chatting, but gotta get to it. Have a good ride." She patted his shoulder, heading in with their empty cups. "Come for supper, soon, will you? If you've wooed the fair Maggie by then, you're welcome to bring her along, too."

"Very funny."

He headed back to find Royal happily grazing in the shade at the side of the paddock.

CHAPTER 10

Later, when Ben returned from a long ride through the scrub at the edge of the foothills, he found Maggie working with a huge monster of a horse in the north corral. She held the reins and walked him slowly. A young cowboy, whom he assumed was her assistant, sat astride the beast, only a blanket for a saddle. Hair pulled back under a baseball cap, Maggie moved with the fluid grace of the horse she led so carefully, her body in synch with his. Watching her, he felt the familiar stirring in his loins. Never in his life had any woman had this effect on Ben Morgan. Maybe, if he'd been sane five years earlier, he'd have held onto her. With a longing he could neither explain nor shake, he watched, knowing he could not walk away without holding her in his arms again.

As Maggie urged the horse forward, the rider remained calm. The horse nickered, whinnied, and flung his head from side to side.

"What d'ya think, Boss? Wanta try the saddle?"

Maggie looked up at him, pausing for a minute. "Are you sure?"

Ben waved and called out. "I'll grab the saddle. Which one?"

They turned toward him and the horse reared up, hooves punching the air. For a horrible second, Ben feared the giant hooves might strike Maggie, but she remained calm. "Okay, boy. That's right. Come on, now."

When the horse had settled, she led him toward the fence, glaring in Ben's direction. After tying up the horse, she helped the rider down and turned to Ben, who had now dismounted.

"Don't ever do that again."

She scaled the fence, dropped down on the opposite side, and headed into the barn.

The rider smiled, hopped over the fence in one fluid motion, and extended his hand. "Hey, how's it going? Jeb Barnes."

"Ben Morgan. Sorry about that."

"No problem. Tabasco's fine. The boss gets nervous he's gonna throw me, but there's really no cause for alarm. He and I know each other."

"He's a beauty. Looks almost like a Clydesdale."

"Must have some draft horse in him. He's one of the mustangs, headed for the Border Patrol once he's broken in. His rider comes tomorrow."

Maggie emerged, carrying a lightweight Western saddle across her arms. She handed the saddle to Jeb, then turned to Ben.

Caked with mud and sweaty from the long ride, Ben Morgan still looked good enough to eat. Had she not been so irritated about his spooking Tabasco, she might have been tempted to flirt a little. *Maggie Williams, what are you thinking?*

"Mr. Morgan."

He tipped his hat. "Ben, please. I think we know each other at least well enough for first names."

"Nice ride?"

"Awesome. Always beautiful with the desert in bloom."

She nodded. "Just starting. Are you going to cool down Royal or are you leaving him for us?"

There was challenge in her gaze as she dared him to act the part of the owner's spoiled son. His eyes registered hurt, and Maggie regretted her confrontational tone.

"Mind if I watch you guys for a few minutes before we go in?"

She shrugged. "Fine with me, as long as you keep quiet."

She moved to take the fence, and he instinctively reached out to support her arm as she climbed up. His touch burned to her core, and Maggie's knees wobbled. Before she could grab hold of the rail, she fell backward, straight into his waiting arms. Firm hands held her steady, holding her against his hard, muscular chest for a few seconds longer than necessary.

"Oh, my God," he groaned softly, burying his face in her hair, lips grazing her neck for an instant. Just as quickly, he released her, propelling her upward and over the fence.

Breathless, Maggie jumped down inside the corral, beet-red, her neck seared and aflame with the imprint of his kiss.

Jeb watched the spectacle, an amused smile on his face. This was a side of his boss he'd never seen—flustered, red-faced, clearly shaken by the encounter with Ben Morgan. He wondered when things between them had started. Grinning still, he watched her fumble with the saddle, a procedure she usually accomplished in thirty seconds or less.

"Okay, Boss?"

"Don't be ridiculous. Of course I'm okay. Why wouldn't I be?"

"No reason."

Jeb winked at Ben. He had worked for Maggie for three years, and for the first two, he had pined away for her himself. After all, she was one of the most gorgeous women in town, even if she appeared to be uninterested in any male from here to Nogales. Then he'd met Stacy, and his ardor for the elusive, older Maggie Williams had cooled.

After observing Jeb and Maggie work to acclimate Tabasco to the saddle, Ben headed into the barn with Royal. He hosed him down and brushed him. Then, as he was feeding the horse oats from his hand, Maggie came up behind them.

"How'd it go?" he asked.

"Very well. Jeb's good with him. We'll be sorry to see the big guy go."

Her eyes, the color of the valley sky, held a warmth that pierced his heart and triggered another wave of longing. She was just near enough that the scent of jasmine caught him off guard.

"Maggie, do you feel it?"

"Excuse me?" She stepped back, knowing exactly what he meant.

"There's something going on between us. You feel it. I know you do. Shouldn't we talk about it? Shouldn't we talk about what happened five years ago?"

He reached out his hand, but she stepped farther away.

"Have dinner with me."

His dark eyes pleaded, and his scent, a mix of spice and musk, overpowered her. Maggie ached to go to him, to fall into his strong arms and let go of all the heartache of the past five years. Shaking herself, she whispered. "I can't. I have to get home."

"I could bring takeout? I'd love to see Ned again and meet your daughter. Or maybe there's a better night this week?"

She paused, staring into his chocolate eyes. It was only fair to tell him, wasn't it? Her father would be only too happy to watch Emma. "Tonight would be fine. Why don't you come by around six, and we can walk into town."

"Perfect." He leaned forward, lips grazing her cheek. "I'll be there on the dot."

She gave him the address and hurried off. Ben watched her go, the hardening in his loins taking his breath away.

CHAPTER 11

Carmela brought lunch to Ben and his parents on the terrace, and they sat sipping tall glasses of iced tea, enjoying sandwiches filled with ripe avocado, fresh sprouts, summer tomatoes, farm greens, and Carmela's secret sauce. She also brought bowls of salsa and chips, and Ben sighed, tasting a scoopful. "They don't have salsa like this in California, Carm."

She smiled and turned back to disappear into the house. Had it been Ben and his dad, they would have insisted she sit and eat with them, but Leonora never encouraged "familiarity with the help."

His father watched him, sandwich poised midair. "So, what ya think? Things around here look okay?"

"Better than okay. Didn't get out to see Raoul, but Beth and Ruthie's operation is amazing."

His father nodded. "They've done a great job. They hired good people, and they all know what they're doing."

"I was surprised to find Maggie Williams at the stables."

Ben Senior laughed. "You know, even as young as she is, she could probably take over the whole operation, but that's still Harley's turf."

Harley Langdon had been Ben Junior's best friend in high school. Harley went back east for college, but they were inseparable every summer. For a variety of reasons, the friends had not kept in touch the past five years, and Ben was embarrassed to realize that he had yet to inquire about his friend. "Where is the man, anyway? Haven't seen him around."

"Reagan Ranch called and wanted a horse man to train a new crew. I let 'em have Harley for a few weeks. He'll be back in a couple of days."

"Will be good to have him back," Leonora said, wiping her brow with a dramatic flourish. "I worry about that girl getting hurt, what with her crippled daughter and all."

"From what I saw, Maggie can take care of herself."

"Darn right," his father echoed Ben's words, patting his wife's knee as he spoke.

"What do men know? She gave up everything, her hopes and dreams, all because of a foolish mistake. Why, if your father hadn't taken pity on her, Maggie Williams would be waitressing at Gracie's."

"I doubt she'd call a beloved child a mistake, foolish or otherwise," Ben said, his irritation rising. This was just the kind of conversation that had driven him out of Saguaro five years ago.

"What kind of life does she have in Saguaro? No education, no husband. The child's father is probably halfway through law school or has launched a career, and here she is."

"You know the father?"

"Of course not, but rumor has it Mommy and Daddy bought her off. Sent her packing from New Jersey so she wouldn't distract Junior's studies."

"And how would anyone know that?"

Leonora waved her hands, standing. "Oh, for goodness' sake. It's just town gossip. I listen with half an ear. Point is, at twenty-three, she's a ruined woman."

"This is hardly the dark ages, Mother. Women do have children out of wedlock without having to wear a scarlet *A* on their breast."

"Don't be ridiculous, Bennie. We're still conservative out here. That's all I'm saying. It's not Tucson or Flagstaff. This is the Valley. Out here, a woman disgraced is damaged goods."

"Nora, honey, that's enough." Ben Senior stood and took the tray from his wife. "Maggie is a good girl and a hard worker. She just had a rough patch."

Leonora turned to her son. "See, see what I have to contend with? Mr. Soft Touch. If I wasn't watching, he'd take in every stray from here to Yuma."

"Is that what Maggie is to you, a stray?" Ben's voice rose, and he could feel his temples throbbing. "She grew up here, for God's sake."

His mother gave him a curious look. "No, darling, Maggie is our employee. As such, we care about her, of course. Why your sudden interest, anyway? She was Kyle's friend, not yours. In fact, you hardly knew her."

"No reason. Just bumped into her this morning, that's all."

His mother stared at him for a moment, clearly unconvinced. Then, with a peck on his father's cheek, she said, "Gotta run. Don't want to be late for Cowbelles. We're in the final countdown weeks to the fair. I'll volunteer you for something, shall I?"

She hugged her son, "See you at dinner, sweetheart."

Ben turned to his dad and gave him an exasperated look. "She doesn't change, does she?"

"No, and I'd watch out. She's been lining up dates for you. I'm sure that'll be a hot topic at today's Cowbelles meeting, too."

Ben Senior referred to the women's organization of which Leonora was president. The group raised a great deal of money for a number of Valley charities and provided much-needed support to the local schools. Their biggest event of the year was the Valley Fair, and it drew people from hundreds of miles around.

"Well, I'm not interested. Please let her know that at dinner tonight, which I, unfortunately, have to miss."

"Hot date?"

"Something like that." Ben winked at his father. "Now let's get over to the Lodge, and I'll help you coddle the city slickers."

CHAPTER 12

Jeb tipped his hat, sweat ringing his forehead as he watched Maggie latch Tabasco's stall. "So, Boss, I'm headin' out unless you still need me?"

It was the end of the workday, horses all groomed, fed, and put up for the night. Cicadas buzzed, piercing the stillness the darkened barn.

Maggie smiled at him. "All set, and the 'Boss' bit ends tomorrow. Harley's due back."

"You're still my boss lady, chain of command and all that. Shouldn't you be headin' out, too, for your hot date?"

"It's not a date."

"Does he know that?"

"No, but I'm going to tell him."

"Good luck with that."

Maggie laughed and swatted him with her hat. "Get out of here! See you in the morning. Tabasco's rider should be joining us, at least for a little while. I think I'll try riding him first."

"I'll miss him. He's—"

"Special, yup. Wish we could keep him. Giant that he is, he's a gentle boy. He'd be great with the kids."

"Even if their parents had a heart attack, watching 'em."

Jeb waved, and Maggie retreated to the tack room to gather her things. Was she stalling because the thought of seeing Ben Morgan thrilled and scared her more than she cared to admit? That one little brush of a kiss had sent her into orbit. Did she trust herself around him? No, she did not, but then maybe a little wanton behavior wasn't a bad thing?

Maggie walked out of the barn, a dreamy smile on her face, and almost ran smack-dab into Leonora Morgan.

"Oh, Mrs. Morgan, hello. Were we expecting you?"

"No, dear, totally spontaneous visit. Just wanted to say hello, see how you, Ned, and Emma were doing."

"Fine, thanks." Maggie regarded the older woman quizzically, wondering what was behind this unexpected visit. Leonora rode with her husband maybe once a year, on their anniversary, and only then to please him. To Maggie's knowledge, since Ben Senior's heart attack, his wife had not come within a hundred yards of the stables.

"Any news about Emma's prognosis?"

"Nothing's changed. There's a doctor in Baltimore who has done surgeries on children with Emma's type of injury, but the expense of getting her back there, not to mention the cost of the procedures themselves, is beyond me right now, especially when the outcome is uncertain. This type of surgery is considered experimental so it's uncertain if insurance would pay for it. After all she's been through, I won't put her through any more, at least not right now. Maybe in a year or two."

"Maggie, you know Mr. Morgan and I would help you. Loans, travel support, whatever you need."

"Thank you, and I'm grateful. Mr. Morgan has offered before, but this is something I need to take care of myself."

"Well, dear, I won't keep you. I imagine you're anxious to get home. Just off to see the Dillons. Rose, their daughter, was very close to our Ben. Rose is back in the area and they're planning a get-together to reconnect. So exciting for our family, the prospect of two Valley families joining. It's always been my secret wish for Ben. They're so suited to one another. Do you know Rose?"

Maggie shook her head and prayed Leonora could not sense the trembling that coursed through her body. "I know the name, but she was ahead of me in school, and she hasn't been around town for years, has she?"

"She's been back east at medical school, then off making her fortune, just like our dear Ben. Now they're both back. Isn't that wonderful? Rose is with a very prestigious pediatric clinic in Tucson. She's a neurosurgeon, you know, specializing in spinal injuries. You should take Emma to see her. She and her associates are highly sought-after, I understand. We're lucky to have them here in Arizona."

"That's good to know, Mrs. Morgan, I will think about it. If there's nothing more, I should get going."

"Of course, dear, sorry to detain you. Have a wonderful evening."

Maggie almost ran to her car. She breathed a huge sigh as she shut the door of the clunker, never so glad of its refuge. Unbidden tears threatened to fall as she backed up, with Leonora Morgan waving her off. *This is why I will not get involved with Ben Morgan again.* Her heart felt as if Leonora Morgan had plunged a knife to its very core. *What was I thinking?* She would not allow herself to be undone again. It wasn't fair to Emma, her dad, or herself.

Leonora watched the disgraceful excuse for an automobile drive away and knew she'd been right to come. After hearing from her husband that Ben wouldn't be home for dinner, she instinctively knew why and with whom he'd be. She hadn't a clue what hold Maggie Williams had over her oldest, but she wasn't about to allow him to throw his life away on a harlot. She had plans for him, and they did not include a relationship with a stable hand.

CHAPTER 13

Ben arrived at the Williams' home a few minutes early. As he made his way up the front walk, he observed that the house needed a coat of paint, but the gardens on either side were well tended and bursting with summer blooms. A small vegetable garden flourished in the side yard, and he wondered if it was the work of Ned or Maggie. His heart raced as he rang the doorbell. The thought of seeing her, being near to her, drinking in her sweet scent, touching her skin as soft as rose petals, was enough to give him a hard-on. *Whoa boy.*

His cell phone rang, and his mother's number popped up. He switched the phone to vibrate without picking up. *Mom, you will not, I repeat, not ruin this evening for me.*

Ned Williams opened the door, stepped out on the porch, and closed the door behind him. "Hey, there, Ben. Good to see you."

Ben grasped the other man's outstretched hand. "You, too, Ned. It's been a while."

"Sure has. You look a little thinner than I remember. Food not so hot in California?"

Ben laughed. "Something like that. Stress seems to be a factor, too, according to my doctor."

"Well, glad to see you home. Your parents must be thrilled."

Ben nodded. "Is Maggie okay? Did she tell you we were having dinner tonight?"

"She did, but something's come up and she wanted me to tell you she's sorry, but she can't make it."

Ben's face fell. His body felt like it was collapsing into itself, breath knocked out of him along with it. "Is something wrong? Can I at least speak with her?"

Ned regarded the younger man thoughtfully. Ben Morgan's distress and obvious disappointment appeared genuine. While he felt sympathy for his daughter's would-be suitor, Ned had been around enough women to know that they were incomprehensible creatures. Men mere pawns in affairs of the heart.

"She's not here, son. She took Emma to Gracie's for dinner. Sorry."

Ben thanked him and turned away. As he walked toward the Rover, Ned called after him. "Give her time, son. Works wonders."

Ben got behind the wheel and wondered what to do. He would not go home to his mother's questions and nagging about the eligible women she had lined up for him to meet. He knew he could go out to eat, to the Grille, just west of town, or, he could go to Gracie's. Why not? Gracie was sure to have a trout special on the menu. He turned the Rover around and headed toward the center of town.

They were in a back booth, Emma's wheelchair parked alongside them. The child sat in a booster on one side of the booth, her mom, back to him, on the other. Emma was a lovely child, with brown curls and chestnut eyes. He noticed freckles sprinkled across her nose as he neared them. She was laughing at something her mom had said, her face lit up with a smile that would melt an iceberg. Ben hadn't spent much time around kids, but he knew a beauty when he saw one. Of course, she'd be beautiful with a mother like Maggie. He wondered about the father, jealous that another man might have a claim on this rare, precious being or her mother. There was something familiar about this little girl.

As he neared the booth, Ben felt as if he were coming home.

Emma spied him first and looked up. Her mother followed her gaze, and her mouth fell open as she spotted him.

Ben slid into the booth alongside the child, since the wheelchair blocked access to her mother's side. "Hey, Maggie. This must be Emma?"

While her mother fought for composure, Emma rewarded him with a shy smile.

"Mr. Morgan, hello. Yes, this is my daughter, Emma. Emma, Mr. Morgan."

Ben turned to Emma and extended his hand. "Pleased to meet you, sweetheart. And it's Ben. Nobody calls me Mr. Morgan except for stuffy old bankers."

Emma chuckled, taking his hand in a gentle handshake. "Hi, Ben. I thought you and Mom were supposed to have dinner tonight.?"

Ben winked at her, then turned to Maggie. "That was the plan, but your mom stood me up for someone far more important."

"We, I, well, we," Maggie stammered as two pair of identical eyes stared at her, waiting for an explanation. "Well, something came up, but here you are."

Emma stared from one adult to the other. "Mom, we just ordered. Can Ben eat with us?"

"Yes, we did. Just order, I mean. Would you, I mean would you like?"

"To join you? I'd be delighted." He waved to Stacy, who had just emerged from the kitchen.

"Hey, Ben. Great to see you again so soon. Want a menu?"

"What's Gracie's fish tonight?"

"Pan-seared rainbow trout with rosemary, corn relish, and polenta. Comes with veggies and a side salad."

"Perfect."

"Something to drink?"

Ben noticed that Emma had milk, her mother water, so he said, "Just water, thanks, Stacy."

Maggie watched his banter with the young, obviously smitten

Stacy. When the waitress disappeared, she said, "You do get around, don't you? Another member of your fan club?"

"Stacy and I are old friends. Met her right after our fender bender. So, Emma, what are you having?"

He directed his attention to the child and kept it there throughout the meal. Maggie watched her four-year-old fall under the spell of Ben Morgan and marveled at his capacity to charm the pants off any female from four to fifty. What hope did she have? In spite of herself, she found herself laughing at his stories, grateful for his antics and kind attention to her precious child. His keen interest in Emma's every word appeared genuine. She hadn't seen her daughter this animated and happy for a long time and, for that, she silently thanked Ben Morgan. Before the meal ended, Emma was feeding him her french fries, and he was sharing his polenta with her.

When the check came, he grabbed it. "My treat. I insist, after I crashed your meal. And," he added, turning to Emma, "if your mom agrees, I think we should mosey on down to the Daily Scoop for dessert?"

Emma turned to her mother, eyes wide as saucers. "Can we?"

"Right, I'm supposed to say no to that?" Maggie laughed, already thinking about what flavor ice cream she would order.

Ben leaned forward, whispering. "But don't say anything till we're outside. Gracie'll be offended if we don't try her pie of the night."

As he settled the bill, Maggie stood, rearranged the wheelchair, and waited for him to stand so she could help Emma into it. With a last megawatt smile at Stacy, Ben turned to Emma. "Okay, kiddo, want a lift?" Not waiting for the child's response, he stood and lifted her in one fluid motion, settling her into the chair. She was light as a feather, the frail body no more than wisp of air in his arms. He hated to set her down, her warmth and sweetness a balm to his baffled, tremulous emotions. He realized with a start, that Emma Williams had already found her way into his heart.

Maggie's heart lurched as she watched how tenderly he treated Emma. When her daughter reached up to touch his cheek with a "thanks, Ben," her heart felt like it might nearly break in two.

"Thank you," she said softly.

"Okeydokey, ladies. Are we ready? Then let's go." Ben's voice was gruff, the poignancy of the moment apparent to all three of them as well as to Stacy, who observed from a short distance away.

Gracie emerged to say good night. As she and her young waitress watched the threesome depart, she said, "There's a history there, mark my words."

Stacy sighed. "Too bad. He's such a hunk."

"What about the young and handsome Jeb Barnes?"

"A girl can dream, can't she?"

CHAPTER 14

Ben pushed Emma's wheelchair as they walked the block to the ice cream parlor. Orders filled, they sat in the shade of the shop's back porch, enjoying their "small cones," each with three heaping scoops of homemade ice cream.

"Mmm," Maggie sighed, as she settled back in her chair.

He watched her lips and tongue as she savored each creamy drop. "What's in that Moose Tracks, anyway?"

"Everything," she murmured. "So delicious. I'd forgotten. It's been over a year since I've had ice cream."

Emma licked her crazy vanilla with sprinkles and dripped as much in her lap as went in her mouth. Ben stepped inside to retrieve a wad of napkins, some of which he handed to Maggie.

"Here, kiddo," he said as he spread the remaining napkins over the growing pool in Emma's lap. She rewarded him with a milky grin.

Maggie watched them, her heart softening at his tenderness with Emma. Still, she reasoned, it was not right to tell him. Not until she knew him better. If he was headed back to California, with or without the beautiful Rose Dillon, she was not about to compromise her daughter's welfare. She would wait and see what kind of stuff Ben Morgan was made of. Watching him, she longed to reach over and touch his strong arm, scoot nearer to feel his heat. When might he turn his gorgeous brown eyes in her direction? Clearly her daughter was smitten. After all her surgeries and hospitalizations, Emma was an outgoing child, but Maggie had never seen her so entranced by anyone except her beloved grandfather.

As darkness fell, mother and daughter nibbled the last of their cones. Ben's had disappeared in what seemed like thirty seconds, but his companions savored theirs. Maggie stepped into the shop for a glass of water, then wet a wad of napkins and did the best she could to clean Emma up. She smoothed Emma's curls from her forehead. "Time to go, Sweet Pea."

Ben watched and realized that he missed them already. How had this happened? He never had a problem saying good-bye. No one, man or woman, had ever affected him this way. After accompanying them to the clunker, he settled Emma into her car seat and strapped her in as if he'd been doing it his entire life.

"You're pretty good at that," Maggie said from behind them.

"Engineering degree. There you go, Miss Emma, all safe and sound. See you later, alligator."

Before he withdrew, he kissed the top of her head.

She giggled. "After while, croc-dile."

Ben winked and closed the door, then turned to Maggie. "What a sweetheart. I think I'm in love."

"Yes, she is. Thank you for tonight. It was special for her, and fun for me."

"Me, too. So, can we do it again? Tomorrow, maybe?" As he leaned nearer, his lips grazed her ear, and Maggie's scent engulfed him. "Maggie, I'd really like to see you again. Emma, too."

He could see the child's eyes watching through the window. Every fiber of his body screamed for her mother, but he held himself at arm's length. Then, mustering every ounce of self-control he possessed, he stepped back.

"Let's see how things go." She did not trust herself to say more, but her eyes betrayed her.

For an instant, he spied the longing in her eyes. "You feel it, too," he whispered. He winked at Emma, still watching their every move.

"I've got an idea. I'll bring lunch tomorrow. I wanta say hi to Harley, and maybe you and I can take a short ride? What d'ya say?"

"No way. I can't. It'll be a crazy day with Harley back and Tabasco's rider coming."

"You have to eat, don't you? Look, I'll come by around one. If you're too busy, you can shoo me away."

Fat chance of that, Maggie thought, and she nodded. "Fine, see you tomorrow. Thanks again."

Ben grasped her hand and sent shock waves through her. "Good night, Mr. Morgan." She wriggled from his grasp and hurried around the car.

Ben watched as they drove away. *Home, I finally found it.* The ache in his heart was surprising and real.

CHAPTER 15

Ruthie Morgan watched as her brother came up the front walk. "Who hit you over the head and left you so starry-eyed? You're in Mom's shit house. Better watch out."

"What're you talking about?"

"Well, first, she's pissed that you were with Maggie, and—"

"How did she find out?"

"Come now, brother dear. You know Leonora, Super Snoop. She has spies everywhere. Harriet Carpenter called her the moment she spotted you at Gracie's."

Ben groaned as he sat down hard in the rocker beside her. "This is precisely why I got out of Dodge. In Santa Barbara, everyone's anonymous. No one knows your business and no one cares."

"She's also pissed because she'd invited the Dillons for a drink and then you weren't here to romance the fair Rose."

"She's relentless, isn't she?"

"Yes, I am." Leonora stepped out of the porch. "And I've invited Rose and her parents to dinner tomorrow. I promised them that you would be joining us."

"What am I, chopped liver?" Ruthie asked.

"Don't be silly, Ruthie." "Fine," Ben said, "it'd be great to see the Dillons. Okay if I bring two guests?"

His sister cringed and slunk down in her chair, mouthing "ouch."

"What are you talking about?"

"As long as we're inviting people to dinner, I'd like to invite Maggie and her daughter, Emma. Maybe even her dad, if he'd like to come?"

Leonora stared at him, mouth agape. "Do you think she'd feel comfortable? I mean, here at the big house when she's our employee?"

Ruthie rolled her eyes. "Mom, Maggie tames wild mustangs. I'm sure she can handle us. Besides, I'll be here, and Ben and Dad."

"And what does that mean?"

"That you're the only scary one in the group," Ben said. "They come, or I don't."

Leonora threw up her hands. "Fine, have it your way. I'm going in to find your father. Good night, you two."

As the door closed behind their irate mother, Ruthie turned to him. "She won't give up, you know."

"Neither will I. Night, Shortcake. Lover boy returns tomorrow. You excited?"

Ruthie laughed and threw a boot at him. "I'll get you for that one."

Ruthie had had a crush on Harley Langdon since elementary school, but he had always treated her like his little sister. She assumed that Harley had no idea of her feelings, nor did he reciprocate them, but her big brother knew better. Ben had seen the way his friend looked at Ruthie during the summers after high school. She was still too young for him, but that didn't stop the older, seasoned cowboy from looking.

CHAPTER 16

Maggie dressed Emma for preschool. The special morning class for disabled children met two days a week in Tucson. Ned drove the child and ran errands until it was time to collect her. Maggie sighed, smoothing her daughter's unruly curls. What would they have done without her dad and the loving care he provided?

Once Emma and Ned were bundled off, she hurriedly collected her things and headed out. On school days, Maggie arrived at work an hour later, a situation that was no problem with Jeb. Today she would have preferred to arrive before her boss, but Emma came first. As she drove up, she spied Harley and Ben sitting on the tailgate of Harley's pickup, chatting.

Tall, handsome cowboys, they looked like a cover of *Western Digest*. She envied their easy camaraderie. They were gorgeous, irresistible, and utterly charming, and they knew it. There wasn't a woman from here to Yuma who wouldn't give her right arm for a fling with one of these cowboys. *This is why you are not going to get involved, Maggie Williams. Do you hear me?*

A head taller and leaner than his friend, Harley had sandy hair that curled at his neck. He hadn't shaved in a few days and dark circles ringed his green eyes, but his smile that made women go weak at the knees did not look the least bit tired.

He waved his hat at her. "Hey, Mags, look who the cat dragged in."

She nodded at Ben, then turned to the other man. "Hey, Boss, welcome back. How's the high life at Reagans'?"

"Kinda boring, if you wanta know the truth. I prefer Morgan's Run and rough around the edges. Too sleek and tidy out there."

Maggie smiled at her boss, so glad to see him. "So we're untidy, are we?"

"Yup, and proud of it."

Maggie sighed. Now she could get back to what she loved, the horses and the riding, and leave the business end to Harley. The mustang training had consumed them the past few months, and they had neglected the riding programs, pony camps, and pack trips that were the ranch's bread and butter. The exclusive pack trips, led mostly by Harley, had put Morgan's Run on the map. The ranch was now a destination for the rich and famous who sought an undiscovered piece of paradise for their vacation. The ranch had seen its share of movie stars, studio bigwigs, and tycoons over the years, their intense need for privacy assured at Morgan's Run.

The now familiar tingle coursed through Maggie as she regarded the two friends, remembering Ben's touch, his lips grazing her neck, the heat that had set her afire and was now settling in her loins. *Get a grip, Maggie Williams!* She slung her backpack over her shoulder and headed for the barn. The sooner she got away, the sooner her heart would stop pounding.

She waved over her shoulder. "Gotta get Tabasco saddled. Rider should be here soon."

"Great. And Mags, when you have a sec, can you show our new coworker the ropes? I imagine Surfer Boy is a bit rusty."

"Ha, ha," Ben said, nudging his friend.

"Excuse me?" Maggie asked, turning back.

Ben answered before his friend could reply. "Yup, I offered my services and was told this is where I'm needed. They've got a corporate group coming in for a pack trip, and thought I could organize it since you guys are busy with the mustangs."

Mouth agape, Maggie stared at her boss.

Harley shrugged. "Don't look at me. Came from the boss man himself. Besides, who am I to argue? Be fun to see this tenderfoot bumble around after years as a beach bum."

"Beach bum?"

"Whatever. Look, Mags, it's a big group. I can use the help, and it'll be great to have him riding with me."

"Fine!"

As she turned on her heel and disappeared, Harley looked at his friend. "What's up with her? You two have something goin' on I should know about?"

Ben grinned. "It's complicated."

"Didn't look complicated to me. More like pure, unadulterated lust, at least coming from you, ole buddy. I go away for a couple of weeks and you've reduced my best trainer to a trembling schoolgirl. What the hell's been happening around here?"

"Nothing yet."

"And?"

"There's an attraction, no denying it."

"Yuh think?"

"We met up when I drove into town. Had a minor fender bender. She freaked out."

"She would, of course, with Emma and all. How did a fender bender turn into carnal lust overnight?"

Ben shook his head. "I don't know. There's just something about her, you know?"

"Oh, I know, Maggie's sensational, but what about Miranda, your beach bunny girlfriend?"

"We split up a few months ago. Wasn't going anywhere, and we were getting on one another's nerves."

"None of your romances go anywhere, buddy."

"Look who's talking."

"Yeah, but I'm still waiting for your baby sister to grow up."

"News flash—she's there, even though I'd never tell her."

"Never mind about my pathetic love life. What's stoked the fires with Maggie and you?"

"Can't tell you, man, but they're definitely stoked. We had a one-nighter before I left. Did you know that?"

"Round-up Night? Yeah, I remember you disappeared somewhere, but I never knew with who."

"I may have taken advantage of her, Harl. I was pretty drunk."

"Maggie's a big girl, and she's tough as nails. If she went along, she knew what she was doing."

"Maybe. Now she's all I think about. Her girl's a cutie, isn't she?"

"Em? Watch out, buddy. She's already taken. Em's my sweetheart. Has been from the day she was born."

"That had to be rough for Maggie, coming home pregnant, then the accident."

"Like I said, Maggie's tough. We almost lost her after the accident. Never left that baby's side. Hardly slept or ate. Got so thin you could almost see right through her. Thank God she has Ned. He's great with Emma. All I'm sayin' is, tread lightly, buddy. Maggie's the best trainer in the valley, and I don't wanta lose her 'cause you break her heart. You break her heart and you'll have me and Ned Williams to contend with."

Jeb drove up, and conversation ceased as Harley began going over the day's work with his assistant.

CHAPTER 17

Maggie brushed Tabasco, her voice soothing as she slipped a saddle onto the massive creature. Ben watched and marveled at her gentleness and courage. He wasn't completely comfortable around a horse that size, yet here she was, apparently fearless, her slender frame pressed against the horse's flank as she went about her work.

"I won't crowd you," he said softly, not wanting to startle her. "I didn't ask for this work, but they didn't need me at the farm, Raoul doesn't need drovers for at least a few weeks, and my parents are king and queen of the hospitality brigade."

A shy smile played across her face as she continued to stroke Tabasco's flank. "We can use the help."

Forgetting his fear of the horse beside her, Ben covered the distance between them until he stood inches from her. "Maggie, I—"

She gazed up, her eyes reflecting the longing he felt. Before he knew it, Ben swept her into his arms and captured her luscious lips and mouth with his, delving deeply as she responded, her tongue circling his. He groaned, already growing hard as he pulled her closer, desire nearly overwhelming him. No woman had ever had this effect on Ben Morgan. He was lost in the agony of wanting her.

Maggie felt his erection pressed against her stomach and she moaned, willing him to lead her to the hayloft and possess her fully. "Oh, Ben, I—"

"Hey, guys, anyone home?" Jeb's footsteps sounded on the barn floor, and they broke apart, breathless and red-faced.

Ben turned to greet the younger man, holding his jacket at his waist to hide his arousal. Maggie moved to adjust Tabasco's halter, her eyes unable to meet her assistant's.

Jeb's eyes moved from one to the other, his expression bemused. "Sorry, guys. Should I come back in a few?"

Maggie handed the reins to Jeb. "Don't be ridiculous! Let's get him outside. Rider'll be here any minute."

Jeb led Tabasco out, giving Ben a wink as he passed by.

When horse and trainer disappeared, Maggie stared at Ben, not sure whether to laugh or cry.

"Well, that was interesting." Ben grinned at her, and they both burst out laughing. "Listen," she muttered, "I've got to get out there."

As she moved past, he touched her arm. "What I should have said is that it was more than interesting. We still on for lunch?"

"I don't know. This is starting to make me a little crazy."

"Me, too, but look, we've got to eat. I've got Carmela making us a picnic. We'll take a ride, eat, and get you back in no time."

THE MORNING FLEW BY. Maggie and Jeb welcomed Carl Delgado, the Border Patrol agent, and introduced him to Tabasco. Today was for paperwork and getting acquainted. Delgado, a seasoned agent and experienced rider, took a long look when he spied the massive draft horse.

"You gotta be kidding. Never seen a mustang that looked like that."

Maggie laughed. "Clearly there was some outbreeding in Tabasco's case."

"We think a renegade from a traveling circus might've found his mama," Jeb said.

"Or one of Budweiser's team." Delgado pushed his wide-brimmed Stetson back to take a full view of his new ride. "You guys sure about this?"

"He's gentle as a lamb, but we have a backup if you guys don't click. We've been working with Pearl for a couple of months. She's a favorite of the owner's daughter, but she's available, if you'd feel more comfortable."

The tall, burly man in tee shirt, black jeans, and worn Justin boots scratched his head. "I'm willing to give him a shot, but can I take a look at Pearl anyway?"

Maggie signaled to Jeb, who disappeared into the barn and returned a few minutes later with a brown-and-white pinto, a beauty that stood at least five hands below Tabasco. Ruthie had already fallen in love with her. In truth, Ruthie rarely had time to ride,

but her father promised if Pearl went south, they'd find another painted horse for her. "Now, she's more like it." Delgado stepped forward without hesitation to nuzzle Pearl's nose and scratch her ears. "Can I?"

Jeb gave him his arm for support, and the short, compact man easily mounted Pearl, settling into the saddle, adjusting the reins and stirrups. It was clear Delgado had found his mount. Maggie watched rider and horse, knowing with certainty that Tabasco was no longer in the picture. Secretly she was glad, as she would have liked nothing better than to hold on to the gentle giant. She might be a bit afraid of him, but he had already captured her heart.

CHAPTER 18

Ben arrived slightly before one, backpack over his shoulder. Maggie noticed he had shed his denim shirt in the midday heat. Every ripple of chest and arm muscle was outlined by the faded blue tee shirt he wore over jeans that fit him like a glove. *Oh, boy, this is going to be a lunch to remember!* Maggie waved and headed in to wash up.

When she returned, he and Jeb had saddled two of the ranch's sorrels, Tara and Raine. "You guys have fun, now," Jeb said, grinning as he gave Raine a swat on her rump.

Maggie was relieved that Harley had gone up to the Lodge. One smirking bystander was quite enough!

They rode up into the foothills on a well-worn trail that led to the ranch's high meadows. Soon those meadows would be home to the sheep now grazing in the lower fields. The deserted fields, green and verdant, stretched as far as the eye could see. The mountains that surrounded them were dotted with thousands of saguaro cactuses and scrub. They rode in silence, neither daring to start a conversation, the searing memories of the morning's encounter still fresh. Finally, Ben spoke as he pointed to their right, at a towering desert willow that stood at the edge of the meadow.

"What d'ya think? Good spot?"

Maggie nodded and guided Tara toward the shady grass. He spread a blanket and opened the pack as she settled beside him. "We used to have a swing on this tree. Wonder what happened to it?" He gazed up, eyes locked with hers.

Maggie shrugged, her breath caught in her throat. *Stay calm. Breathe, Maggie.* "Must've been a while ago, 'cause I've ridden by and never seen it."

He watched her fiddling with Tara's reins, patting her, whispering softly to the perfectly calm horse. *She looks like a scared rabbit. Better back off a bit or risk losing her, Morgan.* "You hungry?"

"Starved," she replied, only partially referring to the food.

"Well, then, let's see what Carmela's whipped up for us." As he began to pull out the sandwiches and a thermos of iced tea, she leaned forward and rested her hand on his forearm. She was trembling, but she had to touch him to ground herself, as if his heat would calm her frayed, raging emotions.

Surprised, he turned to her, food forgotten as he saw the desire in her soft doe eyes. Instantly his arms circled her, and he drew her close. "Oh, my Lord, woman, the last few hours have been torture for me."

"Me, too." She reached up to caress his jaw. *What are you doing, Maggie Williams?* was the last coherent thought she had before his lips captured hers and she was lost.

His tongue plunged and delved, hers entwining, teasing, returning his kisses. Sure hands slipped under her tee shirt and cupped her firm, rounded breasts. His fingers circled and teased her nipples to hardness as he reached around and unclasped her bra, slipping it and her tee shirt off with one fluid motion. Maggie did the same with his shirt. For an instant, they stared at each other in wonder.

"My God, you're beautiful." Voice husky, Ben drank in the sight of her as Maggie's hands ran over his hard, rippled chest, then boldly moved lower.

The size of his erection nearly brought her to climax as Ben began to unbutton her jeans.

"My darling Maggie, I've never wanted anyone like I want you."

"Take me, then," she whispered as they divested each other of their remaining clothes.

His fingers moved over her alabaster skin, untouched by the sun like the rest of her, until he caressed her inner thighs, fingers entering her, finding her wet with desire, more than ready for him. Wanting to pleasure her first, he plunged his fingers in again and again, teasing and stroking her. Instinctively he knew what would send her over the edge, and she climaxed in a clashing moment of pure delirium.

Ben gazed down at her lovely face, transfixed by ecstasy, and knew he was in love. For the first time in his life, he understood what it meant to be hopelessly lost in love for another human being.

"My beautiful sweetheart." He sighed and drew her closer, watching as she touched him, fingers stroking lazily at first, then moving faster, until her touch had aroused him to the edge of madness.

"Take me now," she said. "Please, Ben. I need you inside me."

"Condom?"

"On the pill."

"That's my darling."

Maggie gasped as he slipped her body beneath him, widening her legs and plunging deeply, his moves gentle at first. She matched him thrust by thrust. "Am I hurting you, sweetheart?" He gazed down at the beauty beneath him, his dark eyes soft with passion.

"Never." Her body seemed to draw him in, inviting him to go deeper. Her slender legs entwined his hips as she met him, urged him harder, deeper, until she climaxed again, Ben following her in perfect synchrony.

He groaned, "Oh, my God," then moved to rest on his side, taking her with him, never wanting to sever their intimate connection. "It's never—I've never—oh, my God, Maggie. Thank you." He regarded her, his brown eyes gentle and full of concern. "Are you okay?"

She rewarded him with a dazzling smile that took his breath away. "More than okay."

"You sure we were protected?" he asked, then realized he didn't care. Creating a child with this woman would be an amazing gift.

"I'm sure. I'm on the pill, not because I'm a loose woman. I have irregular cycles. This keeps them regular and predictable. Oops, probably more than you wanted to know."

"I want to know everything about you, darlin'."

Ben nuzzled her neck.

"Mmm." She met his lips for a loving kiss. As the kiss deepened, Ben found himself growing hard again, and her smile widened. "Why, Mr. Morgan, I do believe we may have some unfinished business." Gently she moved to take him deeper, her inner woman caressing and teasing as she moved closer, then withdrew. As his erection grew, he slowly plunged deeper. They gazed into one another's eyes as they scaled new heights and moved to a roaring simultaneous climax.

Afterward they dozed, still connected, arms entwined, until a hawk screeched overhead.

Maggie stirred, rising on one elbow. "What time is it?"

He nuzzled against her. "Who cares?"

"I do. I have to pick up Emma at three!"

"Shush."

He nibbled her ear as he reached an arm over his head to check his watch. "Just short of two. We'll eat something, then head back."

Satiated, neither felt much like eating, but they shared a fragrant mushroom and goat cheese sandwich, made with one of Carmela's fresh baguettes and a hint of her special sauce.

"Heaven," Maggie moaned, wiping a drop of sauce from her chin.

"Oh, no, my sweet. Carmela's a fine cook, but heaven's where you've just taken me. There's a world of difference."

As they dressed, grabbing bites of sandwich, Maggie looked over, marveling at his gorgeous body. "This was crazy. You know that, don't you?"

"Crazy amazing."

"In case you hadn't noticed, your mom's trying to marry you off to Rose Dillon or just about any single girl from here to Albuquerque."

"Ah, but what you don't understand, my lovely desert flower, is that my mother hasn't a clue what I like or whom. Whatever she wants, I've always wanted the opposite."

Maggie pulled down her tee, giving him a look. "Is that supposed to be a compliment?"

"Now, now...don't get all uppity, Ms. Williams. I just mean, my mother is not me. Oh, and that reminds me. I'd like to invite you and Emma to dinner tonight. Your dad, too, if he'd like to come. My parents insisted."

"Yeah, right. Thanks, but we'll pass. And I can't see your mom being enthusiastic about such an idea."

"She is, and you're coming. Please, Maggie, if we're going to be seeing each other, you'll have to see them. Let's get it over with now."

"Now that really sounds appealing."

"Please say you'll come."

"Is that what we're doing, seeing each other?"

"What do you think?"

"I don't know. Boss's son, back from the big city, remembers a roll in the hay and decides to rekindle it for another roll in the hay?"

Ben sat back as if she'd struck him. "Is that what you think?"

Embarrassed to see the hurt in his eyes and know her words had caused it, she said, "Look, I'm sorry."

Unable to meet his gaze, she stared at the ground, emotions roiling. Finally she looked up to find the beautiful chestnut eyes, so like his daughter's, waiting expectantly. "It's just, you're you and I'm me. Morgans don't see girls like me. They see doctors and lawyers and heiresses, people like Rose Dillon."

"Bullshit."

"It's true."

He reached forward and grasped her hand. "Maggie, I know what you're doing. You're scared, and I don't blame you. First your Ivy League boyfriend abandons you and Emma. Then you have to take care of her all by yourself. No wonder you're a little shy when it comes to men, but I'm here, and I'm not going anywhere."

"Yet."

"I'm here for a while. Let's just see where this goes. This is not a roll in the hay for me, I promise. Please come to dinner. It'll be fun."

Maggie laughed and squeezed his hand. "Yeah, right, like a fork in the eye."

"Please say yes."

"Okay, but don't say I didn't warn you. And at the first sign of trouble, I'm giving you a signal and we're out of there. If you don't agree, we're not coming."

"You have my word." He leaned forward and claimed one more deep, lingering kiss. Then he stood, took her hand, and lifted her up, strong arms encircling her for one last embrace.

"How am I ever going to ride?" she asked, laughing and wincing as he helped her into the saddle.

CHAPTER 19

Ben arrived right on time. It was Ned's poker night, so he had declined the dinner invitation. As Ben drove up, he was heading out.

"Take care of my girls." The older man smiled a smile that didn't quite reach his eyes, and Ben spied a challenge there. *You hurt my girls and I'll come after you.*

"You got it. Believe me, at the first sign of distress, we'll make our escape."

Ned laughed. "Hope that's not necessary. I'm trustin' you, son. They're everything to me. Come on, let's get the car seat in."

By the time the two men had installed the car seat in the Rover, Maggie and Emma appeared, the child agog with excitement and her mother pale as a ghost. Ben paused, hating to see her in distress, and wondered if he should call and cancel. After Emma was strapped in, Maggie shut the door and brushed a lock of hair from her face. She had worn it down, the way he loved it, soft waves framing her slender, lovely face. Dressed in a light summer dress that hugged her rounded breasts and slim waist, the pale peach floral skirt flared to just above her knees, she looked good enough to eat. Strappy high-heeled sandals had replaced her cowboy boots, and he marveled at her long, lithe legs and graceful ankles.

"You look incredible."

"Thank you." Maggie's heart skipped several beats as her tall, rugged lover turned to her. His blue cotton dress shirt was open at the collar, and he wore black jeans and what looked like brand-new boots. If only they were headed for a country dance instead of her employers' fortress on the hill.

He reached into his pocket and pulled out his phone. "You sure? I can call and say something's come up."

Hands on hips, she stared at him. "Now you ask me! Did you see Emma's face? She's practically been jumping out of her skin all afternoon, she's so excited. We don't get out much, and she's only been to the ranch once, when she was too young to remember."

His hand grazed the small of her back as he ushered her around and opened the jeep door. "Well, we'll just have to change that, starting tonight."

CHAPTER 20

A group awaited them on the wide front porch as Ben eased the Rover in next to the Dillons' SUV. "Here goes nothing," he said as he leaped out and grabbed Emma's chair.

Ben Senior and Rose came to greet them. She gave Ben a quick hug, and his father bent to kiss Maggie's cheek.

"Hello, hello! Two of my favorite young women!" His son lifted Emma, and the older man gave the child a quick pat and a kiss. "Set her down, boy. I'll take her from here."

Maggie watched the proceedings, then turned to Rose. "Hello."

"It's been a long while." Rose stepped forward to hug her, and Maggie returned the woman's warm embrace.

"Yes, it has."

They followed the men, who had lifted Emma's chair to carry her up the porch steps.

Like Ben, Rose Dillon was eight years older than Maggie and had attended a private school in Tucson from middle school on. The Dillons' property was south of Saguaro, and they tended to socialize and shop in Tucson, so Maggie knew very little about the slender, blonde woman. Rose looked elegant in beige linen slacks, a white linen shell, and matching linen flats, and her silver-and-turquoise jewelry beautifully complimented her understated but clearly expensive ensemble.

Maggie suddenly felt cheap and common. *What am I doing here? They belong together. The perfect couple.*

"Welcome, welcome," Leonora Morgan cried, opening her arms to hug Emma, then Maggie. Martha and Jay Dillon stood up to shake hands with Maggie before turning to bestow a more effusive greeting on the prodigal son.

Jay Dillon slapped Ben's back. "So good to see you, son! Back to stay, we hope?"

Ben Senior draped his arm over Maggie's shoulders. "What can I get you to drink, darlin'?"

Leonora waved her glass. "We're all having gin and tonics."

Maggie hesitated, and the kind man patted her back.

"We've got everything, sweetheart. White wine? Red? Beer? Soft drink?" He winked at Emma. "I bet you'd like a soda, wouldn't you, honey? Coke, orange, root beer, Sprite?"

"Orange soda, please."

Emma gave him one of her hundred-watt smiles and the older man stopped, frozen, staring from the child to his son. It was less than thirty seconds, but to Maggie, it felt like an eternity. Her heart raced, wondering if Emma's grandfather had recognized what she had worked so hard to conceal.

She stepped between Ben Senior and her child, blocking his view. Fortunately, Ben Junior had been wrapped in conversation with Jay Dillon and had not noticed the exchange, but Ruthie and his mother had. "A white wine would be lovely, thank you," Maggie said.

Misinterpreting her husband's behavior, Leonora moved to his side. "Are you alright?"

"Never better." He drew her close and kissed the top of her head.

As Maggie turned away from the elder Morgans, she found Rose's hazel eyes darting back and forth from Emma to Ben. Her expression registered surprise, then understanding. Maggie groaned inwardly. *What a terrible mistake this was.* As she watched, the other woman's eyes looked sad for an instant before the strong emotion vanished behind a mask of affability.

Maggie smiled as Ben Senior handed her a large goblet of wine, then moved to sit beside her daughter. The elder Morgan kept up a lively conversation with Emma about everything from jackrabbits to Barbie dolls, although he 'fessed up that he knew next to nothing about the latter. "Wait'll Ruthie gets here. She can probably unearth her dolls from the attic, since it was just last year when she stopped playing with 'em."

For dinner, Carmela passed around a huge earthenware tureen of vegetable ragout along with farm cheese polenta, fresh breads, and lamb kebobs. She made Emma a cheeseburger, with french fries in a fancy wire basket accompanied by tiny ramekins of ketchup, relish, and mustard. Delighted, the child ate every bite. Dessert was a creamy tart topped with berries. Each course was accompanied by a different wine, most from the Dillons' winery, except the last, a crisp California champagne from the case Ben had brought back with him.

Maggie nursed her glass of wine until dessert, when she accepted a small flute of champagne. Leonora presided at the north end of the table, waving instructions to her husband throughout the meal. Sensing Maggie's discomfort, Carmela flashed her covert smiles as she served and cleared.

Ruthie chatted nonstop with Emma. This left Maggie to converse with Jay Dillon, whose conversational repertoire appeared to be limited to wine grapes, livestock and crop reports. As he droned on, Maggie feigned interest as she stole glances at Ben and Rose. Clearly enjoying one another's company, they fell into the easy conversation of old friends. Like his kind, sensitive housekeeper, Ben Sr. kept his eye on Maggie. As dessert was served, he leaned forward and inquired about the mustang training.

"Poor Tabasco scared him off, I'm afraid, but he took to Pearl immediately."

"Uh-oh." He gazed over at his youngest daughter, now making funny faces at Emma. "There'll be hell to pay when she goes. Have to start lookin' for a pretty painted filly."

As Carmela served coffee and tea, Leonora turned to Rose. "So, your mom tells us you're setting up in Tucson. How wonderful for you and your proud parents. We hear that the clinic is headed for world renown."

CHAPTER 21

As there was still plenty of light when they finished dinner, Ben Sr. suggested a walk to the stables. Instantly Emma's eyes sparkled. Leonora, Jay, and Martha elected to remain at the house, but the rest of the group headed down the grassy pathway behind the house. Ben, his dad, and Ruthie took the lead with Ben pushing Emma's chair, the others pointing out the sights as they progressed. Maggie and Rose followed a short distance behind them.

"She's a beautiful child, and good as gold," Rose said softly. "I know a lot of four-year-olds, and none of them are as well-behaved as Emma.."

Maggie smiled, grateful for the other woman's kindness. "She was getting a lot of attention, and this is a special treat for her. We don't go out much."

"I was so sorry when I heard about your accident. The whole town is pulling for Emma."

"Yes, we've had wonderful support. My father takes good care of her so I'm able to work, thank God."

Rose paused on the path and turned, touching her arm. "Maggie, I don't want to interfere, but have you exhausted all possibilities, seen specialists and all, about Emma's injury?"

Tears stung Maggie's eyes. "Let's just say, we've exhausted the possibilities in the southwest, Phoenix, Tucson, even the research center in Santa Fe. We haven't yet gone east, but there's a surgeon in Baltimore who came highly recommended by Emma's doctor in Tucson. Right now, the cost to get her back there, not to mention the surgery itself, is beyond my means."

She brushed tears away. "Sorry, it's literally all I think about night and day, but so far, all I'm able to do is think. I try to take the best care of her I can. My dad drives her into Tucson for PT twice a week. We're trying to keep her legs strong and limber. Her voice trailed off as she watched Ben sweep Emma from her chair and carry her into the barn.

Rose followed her gaze. "He's great with her, isn't he?" Maggie nodded. "Maggie, I'm not sure if you were listening to the dinner conversation about my job, but Dr. Heavers, my mentor and now boss, is one of the best pediatric neurosurgeons in the world. He moved out here to start the clinic, thinking about retirement in five or six years, but he's still at the top of his game."

She reached into her pocket and pulled out a business card. "I brought this for you. I would trust Dr. Heavers with my child in a heartbeat. Please think about coming down to see him." When Maggie's eyes registered surprise, she added, "Ben called this afternoon and told me you'd be here."

"Thank you." Silently she wondered about the communication between the childhood friends, but was nonetheless grateful for Rose's concern. The beautiful couple could ride off into the sunset for all she cared, if Rose's mentor could help her Sweet Pea to walk again. Like every other avenue she had explored, the Heavers Clinic's costs would, no doubt, be prohibitive, but for Emma's sake, she would think about it.

Harley greeted them inside the barn. "Sorry to miss dinner at the big house, guys, but isn't this my lucky day? A whole bevy of beauties and Rosie, our prom queen and girl of my dreams, back in the fold. Your folks must be in heaven." This pronouncement received a scowl from Ruthie.

Rose laughed, hugging her high school classmate. "Good to see you, Harl."

Maggie went to join Ben and Emma, who were getting acquainted with Sunny, a sixteen-year-old Shetland, the ranch's unofficial mascot. She had been the younger Morgans' first mount. Nowadays she mostly grazed and followed Maggie, Jeb, and Harley around. Occasionally, one of Carmela and Raoul's nieces or nephews came for a ride, but mostly Sunny was retired, though not by choice. She was practically dancing over Emma's attention, every fiber of her body screaming "ride me!"

"She likes you," Ben said as they petted Sunny and fed her handfuls of oats. Emma's arm circled his shoulder, and he held her close. He was so in love with this frail, spunky little girl. "We oughta get you out here for a ride."

Emma looked at Maggie, wide-eyed. "Can I, Mom, can I please?"

"I don't know, sweetie. It would have to be with one of us, and I'm not sure Sunny could handle the weight. She's an old girl now."

Ben started to speak but then stopped, not wanting to contradict Emma's mom. His mind was already racing with possibilities as he stood beside the woman who had rocked his world earlier in the day. Casually he draped his arm round her shoulder and was relieved that she did not pull away. His chest swelled with pride.

Ben Sr. leaned to whisper in his daughter's ear. "Now, that's a mighty nice picture, isn't it? Never thought I'd see your brother head over heels with a lady, did you?"

Ruthie tore herself away from her surveillance of Rose and Harley's conversation. *What chance do I have when she's around?* "Yup, big brother is certainly smitten."

"Always liked Maggie. Level-headed, feet on the ground."

"You know Mom's having fits over this?"

"Oh, she'll settle down. It's just new and so soon after she's gotten him home. She'll get used to it with time."

"Yeah, right. You wait. She's got dates lined up for him every night for the next month. She's probably been on the matchmaker hotline all day."

"Your brother can handle her. 'Sides, it doesn't look like her first idea panned out too well." He gazed at Rose and Harley, who were outside now, talking and laughing. "Have we got ourselves another romance in the making?"

His daughter scowled. "Humph! Now, what about my horse? When can we start looking?"

Surprised at her youngest daughter's change of mood, he gave her a look.

"You know, honey, I was looking at Emma earlier. She's...I mean... she looks like...do you see any resemblance to—"

"Oh, my God!" Ruthie exclaimed. "She's been in town five minutes and she's already flirting with every man she sees!"

"What's that, honey?" But Ruthie had already stalked off. As she headed back to the house, her father joined the others.

Maggie smiled as the elder Morgan approached. "This has been a lovely evening, Mr. Morgan, but we should be heading home. Thank you so much."

Ben Sr. winked at her. "Lots more get-togethers in the future, I expect."

CHAPTER 22

Car seat stowed back in Maggie's car, Ben walked them to the door, where Ned waited.

"Hey, you three. I was getting worried."

"Night, Em," Ben said, giving the child a hug, which she returned. "See you later, alligator."

"After a while, croc-dile."

When she smiled up at him, adoration shone in her dark eyes.

Ned wheeled the chair in and closed the door behind Maggie and Ben.

As soon as the door closed, Ben swept her into his arms for a deep, lingering kiss. "Wasn't too terrible, was it?"

Breathless and weak-kneed, Maggie nodded as she ran her fingers along his strong jaw. "Thank you. It was very special for Emma." "What about you?"

"It was fun to see her happy."

"And her mom?"

"Do you want the truth?"

"What do you think?"

"As one of the hired help, dining at the big house was a bit uncomfortable. Your dad's great and all, but it feels more than a little strange. Why do you think Harley begged off and ate in town?"

"He was busy."

"Maybe." She gave him a wry smile. "Look, it's no big deal, but you and I grew up in different worlds. I didn't hang out at the Rancho Mirage Club, playing tennis, golf, or whatever they do there."

"Neither did I."

"Never?"

"Well, I might've spent a summer or two there."

"Hmm, and I suspect many evenings with young adoring ladies at your side. You do have a bit of reputation, you know."

"That was a long time ago. That's my mother's world. I walked away from it in my early twenties and never looked back. My father's never been comfortable off the ranch."

"A ranch that counts celebrities and the A-list of the rich and famous among its regular guests."

"Again, not me." He felt her stiffen in his arms and decided to change the topic. "Emma loves horses, doesn't she?"

Maggie nodded. "I should bring her out more often. It's been so busy with the mustangs."

"Now that I'm here, that can change. I'd be happy to take her riding. Probably not on Sunny, but I could take her on one of the quarter horses."

"We'll see."

"Please let me do this, Maggie. I didn't want to say anything in front of Emma, but I'd be thrilled to take her riding."

"It's not that," she said quietly. "I trust you. I haven't taken her because I don't know if it would be safe, with her injury. I wouldn't want to cause more damage if there may be hope someday."

"Of course, I'm sorry. I didn't think."

She reached up again to stroke his cheek. "It's okay. I was talking to your friend about Emma's injury. She suggested I come to her clinic."

"You should. She works with the best, or so I'm told."

"She's nice, your Rose."

"Yeah, Rose is a nice person, but she's not 'my Rose.' She's an old family friend."

"Hmm."

"Do you honestly believe I could be interested in another woman after today?"

"Hard to tell. Maybe that's what you do with all the female help."

He stared down, ready to do battle until he glimpsed the teasing in her eyes. "I'll get you for that, Maggie Williams. In fact, if we weren't standing on your front stoop, I'd have my way with you right now."

With one long, sensuous kiss, tongues entwining, teasing, and caressing, they said good night, and Maggie went in.

"Hot date," Ned said, smiling as he watched his daughter close the door.

Maggie blushed crimson. "Something like that."

"Sounds like Emmie had a ball?"

Maggie nodded.

Her dad said, "She's waiting for you."

CHAPTER 23

Within a week, they wondered how they had ever managed without Ben. More mustangs were delivered, and Carl Delgado's work with Pearl took most of Maggie's time. Harley and Ben spent their days running between the Lodge and stables, working with Ben Sr. to plan the corporate pack trip scheduled for the following week. Ben took Emma, Maggie, and Ned to supper at Gracie's one night, but other than that, they'd seen little of each other except in passing.

After the dinner at the big house, Maggie had asked for space to work, to catch up at home, and think things through. It was torture for her and for Ben. He nonetheless respected her request until the day before the corporate group's scheduled arrival.

After an exhausting day, Maggie saddled Tabasco. The gentle giant had had little attention since Carl Delgado's rejection. He nickered softly as she adjusted his harness, nudging her as if to say, "Hurry up."

"Okay, boy, I'm going as fast as I can," Maggie said, ruffling his mane, patting his shoulder.

"Want some company?"

She jumped at the sound of Ben's voice. "If you like, but it's gonna be a quick ride. No stopping along the way."

"Fine with me. Meet you outside?" As he moved away, Ben took a few seconds to drink in her sweet scent, thinking how much he missed her.

They took the Falling Water Trail but did not ride out far enough to reach the falls, which were a trickle at this time of year. The trail wound north through a forested area, so they were in shade for most of the time. Tabasco trotted merrily and seemed thrilled to have escaped the confines of barn and corral. Despite his size, he was agile and steady. Maggie thought again how glad she was that Carl Delgado had chosen Pearl. If she had the money, she'd offer to buy Tabasco in a heartbeat.

Ben rode Rowdy, the stable's resident "wild stallion." A ten-year-old quarter horse, he was the mount most often favored by his brothers and men wanting lessons on a feisty mount. A beautiful sorrel, he was sure-footed and dependable as long as his rider used a firm hand. Ben had already decided that Rowdy would be his mount for the pack trip. Harley would be riding Pepper, his five-year-old Appaloosa. Since Rowdy and Pepper did not always see eye to eye, Maggie had suggested he take Royal, but Ben had assured her that with two experienced riders who would no doubt be at opposite ends of the group most of the time, there would not be a problem.

Watching her, he marveled at her ease in the saddle as she guided the enormous horse up the narrow trail. She barely moved a muscle, her curvaceous body one with the horse as they moved in perfect sync. Ben had been riding his entire life, but if he were being truthful, Tabasco's size and wildness scared the heck out of him. Yet here was this slender, lithe creature riding him as if he was the old gray mare. Her hair was tucked under her hat, and a long chestnut braid trailed down her back.

When they reached the ridge, they paused at the overlook to gaze down the valley, farmlands and pastures stretched out before them.

"Time for this city slicker to take a quick break," he said.

She laughed and dismounted alongside him. "If you need a break after twenty minutes of easy riding, you'd better bring knapsacks full of panty hose and Advil with you next week."

"Don't I know it."

"Harley'll give you no end of grief about it."

"I'm prepared. I've got a few tricks up my sleeve to distract him."

She laughed. "Good luck with that."

Maggie leaned back against the red clay outcropping and gazed toward the mountains. "This is one of my favorite places on the ranch. Best views in the valley."

"The best view anywhere, and I'm not talking about the mountains." Gorgeous eyes, dark and smoky, gazed down at her. "I've missed you, Maggie. Can we plan something special when I get back?"

Maggie felt her resolve crumble as her body cried out for him. "Ben, I'm not sure this is a good idea. I work for you. Your mother's got you married off to half the women in the county, and I have so much going on with Emma and work."

"Hush, my sweet."

He leaned down and captured her full, trembling lips in a deep kiss, his tongue probing, hers swirling to meet him. Strong arms lifted her and he wrapped her legs around his waist, his erection pressed against her.

"Sweetheart, please don't pull away. I can't live without you. Forget my mother. I certainly do. There's no one else for me."

Her arms circled his neck and Maggie let go, giving in to his embrace as his hands grasped her shirt and pulled it free, fingers slipping under her bra to rub, caress, and tease until her nipples grew hard, and she moaned with pleasure.

"Oh, Ben, I can't live without you, either."

With several swift movements, he loosened and removed her jeans and panties, unleashed his erection, and lifted her higher to plunge into her wet, warm depths. He moved gently and slowly at first, then faster and harder as she urged him on. Breathing as one, they spiraled skyward until Maggie's climax shattered her and his followed right behind.

Ben's hands and arms cushioned her body against the hard clay as he cradled her buttocks, taking care to maintain their intimate connection. As he massaged and caressed, his fingers crept upward to her sweet spot. He stroked and teased, arousing her again as he grew hard inside her.

Maggie squeezed him deep inside and moaned, "Ben, no," knowing full well that her body was screaming, *Yes, yes, take me again.*

This time he moved slowly, plunging and withdrawing, over and over again in agonizing rhythm. His kisses delved deeper, then trailed down her neck to capture her rounded breasts.

"Let me love you, Maggie."

"Yes," she gasped, and they moved as one, each crying out as they climaxed together, bodies flush with the fury of their passion. As they caught their breath, Ben brought her with him as he lay back against the outcropping. He held her close and drank in the scent he adored, endeavoring to memorize every sensation, already missing her for the week he would be away. "You okay?" He kissed her forehead, tenderly brushing a lock of hair to the side.

She nodded and reached up, and her slender fingers cupped his face. "I'm perfect, but also late. We've got to go."

Later, as they exited the narrow trail and came into the open, Ben brought Rowdy up beside Maggie and Tabasco. "You're incredible with him. "

She flashed him a beautiful smile. "To be honest, I was scared to death of him at first, but he's a marshmallow. Wish we could hang on to him. If I had the money, I'd buy him."

"Why don't I talk to Dad? It's not as if he went to Kentucky and spent half a million on him. He was headed to the glue factory. My guess is that—"

"Don't you dare. The ranch has invested a ton in these mustangs, and I do not accept charity."

"So, how about we lobby to keep him as a stable horse?"

"For what purpose? Most people are scared to death of him."

"Not you."

"But I'm not a customer paying eighty dollars an hour for lessons."

"Still, it doesn't look like he's goin' anywhere in a hurry. When's the next Border Patrol agent due in for training?"

"Two will be here in three weeks."

"A lot can happen in three weeks. Just out of curiosity, what would you do with him if you had him?"

"Ben, I'm serious. I am not discussing this!"

"Promise, scout's honor, I will do and say nothing. I just wondered what you'd do with a brute like him."

"Well, ride him, for one thing. And, my dream is—" She stopped short and stared ahead before turning to him.

"I won't tell, promise."

"My dream is to open a riding camp for disabled kids. The children at Emma's day program would love a place like this."

"That's a terrific idea. Does that mean you're ready to let Emma ride?"

"Not until I'm sure it won't cause more damage to her spine."

"About that. I know it's none of my business, but have you exhausted all possibilities? There's so much research going on with spinal injuries. I'm not minimizing the extent of Emma's injuries, but kids' bodies are pretty resilient. As someone who broke a lot of bones before my teens, I can attest to how easily we youngins bounce back."

"I made an appointment with Rose's clinic. She was kind enough to get us in next week."

"That's terrific news." As they circled the corral, he reined Rowdy in. "Hold on a sec, Maggie."

Without missing a beat, Tabasco stopped and waited, still and steady. Maggie looked quizzically at Ben. Her heart melted as the rugged, handsome cowboy took her hand. Ben Morgan had rocked her world to its foundations. How could she resist him?

"Maggie, please, I'm begging you. Let me help you. My partners and I have made a ton of money with our companies. They both have families and two and three homes, but I have nothing and no one to spend my money on. Please let me do this for Emma."

"I can't."

"But there may be a limited window of time for her before it's no longer possible."

Maggie slipped off Tabasco and draped his reins over her shoulder as he followed her. "I appreciate the offer, Ben. I truly do, but I can't."

Ben jumped down and tied Rowdy to the fence as he moved to stand in front of her. "Okay, okay, I get it, but please promise me this. If Rose and her colleagues see hope and there's a time frame for corrective measures, you will at least consider a loan. I could arrange very favorable terms."

Maggie gazed into his kind eyes. "Thank you. I mean that sincerely. I promise to think about it."

CHAPTER 24

Black clouds hung over the valley as the group of twenty-two assembled at the stables. The previous evening, they had been wined and dined by Leonora and Ben Sr. as their handsome guides mingled among them, charming the pants off everyone, especially the six women in the party. As she listened to the banter, Maggie rolled her eyes, glad to be in the background as the group prepared to ride.

"So, honey," a buxom, blonde beauty drawled, batting her eyelashes at Harley. "Looks like rain. Where should I stow my jacket so it's handy?"

Harley flashed his most dazzling come-hither smile. "It's good luck starting a trip in the rain. Don't worry about jackets. We carry ponchos for everyone. If the skies open up, you'll be fully covered."

"Sugar, you can cover me any ole time."

"What d'ya wanta bet that accent is less than five minutes old?" Ben whispered, startling Maggie.

"Well, you'd better watch out for that accent and her friends, too."

"Honey," he drawled, "I'm all growed up. Kin take care of myself with the likes of her."

"Very funny." Would there ever be a day when women were not

throwing themselves at Ben Morgan and his equally gorgeous friend? How did she and Ruthie stand a chance?

"Will you miss me?"

She was afraid to answer truthfully when her heart already ached at the thought of their week's separation. "Not with all the extra work Jeb and I will have to pick up in your absence."

"So, I'm already indispensible? I like that."

"Take care of yourself, cowboy," she whispered, then headed over to help with the pack horses.

Well, that's something. As Ben watched her retreat, he felt the now familiar longing in his loins and his chest. As the group started up the trail, a week seemed like an eternity, and he realized he would miss her more than he had ever missed anyone in his life.

CHAPTER 25

Early Tuesday morning, Maggie dressed Emma, and the two of them headed to Tucson for their nine o'clock appointment at the Heavers Clinic. Ned had offered to go with them, but Maggie suggested he take the day off and hang out with his buddies. After some grumbling, he had acquiesced, understanding that this was a trip Maggie wanted to take alone. They had barely checked in at Reception when Rose appeared and ushered them to her office, passing a full waiting room of young patients and their caregivers.

Almost immediately, Dr. Heavers appeared, and they spent nearly forty-five minutes talking. He informally assessed Emma's mobility and discussed possible next steps. Maggie had sent copies of all Emma's medical records to Rose, and it was clear that he had read them carefully. At the conclusion of the visit, he moved his chair close to Emma's wheelchair and smiled, a kind, genuine smile, as he took her hands in his own.

"If you're willing, young lady, I'd like to do a few tests, take some pictures, and see how your back's doing."

Emma smiled shyly. "Will it hurt?"

"Not if I can help it."

"I can do it."

Tears sprung to Maggie's eyes as her brave four-year-old agreed to yet another agonizing round of poking and prodding. Rose leaned forward and squeezed her hand. Maggie smiled gratefully, accepting the tissue box the other woman held out to her. While she might be a rival for Ben Morgan's affections, Rose Dillon had brought Maggie and Emma to Dr. Heavers and had given them hope for the first time in two years.

She turned to Rose. "Would it be possible for Emma to look at all those great books in the waiting room? She spotted them when we came in."

Her daughter gave her a puzzled look, but before she could speak, Rose stood. "Wonderful idea! Shall we, Emma? I'll show you my favorites!"

When the door closed behind Emma and Rose, Maggie turned to Dr. Heavers. "I am so grateful for your time, but there is an issue of cost. There is no way my insurance or my bank account could ever pay for extensive tests, treatments, and surgeries. I've been trying to save, but at this rate, Emma will be an adult before I have half enough to cover your fees."

Kind eyes gazed at her. Then he reached out and covered her trembling hands with his own.

"My dear Ms. Williams, perhaps Rose didn't explain. This is a research institution. There would be little or no cost to you should Emma receive treatment here. I'm not going to lie to you. I've studied her charts. The damaged area of her spine is very difficult to repair. The success rate is slim, but we have several new techniques and ways to regenerate the tissues that show promise. She's young, and her growing body will actually help us. I'd like to take a closer look. Then we'll talk again. Would that be acceptable to you?"

Tears spilled over as Maggie slumped forward, head in hands. He patted her shoulder while she sobbed and wondered if this was all a dream. Finally she sat up and hiccupped back the tears. "It's been such a terrible two years of surgeries, tests, and hopes raised, then dashed. Promising treatments completely out of our reach because of money. Through all of it, Emma has been such a trooper, never complaining, always smiling. They call her Sunshine at her care facility because she keeps everyone, children and adults, smiling."

"She's a lovely child. You have reason to be proud."

"I am proud, but more than anything, I'm scared. Scared that we'll raise her hopes only to dash them again."

"Then why don't we say we're doing this round of tests to see how she's growing and to decide what kinds of chairs and equipment she'll need soon? Does she even remember when she could walk?"

Maggie shook her head.

"Then, like so many childhood milestones, if it happens, it will seem like a miracle. If it doesn't, perhaps she is accustomed to the life she has? I will have my clinical coordinator schedule the tests, and she'll be in touch. In the meantime, can I answer any other questions for you?"

"I wondered—with what you've looked at with her x-rays and other reports, do you think it would be dangerous for her to ride? I work as a horse trainer at Morgan's Run in Saguaro. Emma adores horses and has been begging me to let her ride."

"It might be fine, but I'd rather take a look at the new test results and see what's going on with her spine before I say yes. Would that be okay?"

Maggie thanked him, and found Emma and Rose sprawled on the waiting room floor reading *Sheila Rae, the Brave.* Rose read expressively as Emma stared wide-eyed and entranced by the story.

Emma looked up and waved. "Hi, Mom. Can we finish the story?"

Maggie nodded and took a seat beside them as Rose finished reading the story animatedly. A few minutes later, she walked them out. After Maggie had settled Emma into her car seat, she closed the door and turned to the other woman, giving her a hug.

"Thank you. I cannot tell you how grateful I am."

"Dr. Heavers is the best. Back east they called him the Miracle Worker. If there's anything that can be done for Emma, he'll find a way to do it."

CHAPTER 26

Jeb leaned against an open paddock door, watching Maggie as she flew around the barn, grabbing tack and hurling instructions to the summer workers mucking out the stalls. "Hey, Boss, who lit a fire under you?"

Since Harley and Ben Morgan departed, Maggie had been a bit on the manic side, but today, she was berserk. The first day of summer pony camp was always hectic, and they were also juggling a bunch of private riding lessons. Four college kids had joined them for the summer months and Jeb watched as the four scurried around, attempting to do her bidding.

Annoyed at his laissez-faire affect, Maggie stopped long enough to glare in her assistant's direction.

"They'll be here any minute! Where are the training straps, for Christ's sake! I told you we needed all of them out here!"

"Whoa, whoa. It's the advanced camp this week, remember? Beginners are next week."

One of the college workers, Jill approached them, pushing a wheelbarrow full of soiled hay. "A couple of cars just pulled in."

Maggie threw up her hands. "Oh, great, and we're not even close to being ready!"

"Thanks, Jill," Jeb said, then turned to face his boss. "I'll go out and meet 'em. Where are we gathering, picnic tables?"

"Fine."

Maggie glanced at Jill, frozen and clearly afraid to make a move. *What is wrong with you, Maggie Williams?* She took a deep breath. The constant worry about Emma's upcoming tests and the ache in her heart at missing Ben were literally driving her crazy.

"Sorry, guys, I've been a bitch on wheels. Jill, why don't you dump that and go out with Jeb? He can take the first group around, and you can direct the others as they arrive, okay?"

Jill nodded and followed Jeb as Maggie headed back to the stalls and directed the others to come out to the meeting area when they completed their mucking out chores.

CHAPTER 27

True to his word, Dr. Heavers's clinician called the day after their initial visit, and Emma's marathon of tests began the following day. At Rose's urging, they had pushed her to the front of the line, a testament to the high esteem with which Dr. Heavers regarded his young protégé. By the time the pack trip straggled in after eight days on the trail, Maggie, Emma, and Ned had made several daylong trips to Tucson and one to Phoenix, to labs, clinics, and special diagnostic centers.

As she and Jeb watched the line of riders wend their way down the pass, Maggie reached into her back pocket and pulled out the message Jeb had taken for her an hour earlier. Dr. Heavers wanted to schedule a few additional tests the next day. He had also requested that they find a time for him to meet with her alone, without Emma.

"You're worried, aren't you?"

"It's hell, if you want to know the truth."

"No matter what, Em's gonna be fine. You believe that, don't you?"

Maggie nodded, patting his forearm. "Thanks, partner. Let's get cracking. These guys are gonna be whipped and probably need help dismounting. Call the others and pull out the steps and crates."

Ben led the group, with Rowdy, spirited as ever, chomping at the bit to get home. Even with his face covered with trail dust, her lover was drop-dead gorgeous, tanned after days on the trail. Maggie's heart fluttered as he caught sight of her and waved.

As Ben caught sight of her , he could see something was wrong. Her lovely face was drawn, her color ashen. His beloved looked as though she'd lost twenty pounds. A moan from behind pulled his attention away. Cassie Breedmore fell forward and nearly slipped from her mount.

"Hey, girl, hold on. Almost there."

Ben dismounted and rushed back in time to catch the petite redhead as she slipped from the saddle and swooned into his arms.

Maggie turned to Jeb. "Better get the jeep. Clearly some of this lot won't be able to walk to the Lodge."

WHEN THE LAST of the group had departed by foot, jeep, or ranch's van, the four college workers cooled down the horses, stored the gear, and sorted the equipment for cleaning or storage. After Cassie's collapse, there had not been a minute even to say hello, but as Maggie packed up to go, Ben stepped into the office.

"Hey, stranger. You okay?"

Before she could stop to think, Maggie crossed the distance between them and threw herself into his strong arms, drinking in his familiar scent, comforted by his heat and nearness.

"Oh, Ben, it's so good to have you back."

"Mmm, that's what I like to hear. Sweetheart, I missed you big time. I am never doin' that again."

In spite of her worry and fatigue, Maggie laughed.

"Oh, yes, you are. There's another group coming in three weeks."

"Well, I'm looking into helicopters, so I can come back midweek and see you." He buried his face in her hair and inhaled her sweet jasmine and citrus scent, so fresh and clean compared to the heavy odor of the perfume favored by Cassie and the other women. Almost every one had propositioned Harley and him at some point during the trip. "Maggie, Maggie, Maggie," he sighed, loving the feel of her soft body against his.

They held each other a long time, no passion, just the tender closeness they both needed. On the trips back and forth from the Lodge, Ben had given Jeb the third degree about Emma's tests. It was clear that accounted for the pain and worry etched on his beloved's face. He said nothing until they were saying good night. After a deep, tender, loving kiss, he cupped her chin, dark blue eyes staring down at her.

"She's going to be fine. Whatever happens, we'll face it together, okay?"

Maggie nodded and held on. She desperately needed his strong arms around her for a few minutes longer. *How have I lived without this amazing man?* As she drank in his warmth and the earthy scent of the trail, she told herself it was time. She must tell Ben Morgan the truth about his daughter. He deserved to know and he deserved to be there, to hear what Dr. Heavers had to say.

CHAPTER 28

Dressed in pale linen slacks, a silk blouse and pearls, Leonora Morgan breezed into the dining room, where she found her eldest polishing off a plate of Carmela's huevos rancheros from the sumptuous brunch the housekeeper prepared for the household each Sunday. The brunch was timed to coincide with the elder Morgans' return from church services, but the entire Morgan's Run community, including all workers and staff, was welcome. Most weeks only a smattering came unless they happened to be working.

Ben Senior followed his wife in, loosened his tie and draped a sport coat over an empty chair near the door.

"Hey, traveler, good to see you!"

As his father clapped a hand on Ben's back, Leonora leaned down and gave him a peck on his cheek. Away the previous day at one of Leonora's Cowbelles charity events, neither had had a chance to greet the returning riders. The host and hostess would, however, preside over tonight's farewell banquet .

"Good trip? Didn't hear from Harley last night, but didn't have any complaints on my voicemail this morning."

Ben strolled up to the sideboard and grabbed a piece of toast and a second cup of coffee.

"Good trip, pretty good weather, except the first day and night.

Just as well you didn't have the banquet last night. Some of them wouldn't have been able to sit."

"Ouch! Newbies?"

"You could say that." Ben grinned, remembering the first two days when Harley had had Cassie Breedmore glued to the back of his saddle. After three hours on the trail, she was sobbing so uncontrollably that it was either put her up with Harley or turn back. She had been too scared even to flirt.

"Next time, if we don't know their riding experience, we'd better plan a route that lets us double back with people who really shouldn't be out there."

As Ruthie came in, his mother brought her plate to sit beside her eldest.

"Were the women interesting?"

"I just told you, they were too scared to flirt, and in their few calm moments, they seemed gaga over Harley, not me." As Ben saw his sister's face fall, he regretted his words and added, "But after a couple of days, they were all too busy moaning and groaning to be interested in romance."

"That's not good," Ben Senior said.

He took a seat at the head of the table, his plate laden with food. Leonora scowled at the overflowing plate but said nothing. His parents thought he was in the dark about his father's heart attack, and Ben resolved to speak with them as soon as possible.

"It was fine. The bigwigs had a great time, and they loved pretending to look after the little women. My guess is, you'll hear good reports tonight."

"What're you doing today?" Ruthie asked. She wore a frayed chenille bathrobe, hair still rumpled with sleep.

"Taking Maggie and Emma to the zoo in Tucson. Wanta come?"

"Would love it, but I have a date."

"With whom?" Her parents and brother spoke in unison, all eyes trained on her.

"Don't look so shocked. There is life outside Morgan's Run, you know."

Leonora raised her coffee cup in toast. "We know that, darling. We just didn't know you did."

Her father smiled and clinked his mug against his wife's. "Who's the lucky fella? Can't have my baby going out with just anyone, you know."

"Well, technically, I haven't met him yet."

"Oh, God, here we go," Ben mumbled. He had a pretty good idea what was coming next.

"Now, don't everybody freak out. I met him online. We've been corresponding for a few weeks. We're meeting for coffee, in, oops, half an hour. Sorry, no time to chat, gotta go. Don't worry, it's a public place. If I'm not back in three hours, you can send out the posse."

"In three hours, you could be in Guatemala."

"Ha, ha. Thanks for you support, big brother." Ruthie whacked his head with her napkin and disappeared before her parents could utter a word.

Ben rose. "She'll be fine. Ruthie's tough."

Leonora sniffed and inclined her cheek to receive her son's kiss. "Hmm, some Sunday brunch this turned out to be."

Five minutes later, as the elder Morgans watched the Rover spin out of the drive, Leonora shook her head.

"Thank goodness I've lined up Daisy Randolph for tomorrow night. We've just got to get him interested in some suitable women."

Her husband leaned over and patted her hand. "Leave him be, Nora. He's in love with her. Ain't nothing you can do about it. Time to get used to it."

"The heir to this ranch and a stable hand? I don't think so!"

"Well, I like her. A lot. She makes him happier than I've ever seen him before. 'Sides, Maggie's a hell of a lot more than a stable hand. It's her choice to stay where she is, remember? She's bright and extremely capable, as you've said yourself many times."

CHAPTER 29

Ben, Emma, and Maggie spent a few hot but fun hours at the Tucson Zoo, actually a zoological park within the larger Reid Park with its ball fields, hiking trails, playgrounds, lake, and even a children's train, which Ben rode four times with Emma. The tiny cars held only two people, so Maggie stayed behind with the wheelchair. Usually when Maggie brought Emma to the zoo, Ned came, too, and they took turns riding the train, but since Ben and Emma were clearly enjoying themselves, she happily waved them off and sat in the shade. She needed the time to think.

When Ben had arrived at her house in shorts and a tee shirt, looking handsome and tanned after his time on the trail, she considered asking Ned to watch Emma for a few minutes so she could tell Ben about his daughter before their day at the zoo, but Emma was jumping out of her skin with excitement, so she delayed again.

After the zoo, they ate at a sandwich shop that Ben loved near the university, then headed home. As he helped Emma from the Rover, her thin arms circled his neck, and she pulled closer and kissed his cheek.

She gave him one of her shy, beautiful smiles. "Thanks, Uncle Ben."

His eyes filled as he gazed down at the brave little girl he loved as much as he did her beautiful mother. His parents had provided him with a home filled with love, but something in Emma's eyes called to him, a familiar feeling and a sense of being truly home for the first time in his life.

"Hey, you two, should I be jealous?"

Maggie bent over to unstrap Emma's car seat. Without a word, Ben grabbed it and walked toward Maggie's car to reinstall it. By the time he finished, Ned was already wheeling Emma into the house.

"See you soon, kiddo."

"Yup, alligator!" she called as the pair disappeared inside.

Maggie watched him, her expression unreadable. In a pale blue sundress that hugged her in all the right places , floppy straw hat, her canvas purse slung over one shoulder, she looked as beautiful as he had ever seen her. Ben longed to take her in his arms for a deep, passionate kiss, but settled instead for a chaste one.

"Thanks. This was a fun day for Emma and me."

"Me, too. I loved every minute. She's such an amazing little girl."

Maggie was startled to see his eyes fill with tears. *He loves her. No matter what happens with you, Ben Morgan is crazy about his daughter.*

"Yes, she is. Ben, I have something to ask."

"Anything."

"Are you busy tonight?"

"What'd you have in mind?"

"I wondered if you'd be able to meet me for a drink, or early dinner? Just the two of us? There's something I need to talk with you about."

"What is it? Are you okay?"

"No. Yes. I mean, things happened. I'd like to tell you about that, but this is something else. Please let's wait for when we can talk alone, okay?"

They agreed on dinner, and he said he would make a reservation at a small inn about ten miles south of town.

CHAPTER 30

Nestled in the foothills, miles from the nearest home or business, Red Mesa Inn was a popular honeymoon spot for those desiring seclusion and privacy. The inn's terrace bistro was one of a handful of five-star restaurants in the southwest. Despite its rating, the food was casual, as was the dress. Ben had booked them a corner table with a spectacular view of the mountains. He wore a blue sports shirt, open at the collar, and dressy jeans that were so sexy Maggie nearly forgot the purpose of the evening. She gasped when she opened the door, so perfect was her lover in every possible way.

Ben whistled, taking in every inch of her strapless summer dress, the neckline providing a delicious peek at her soft, rounded breasts. With a wink at Ned and a wave to Emma, who sat eating pizza with her grandfather, they departed and were now sipping delicious sangria, their dinner orders in. They oohed and aahed at the view, remarked about the weather and engaged in a host of other small talk, all the while staring into each other's eyes, leaving no doubt as to their respective feelings. Finally Maggie set down her glass, her mouth set.

Before she could speak, he said, "You've never looked lovelier."

"My girlfriend Jeanie went shopping with me a month ago and made me buy this dress."

"I love Jeanie."

He smiled as he took her hand, and his chestnut eyes drank in the sight of her.

Swallowing, Maggie cleared her throat. *Here goes nothing.* "Ben, there's something I need to tell you. Something I should have told you a long time ago."

"Uh, oh, you're married?"

She shook her head.

"Secret lover?"

She reached out to take his other hand. "Please, let me say this, okay?"

"Sorry, of course." He leaned forward, eyes riveted on hers.

"You've never asked about Emma's father."

"I figured you'd tell me if you wanted me to know."

"Well, I want you to know. You deserve to know. You deserve to be with your daughter as she goes through the next few weeks. She's crazy about you, and I know it will make things easier for her."

Shock registered in his eyes, and Ben sat back as if she'd struck him. "Are you saying what I think you're saying?" She nodded, frightened by the fire in his eyes, the emotion behind it unreadable. "Why didn't you tell me? Why didn't you get in touch when you knew you were carrying our baby?"

"You were gone. I was in New Jersey. What was I supposed to do? Call you up and say 'Hey, Ben, our one-night drunken roll in the hay has knocked me up?' You left for California without even saying good-bye. That sent a pretty clear message about our one-night stand. Can you honestly tell me you would have rushed to my side if I'd called?"

He stared at her for several minutes, then shook his head, eyes a million miles away. "Hell, Maggie, I don't know what I'd have done, but I still deserved to know."

Their dinners arrived and went largely untouched. Neither could swallow more than a few mouthfuls in the yawning silence. They declined dessert. Ben asked for the check and waved away her offer to split the bill.

When the Rover stopped alongside her house, Maggie turned to him.

"Ben, I'm sorry. I was a scared eighteen-year-old, impregnated by an older guy I barely knew. I needed to figure out what I was going to do without other people swooping in and taking over."

"But I'm not other people, Maggie. I'm Emma's dad, and I've missed four years of her life. Look, I get it. I was an asshole back then. I can see why you did what you did. I just need some time. Absolutely, I want to be at Emma's appointments. I think you know that I'm crazy about her. I'll be there to take you guys Tuesday morning. With apologies for the psychobabble, I need time to process this."

Maggie struggled to hold back tears. Where was the man she loved and trusted? She felt like she was sitting next to a stranger—a cold, unfeeling stranger.

"Will we see you tomorrow?"

"Probably not. I've got to run into Phoenix to take care of some stuff, and my parents have got something tomorrow night. Why don't we say I'll see you Tuesday, okay? Say hi to Emma for me."

He turned away, staring straight ahead.

"I have no right to ask this, but until you think things through, I'd rather not tell people about Emma and you. If that's okay?"

"No problem here. See you Tuesday." Still staring straight ahead, he waited until she got out of the Rover. Then, without another word, he drove off. Stunned, Maggie watched him go, her chest aching and her heart broken into a million little pieces all over again, just as it had five years earlier, and just as it had after the accident. *What a fool I've been, letting myself fall in love with Ben Morgan again.*

CHAPTER 31

Angrier than he'd been in his entire life, Ben raced through town. He wasn't sure if he was angry at Maggie, himself, or the world, but he knew if he spoke to people at that moment, he'd most likely punch out their lights. He stormed into the house, grabbed a bottle of Jack Daniels, and headed for the stables. His mother called from the living room, but he ignored her and slammed the back door behind him.

When Harley found him, he was slumped in the hayloft above the stables, having polished off half the bottle of whiskey. "Never a good idea to drink alone, buddy. Lemme have that." He wrenched the bottle from his friend's grasp and sat down beside him.

Ben leaned back and closed his eyes. "Go away, Harley." "No can do. Did you know your little sister's Internet dating?"

"If that's your only worry, you're a lucky man."

"You're slurring bad, ole buddy. Never could hold your liquor, Morgan. Wanta talk about it?"

"Nope."

"Might help?"

"Doubt it."

"Does it have to do with my trainer?"

"What d'you think?"

"She dump you?"

"Nope."

"So what's the prob?"

"She had my child and is just getting around to telling me about it almost five fucking years later."

"So, she told you about Em, huh?"

"You knew?" Ben sat up, eyes blazing.

"Hold on, hold on. Don't start swinging, you moron. Anyone who takes a long, hard look at Em knows she's a Morgan."

"And no one thought to tell me?"

"No one knew for sure, or even which Morgan. There are a few of you around, you know."

"Is it common knowledge in town?"

"No, it isn't common knowledge anywhere, you dope. Maggie's never breathed a word, but anyone with working eyesight can see it. Have you ever looked at Em's eyes? They're yours, man."

"She should have told me."

"Don't judge her too harshly. She's had a rough time."

"Four years, Harley! Four years of not seeing her sit up, crawl, toddle, walk, cut teeth, start talking, all those times a dad should be there for."

"You seem to know a lot about kids."

"Both my business partners have kids. I've spent many days and many hours around toddlers the past few years. And, in case you've forgotten, I am the oldest Morgan."

Harley smiled, knowing his friend had not exactly been Big Brother Nanny to his siblings.

"Give her a break, man. She went through hell when she came back. This town's ultraconservative, as you well know. Do you think your mom would have welcomed her with open arms? I seriously doubt it. Your family's pretty formidable, buddy, especially to us lowly worker bees."

"Don't give me that lowly bullshit. I know you've got investments and enough socked away to buy Morgan's Run twice over." Harley laughed and took a swig of whiskey, then handed Ben the bottle. "You really do live in a fantasy world, don't you?"

Ben set the bottle down. "You can fool everyone else, Langdon, but you forget, I've seen your portfolio."

"You took an oath of secrecy about that."

"Cool your jets. I'm not going to blow your cover, Mr. Buffett. Just like you won't say a word about Emma. Maggie's asked me not to tell anyone."

"So much for you being able to keep a secret. What's it been, two hours since she told you?"

"You don't count. I've kept your secrets all these years, haven't I?" Ben sighed and leaned back, closing his eyes. The world spun, and he felt bone-tired.

"Give her a break, Morgan. That's all I'm sayin'. She's been through hell, especially after the accident."

Harley's words were lost on his friend, who had passed out. He grabbed a blanket from one of the stalls, threw it over him, then climbed back down, taking the Jack Daniels with him.

CHAPTER 32

Maggie dreaded going to work but dragged herself in Monday morning, just in time to spy Ben's Rover heading out the front gate. He waved but did not slow down, expression grim. She had only a quick glance, but he looked like he hadn't slept in a week.

It was a busy day. They had back-to-back lessons and two training sessions with Carl Delgado and Pearl. Agent and horse had bonded, and Maggie and Jeb agreed that they would be ready to roll by the end of the week. Just in time, too, as two of his fellow agents would be arriving the following week. Initial training of their horses, and Tabasco, had been largely Jeb's responsibility since Harley had been busy with other projects and Maggie and her college kids were running the pony camps.

They had all agreed that the other agents' reaction to Tabasco might be similar to Delgado's so they were training two other mustangs. They planned to introduce Tabasco as a third alternative. Ben Morgan's job seemed to revolve around trips to town and meetings at the Lodge, so they were unlikely to see much of him. The ranch was gearing up for three pack trips over the next two months. Most of that planning now fell on Ben's shoulders.

Following their usual Monday routine, Harley drove in at noon with sandwiches and cold drinks for the crew. The crew was assembled, eating in the shade, the pony campers at the picnic tables across the yard, when Leonora Morgan drove up in one of the golf carts they kept for guests and workers to get around the ranch.

"Hi, everyone! Harley, have you got a minute?" Their boss was dressed in lime-green capris and a floral blouse, her ash-blond hair held back in colorful scarf.

"Sure, Mrs. M." He set down his sandwich and strolled over to the cart.

"I hope Ben told you about dinner tonight. We're expecting you, dear. We have two lovely ladies joining us, so we need you to round out the table."

Harley tipped his hat. "I'll be there. What time?"

"Six-ish is fine. See you then!" With a wave at Maggie and the others, she drove off, leaving a cloud of dust in her wake.

Jeb whistled as Harley sidled back to join them. "She's got your number, Boss."

Maggie rose, face flushed, and tossed her sandwich wrapper into the trash on her way into the barn. "Thanks for lunch, Harley." Another word and she would burst into tears.

A short time later, Harley found her in the office, pretending to do some paperwork. "Mags, you okay?"

"Yes, why wouldn't I be?" She looked away, hoping to hide her tears.

"Oh, I don't know. Maybe 'cause there's trouble in paradise?"

"Stop it, Harley."

"He's a good guy."

"If you say another word in his defense, I will quit right now."

"Well, okay, how about this? Em deserves to have a dad, and you could do a hell of a lot worse than Ben Morgan."

"So much for my asking him not to tell anyone. What a stupid, stupid fool I've been. To trust him, to be taken in by him again!"

"He didn't tell me, Maggie. I've known about Emma since the first time I laid eyes on her. I was there the night of the barbecue, remember? I saw you guys go off, drunk as skunks, already all over each other. And I can count. Nine months later, Em was born. Doesn't take a genius to put two and two together and realize you didn't hook up with some Princeton guy that quickly."

"Then why didn't you say?"

"Not my business. I figured you'd tell me if you wanted to talk about it."

"Does the whole town know?"

"Not that I've ever heard." Harley decided not to mention Ruthie's occasional comments to him over the past several years, or the way Ben Senior looked at Emma.

"So what's tonight all about, anyway? Who's Leonora throwing in front of you and Ben this time?"

"Search me. Probably some sorority sisters she's dredged up from her Cowbelle network."

Maggie groaned.

"Look, the boss lady's dinner is nothing. I've known Ben Morgan since we were in diapers, and I've never seen him talk about a woman like he does you. *Obsessed* is the word that comes to mind, and my friend, the playboy doesn't get obsessed with women. He's crazy in love with you."

"Says you. I don't know that. Not a word since I told him about Emma."

"Give him time. He'll come around."

Jeb poked his head in, gazing from one boss to another. "Hey, Maggie, want me to get the campers started?"

"Thanks, Jeb. I'll be right out. I thought we'd take them on a short trail ride. They're ready, don't you think?"

She brushed by Harley.

CHAPTER 33

Monday evening, Maggie, Emma, and Ned went to Gracie's for dinner. Ned and Emma kept up most of the conversation while Maggie moped, trying to smile at appropriate intervals. All she could think about was Ben, Harley, and the sorority sisters, wining and dining at the big house. Her heart ached with sadness and loss.

Doing a credible imitation of the Queen Mother, Leonora Morgan presided over the dinner table. The party included Ruthie and her new boyfriend, Chas, Ben Senior, Ben, Harley, and their "dates," Joanie Suttell and Sally Skeffington. Joanie and Sally were, indeed, newly recruited Cowbelles. Both held good jobs in Tucson but lived in Saguaro. Their families were part of Leonora's country club set, and both had grown up with their handsome tablemates, albeit admiring them from afar, as they were seven years younger.

All Ben could think about during dinner was Maggie and how much he had missed her. Miracle of miracles, he had a daughter, a sweet, brave child. The realization filled him with awe and profound gratitude to her sexy, gorgeous, infuriating mother. Lost in thought, he was startled by his mother's poke.

"Bennie, Sally is asking you a question!"

"Oh, sorry, what?"

Knowing full well what was on his friend's mind, Harley came to his rescue and made up a story about a difficult problem they had been wrestling with that day. As he prattled on, talking complete gibberish, Sally and Joanie hung on his every word. Gorgeous Ben Morgan might be in La La Land, but his hunky friend was not.

Joanie leaned toward the handsome cowboy, her skin-tight lemon-yellow top revealing a wide swath of cleavage. "Oh, Harley, your work sounds so fascinating. I've been dying to take some riding lessons. Haven't ridden since my pony camp days. Do you and Ben give private lessons?"

Oh, please, Ruthie thought, watching the performance going on at the other end of the table. *Could Harley be any more sickening? Where has Leonora found these airheads?* Sally was pretty, in a preppy, stick-up-your-ass way, her shoulder-length blond hair pulled back in a simple floral headband that matched her summer dress, but Joanie? Could the woman be any more of a floozy with her fake boobs hanging out of a skin-tight V-neck top and white slacks that looked as if they'd been painted onto her long, shapely legs? Joanie's auburn hair was tied carelessly back in a loose chignon, curls framing a heart-shaped face. Her jewelry was clearly high-quality and expensive, but the woman was a slut!

Ruthie turned back to Chas, feigning flirtatious interest she did not feel. He was a nice guy, but dull as dishwater. A CPA from Tucson, with short, dark brown hair, pale-skinned from a life spent indoors hunched over a computer, he looked sickly beside the two cowboys at the table. His photo on the dating site had shown him kayaking, but it was clearly false advertising. He wasn't the outdoorsy type. Ruthie decided that he looked particularly dorky tonight in a green polo shirt and pressed khakis.

Leonora clapped her hands. "Riding lessons, what a wonderful idea! Ben has been looking for projects, and I'm sure Harley could take a break this week and help out. Make them take you out on the trails. They're beautiful right now with the desert in bloom." Not bothering to ask Harley and ignoring her son, who was clearly a million miles away, she asked, "Do you two have a day that works for you?"

Sally and Joanie proposed Thursday, and before Harley could think up an excuse, the boss lady had set up a riding lesson for ten in the morning. He wasn't even sure Ben had heard, but he would tell him later. Between them, they'd figure out an excuse not to take the two Barbie dolls out for a ride.

CHAPTER 34

The next morning, Ben, Ruthie, and their parents were sitting at the breakfast table when Leonora waved a piece of toast in her son's direction.

"Tell us again why you feel you need to take a day out of work to chauffeur Maggie Williams and her daughter to doctors' visits? I'm sure she's used to doing this herself, and I'm certain Harley can use you at the stables, or your poor father could use help with all the bookings coming up."

"Leave him be, honey."

Leonora turned to glare at her husband.

"I'm fine," Ben Senior said, "and the stables have been running just dandy for five years without Ben. Besides, we can't get too used to him being around. Even though I'd give my right arm to have him stay forever, he has a business to run in California."

"Don't be ridiculous. He's not interested in that now that he's home, are you, darling?"

Ruthie watched her brother and cringed. Their mother was doing it again, driving her brother away. If looks could kill, Leonora would be lying flat on the dining room floor. Deciding a change of topic was in order, she said, "That was an interesting dinner last night, wasn't it? Chas was treated to quite a show."

"Really, Ruth, bringing an Internet date to our table! I mean, the boy seemed nice enough, but what were you thinking?"

"Mom, you're forgetting that I'm an Internet date, too. And you should talk, inviting those two airheads Joanie and Sally. If they'd drooled over Harley and Ben any more, they'd have needed bibs."

"Don't be fresh! It's unbecoming."

"Well, I, for one, think my brother and I are more than capable of finding our own dates and certainly don't need help from you, nor do we need your permission."

Ben rose, grabbed his plate and headed to the kitchen. "We should be back midafternoon. If there are things you need, make a list, okay, Dad?"

"Thanks, son."

On his way by, he gave Ruthie's ponytail a flip. "See ya, Shortcake. Thanks for breakfast, Mother."

Leonora stared at the door Ben had closed behind him. "Where's he off to in such a hurry?"

"Leave it be, sugar. I've gotta get cracking." Ben Senior stood and gave his wife a peck on the cheek and Ruthie a kiss on top of her head.

Ruthie followed the two men out of the dining room, leaving Leonora Morgan alone.

CHAPTER 35

When the Rover pulled up, Maggie and Emma were waiting on the front walk, car seat on the ground.

Ben waved at his daughter. "Hey, Emma."

"Hi, Ben!" She was dressed in shorts and a tee shirt, a white teddy bear in her lap.

Maggie nodded and said, "Good morning," allowing Ben to load her daughter into the car seat.

Emma chatted all the way into Tucson, pointing out javelinas, jackrabbits and other sights along the way. The two adults responded with enthusiasm to her but said little to each other.

It was agony to be so near to him, yet feel the yawning chasm that had grown between them. Maggie longed to take his hand, to feel his strength and warmth, to draw comfort from his heated touch.

Ben drove, remaining silent except for the occasional comment to Emma. He was still sorting through complicated feelings about the woman beside him. He loved her—of this he was certain—but with that realization came what he regarded as her betrayal. He no longer trusted his feelings when he was around her. Pale and drawn with worry, she looked lovely. Her intoxicating scent filled the car and her nearness aroused all his senses, even as he waged an inward war with his feelings.

Once they reached the clinic, the atmosphere lightened as both focused their full attention on Emma. Ben insisted upon carrying the child in, proudly holding her as Maggie pushed the wheelchair into Reception. Emma was scheduled for blood work and physical exams with several specialists. Through it all, she remained mostly cheerful, except when they drew blood. As Ben held her still, he feared he might pass out, watching them stick his beloved child. In fact, he turned so green that Maggie stepped in and urged him to look away. After the first blood test, she asked for a damp cloth for his forehead and insisted the second round be conducted while Emma sat in her wheelchair.

At noon, Rose came upon them in the cafeteria grabbing a quick bite.

"Hi, guys. How's it going? You holding up okay, Emma?"

Instantly the child cowered in her mother's arms. After a morning of being poked and prodded, she was enjoying the respite in the busy, colorful cafeteria, surrounded as they were by other families with children of all ages. Rose reached into her pocket and produced a whistle and a small puzzle, which she set down on the table near Emma. Maggie looked up at Rose and smiled, at the same time stroking the child's hair. "Thank you, Rose, for everything. Would you like to join us?"

"Thanks, but I won't disturb your lunch. I've got some paperwork to take care of. Maggie, when you're finished, do you suppose you could stop in to my office? There are a couple of forms they neglected to give you at Reception. It's on the second floor, room 203."

"Of course. Would you like me to come right now? Ben could sit with Emma."

"No, Mommy, I want you!"

"No rush. Take your time. We can wait until the end of the day, if you cannot get away."

Ben watched the interplay between the women and his daughter's obvious distress. "We'll make sure she gets up there. Don't worry."

When Rose had disappeared, Maggie turned to him. "Thank you for coming today. It's been great having another pair of hands."

He smiled warmly as he gazed from mother to daughter. "Wouldn't have missed it for the world. Now, who's ready for some ice cream? They have a soft-serve machine and sprinkles." He reached out his arms and Emma went to him, her thin arms circling his neck as he carried her off. Over his shoulder, he looked back at Maggie, motioning with his head for her to go. "We'll be fine."

Rose was just sitting down when Maggie knocked. "That was quick. Come in, please." She cleared a chair near hers and invited Maggie to sit. "How did the morning go?"

"Pretty good. After all she's been through, Emma doesn't like needles, so the blood work's always challenging. Then there was the near-fainting episode with your school chum."

"Oh, dear, is he okay?" Maggie nodded as they giggled, their laughter easing the tension.

"Maggie, I asked you up here because there is one more piece of information that may potentially be really helpful as we assemble all of Emma's paperwork and test results. You are no doubt aware that her blood type is B?" Maggie nodded. "So, you also know it's quite rare? According to Emma's records, you are O positive, so Emma's dad may have her type, or not."

Maggie shook her head. "I don't understand why this is important."

"Of course, sorry, I should have explained right away. When considering surgical options, we try to type both parents and close family members before making recommendations. In Emma's case, should surgery be recommended and should you choose to go ahead, we would need a good supply of plasma available. Some we can take from her ahead of time, but with a child that young, we cannot take a lot of blood. We need donors."

"What about my dad?"

"It's a possibility. Do you know his type?"

Maggie shook her head. "I don't think it's B. I would have heard that sometime with all his injuries through the years."

"I don't mean to pry, and would never ask if it wasn't critical, but are you still in contact with Emma's biological father?" Maggie hesitated, then nodded. "Would he, do you think, be willing to be tested and give blood?"

"Yes, I'm sure he would."

"Does he live locally?"

Maggie stared at Rose's green eyes, waiting and watchful. "It's Ben, Rose. Ben is Emma's dad." Her companion nodded, making a note. She did not appear at all surprised at the revelation. "You knew?"

"She resembles him in so many ways."

"Yes, she does. We haven't told anyone, and I'd appreciate it if you didn't either."

"Of course not. I would never have asked except we will need him. We will need him acutely if Emma is a candidate for surgery."

They talked a while longer, and Rose handed her a lab order for Ben. They also made an appointment for the following week to review all the tests with Dr. Heavers and the team. As she rose to go, Maggie turned back. "You were in love with him, weren't you?"

Rose smiled, a wistful, sad smile. "All through high school and beyond. But he never paid me much mind. A few casual dates here and there, but Ben was a real ladies' man."

"I remember well, watching the big kids' crowd. He was always at the epicenter, wasn't he? One or two admirers hanging on his arms?"

Rose laughed. "He was bad, wasn't he?"

"Still is."

"You guys seem close." "Yes, well, looks can be deceiving."

"Maggie, for what it's worth, I've never seen Ben Morgan look at a woman the way he looks at you."

"Thanks, Rose. I'll see you next week."

WHEN THE ROVER pulled up to the house, they looked back to spy Emma fast asleep. "Poor baby," he said. He unhooked the car seat and lifted the sleeping child out, carrying her into the house.

Ned opened the door as they approached. "Hey, guys, I've got chili."

'Thanks, Ned. Not for me." Ben set Emma's car seat down gently next to the couch as Maggie unfolded the wheelchair. He turned to her. "I gotta get going. See you tomorrow?"

Maggie gave her dad a look, then followed Ben outside and closed the door behind them. "Thank you for taking us, and for taking the blood test."

"She's my daughter, Maggie. What'd you expect?"

"I-I don't know. I just know I'm grateful, that's all."

"And now we wait."

"Yes."

"I'll let you go."

Dark eyes unreadable, he tipped his hat and turned away.

As Maggie watched him walk away, a lump rose in her throat and tears sprung to her eyes. She waited for him to look back, but he drove away, eyes straight ahead.

CHAPTER 36

The week was a blur of activity. As Harley and Ben prepared for another four-day pack trip, Maggie and Jeb and the college crew ran the pony camp and gave private lessons in between. Harley's attempts to get them out of the private lessons with Joanie and Sally had failed miserably so both he and Ben were tied up for several hours on Thursday and Friday with the adoring ladies.

Friday morning, Maggie and Jeb were headed for the picnic table area, where nine morning campers awaited them. "Just look at them," Jeb said to her as Ben helped Sally into the saddle.

"I'd rather not, and I could also use your help here, if you're finished ogling."

Despite her pronouncement, Maggie had noticed Ben's hands all over the petite, perky Sally, decked out as she was in jodhpurs and what appeared to be brand new boots. *Hands that were all over me, sending me to the moon, only a week ago.*

Except when he checked in to see if she'd heard anything about Emma, Maggie and Ben had barely spoken in days. The following week, he stopped by the house on Wednesday evening to take Emma for ice cream. Maggie declined to accompany them, claiming she had a headache.

Ben treasured his time with his daughter, even as his conflicted heart ached for her mother. Maggie was visibly shaken and no doubt terrified about the prospect of more surgeries and hospitalizations for Emma.

"Come with us, Maggie. "

"Not tonight, thanks." She smiled at Emma and closed the door before he could glimpse the tears in her eyes.

Ben and Emma took their cones to the park near the Daily Scoop and sat side by side in the shade of a mesquite tree, watching a group of children about her age playing on the slide and jungle gym.

"Hey, Peanut. After we finish our cones, how 'bout a slide?"

"I can't."

"Why not?"

"Mommy doesn't let me. 'Sides, I can't climb up."

"What if I helped you, or we go together?" he asked, mentally calculating if he would fit on one of the several sturdy slides that branched octopus-like from the playground structure.

Emma gazed from the slides to Ben, her soft brown eyes studying him. "Okay."

Having observed Emma with ice cream on their previous outings, Ben had brought a bottle of water and wad of napkins. He soaked the napkins and cleaned up her hands and face. After discarding them, he came back to the bench.

"Ready, kiddo?" His heart nearly broke when he saw the terror in her eyes. "Hey, sweetie, we don't have to slide."

Chin jutted, she let go of her white-knuckled hold on the bench and reached her arms up to him. "I want to. Let's go."

Gently he lifted and carried her to the shortest and widest of the four slides. "Let's try this one first, okay?" He climbed the steps and sat down with her on his lap, holding her against his chest. As she wrapped his arms tighter, Ben could feel her heart beating. "Okay, Em, you say go." He craned his head around to see her face and saw that her eyes were shut.

"Okay, ready!"

Her hands gripped his forearms, and off they flew for the first of many slides together. Finally she asked to go alone, with him holding her from the side. They lost track of time as they graduated from the shortest slide to the longest, which Emma insisted upon going down alone on her first try.

As darkness descended, Maggie grew worried and walked the two blocks from the house to the park, assuming that's where they would be. As she approached, she heard Emma's laughter, her delighted cries of "again, again, again" punctuating the evening stillness. They were the only people still in the park, and it was clear as she watched that Ben was having as much fun as her daughter. *This is what I took from him. No wonder he hates me.*

They hadn't noticed her approach, so Maggie leaned against a shade tree and enjoyed this rare glimpse of her daughter at play. Tears rimmed her eyes as she watched them, talking and laughing as he lifted her again and again, carting her from one slide to the next. Since the accident, this was what she had not been able to give Emma —play and the free-spirited abandon every child deserved. *Thank you, Ben Morgan.*

Emma spied her at last and waved. "Hi, Mommy!"

Maggie waved and came to greet them. "Hi, you two. I was beginning to wonder if you'd been carried off by javelinas."

"Look at me!" Emma cried, holding Ben's arm at the top of the tallest slide.

"Wow, such a big girl!"

Maggie watched, heart in her throat as Emma pushed off and flew down the slide into his waiting arms.

They walked home in the dark, Emma on Ben's shoulders, chattering away, Maggie pushing the chair.

"Wait till Grandpa hears! Can we go tomorrow, Ben? I'm gonna tell my friends at school."

Ben set Emma in her wheelchair at the end of their walk. "Hey, sweetie. I have to work tomorrow, but maybe I can come by and we can slide after dinner, if Mom says it's okay?"

They made arrangements to meet the next day at the stables for the drive into Tucson. This time it would be just the two of them. Their appointment with Dr. Heavers and his team was scheduled for 1:30. Ben said good night and headed right out.

CHAPTER 37

Thursday morning Maggie arrived at work just in time to see the cozy foursome, Harley, Ben, Joanie, and Sally, heading out on a trail ride.

Jeb crossed the yard, having helped "the girls" into the saddle. "Hope they have their cell phones. Poor babies."

"They flirted their way into this," Maggie said, "so they deserve whatever happens."

"I wasn't talkin' about Harley and Ben. I'm worried about Tara and Raine. Those two bimbos have no business being within fifty miles of a horse."

In spite of her irritation, Maggie laughed. "I can't disagree with you there. Come on, let's get started. You know I'm only here until noon?"

Jeb nodded and followed her into the barn. His boss wore the same haunted look she had since the day after Emma's tests, worry shining in her sky-blue eyes.

At noon, Maggie changed out of her work clothes, washed up as best she could. She met Ben by the Rover, Joanie and Sally long gone. They had arranged to grab sandwiches along the way. She had no appetite and wasn't sure she could eat anything, but nodded when he suggested a café in Tucson not far from the clinic.

Maggie's buffalo chicken wrap was delicious, and the sweet iced tea she ordered settled her stomach. Ben ordered a large wrap stuffed with avocado, mixed greens, and a colorful variety of vegetables. They ate in silence for several minutes before Maggie put down her sandwich, pushed her plate away, and sipped her tea. Tears rimmed her eyes and she gulped hard, trying to stop them.

He reached across and took her hand. "Hey, Maggie, it's gonna be okay. Whatever they say, we know Emma's perfect just the way she is. Nothing can touch that. We'll get through this together, okay?"

She turned away to gaze out the window, wishing she had come alone. "I think Sally might object to that."

"What are you talking about?"

"How was your ride this morning?"

"Jesus, Maggie, you don't think there's something going on with Sally, do you?"

"We need to go."

She rose and asked the waitress to bring the check and a takeout box. Not waiting for either, Maggie grabbed her iced tea and hurried outside.

Ben threw both their sandwiches into the box, paid the check, and followed her, catching up at the Rover. "Wait a minute! Maggie, hold on."

Before he could stop her, she hopped in and shut the door in his face.

He came around, slipped into his seat, and closed the door. "What's the matter?"

"Please, Ben, start the engine. It's boiling hot and we're going to be late. Let's get this over with and go home. It's clear from your behavior this past week that you've moved on. We share a daughter, whom we both love, but aside from that, I don't have a claim on you. If you and Harley want to behave like lovesick adolescents, that's your business. Let's just focus on Emma and not pretend to be anything more than coworkers and casual acquaintances."

He tried to take her arm, but she pulled away. "You know that's not how I think of you."

"Do I?" Her eyes blazed. "You've barely spoken to me since you found out about Emma, and now you're mooning all over Sally Skeffington. What am I supposed to think?"

"That I'm giving riding lessons to a paying customer. I couldn't very well say no. And as for the rest of it, I told you, I need time. It was only a few days ago I found out I'm a father. I'm crazy about Emma and as worried as you are about what's ahead."

Gazing into his beautiful eyes, Maggie knew what he said was true. He was as terrified as she was. She ached to reach out and fold herself into his arms, to feel the comfort of his strength and warmth.

"Can we just go? I want to talk about this, but not now."

ROSE MET them at Reception and led them back to a conference room, where they found Dr. Heavers and three other doctors who had examined Emma the previous week. Dr. Heavers began, taking them through the results of all Emma's tests. Finally he paused, and his kind eyes regarded Maggie.

"I think your girl has a good chance of walking again, my dear."

Stunned, Maggie and Ben stared at him, waiting as he went on.

"I asked Harry, Miguel, and Claire to be with us because, should you decide to go through with the surgeries, they would be taking part. These spinal cases require a team of surgeons, and you are looking at the best. I cannot give you a guarantee, but her spinal cord looks healthy, and the bone replacement will be minimal. The nerve repair is the tricky part and takes time, a good deal of time. Because her injuries are in several places, we will all be working on Emma simultaneously."

He went on to explain the surgery in detail. As they listened, Maggie held Ben's hand in a death grip.

When the doctor finished, Ben asked, "What are the risks?"

"There are risks, of course, as there are with any surgery. It's a very long operation, at least nine to ten hours, which itself carries risks. It's also very hard on the parents."

Maggie shivered, picturing her precious child on a cold operating table for ten hours.

"Ten hours! She's never gone through anything like that."

"I expect she hasn't. It's a very delicate series of procedures. This is not something we want to rush. I must tell you that while the chances are very slim, because of the neural networks involved and what we must do, there is always the chance that in trying to repair the nerve damage, we may do more harm than good. While the chance is remote, your daughter could come out of this surgery having lost the use of her arms."

Maggie clapped her free hand over her mouth. She shook her head from side to side, her body trembling. "No, no, no."

Ben folded her in his arms and drew her closer.

Claire spoke for the first time. "I know this is a lot to take in. This is something that you, as her parents, have to decide. Take the time you need. I will tell you that Dr. Heavers is the best. We have been very successful with these surgeries the past year. Emma's injuries are extensive, but her bones, tissues, and neural pathways are strong and healthy. She is an ideal candidate for what we do."

Warmed by Ben's nearness, Maggie sat up and stared at the young, slender surgeon in a white lab coat. Her dark brown hair was cropped short, her blue eyes gentle. She looked about twelve years old.

"How long would she be in the hospital?"

"Two to three weeks, maybe less. We have to keep her completely immobilized for the first few days, and that's impossible to do at home. Then there's the physical therapy. We would want to get those routines well established before she leaves. We also need time to train you, her caregivers."

Claire handed them a folder of paperwork. "Why don't you read through this, talk together, and let us know."

Before Ben could assure her and everyone that, if there were any costs, whatsoever, they would be covered, Heavers said, "Remember, my dear, as I told you before, this is a well-supported research hospital. The decision is yours, of course, but cost should not enter into your thinking."

They talked a while longer and then said their good-byes, promising to be in touch soon. There would be a great deal of pre-op preparation ahead for Emma, then many months of intense physical therapy. The latter, of course, depended upon the outcome of the surgery.

They drove back to Saguaro in silence. When Ben pulled next to her clunker at the stables, he turned to her. "Want to talk about it?"

"Not now. I'd like to see her, sleep on it, and talk later, if that's okay?"

He reached across, his hand cupping her chin as he drew nearer. "Maggie, I love you and Emma. I will support whatever you decide." His lips touched hers for a gentle kiss. Then, with a kiss on her forehead, he let her go.

"I'll be in touch," she said softly.

CHAPTER 38

Saturday morning, Maggie was doing laundry, cleaning, and packing a picnic for Emma and her to take to the park when the doorbell rang.

She was stunned to find Ben Senior waiting on her doorstep.

"Mr. Morgan, hello. Is everything alright?"

"May I come in?"

Maggie blushed and stepped aside. "Of course, please come in. I'm doing housework, so I'm afraid the house is in chaos. Dad has Emma in the backyard, splashing in her pool."

"It's you I came to see, my dear."

"Oh? Can I get you something to drink? Water? Iced tea?"

Kind eyes smiled down at her. "Wouldn't say no to a glass of sweet tea." Maggie's hands shook as she poured the tea and brought two glasses in on a tray with a plate of cookies. *What have I done? Is he going to fire me?* She couldn't think why her boss was paying her a visit, something he had certainly never done before.

She settled herself beside him on the long couch. "How can I help you, Mr. Morgan? Is there trouble at the ranch?"

"No, no, all's well. I wanted to talk to you about Emma."

"Excuse me?"

"She's my grandchild, isn't she?"

Maggie's jaw dropped and her mouth went dry. "How did...who did...?"

"No one told me, my dear. Fact is, I hadn't seen Emma since you were pushing her around in her stroller. I'm ashamed I didn't come to see you and her after the accident. But one look at her the other night at dinner and I saw my son. She's remarkably like him in so many ways. Does he know?"

Maggie nodded. "I told him last week, because after talking with Rose Dillon about her clinic, I decided to explore the possibility of more surgery for Emma, surgery that might help her to walk again. As her father, I thought he should know. He went with Emma and me the day she had all the testing, and he came with me to hear the doctors' findings."

"And?"

"They think she has a good chance."

He clapped his hands. "That is wonderful news!"

"I haven't decided yet. There are lots of considerations, and I'm not sure if it's feasible."

"My dear," he said, setting down his tea and reaching out to take her hand. "I am ashamed our family seemed so unapproachable that you couldn't tell us about Emma, but I want you to understand that I will spare no expense if it will help my granddaughter. I want all her bills sent to me."

"Thank you, but that's not necessary, Mr. Morgan. Dr. Heavers has assured me that money should not enter into the decision, and I trust him."

"You are a strong, courageous gal, Maggie Williams, and I will respect whatever you decide. I just wanted you to know that our resources are yours."

"Does Mrs. Morgan feel the same?"

He smiled, taking a long drink before replying. "No, I'm not telling her until you say it's okay. Just know that if and when the time comes, she'll be over the moon at having a granddaughter, especially Ben's daughter. Even though parents aren't supposed to have favorites, he is, and always has been, her favorite child."

"Mommy!" Emma called as Ned wheeled her into the living room.

Ben Senior rose and approached the girl. "Hey, honey, how's the water?"

"A little hot, but grandpa cooled it."

He nodded to his fellow grandparent. "Ned, hello. Good to see you."

Ned Williams shook Ben Morgan's, not entirely successful at hiding his surprise. "Been a while."

"Too long."

They chatted for a few minutes about the price of feed, the Sonoita Rodeo, and how well the mustang program was going before Ben Senior took his leave.

"Thanks for the tea, Maggie. See you around the ranch. Ned, if you ever want to take a ride with an old cowboy, come on out."

When the door shut behind him, Maggie turned and mouthed "he knows" to her father before heading to the kitchen with their empty glasses. "Em, I'll be back to get changed in a minute, and we can go to the park."

Ned kissed Emma's head and followed his daughter to the kitchen. "Son tell him?"

"No, he guessed. As you well know, they look like twins."

"Who has twins?" Emma called from the doorway.

She had forgotten Emma's incredible hearing. "No one, sweetie. They think one of the mares may be having twins." She hated lying to her daughter.

"Oooh, can I go and see them?"

"Of course you can. It may not be twins, though, so don't get too excited."

"I want to take riding lessons. Please, can I?" This was a familiar refrain. Every time Emma asked, Maggie's heart broke all over again.

"Let's see what the doctors say. Maybe in the fall."

CHAPTER 39

Enjoying a leisurely breakfast with his mother, Ben was surprised to find his father gone. "Where's Dad so early?"

His mother shrugged and pushed her breakfast plate aside. "Errands, he says. Probably headed for one of the greasy taco shacks on the edge of town to eat something he's not allowed to."

Ben grabbed a piece of Carmela's corn bread and a bowl of fruit and had just sat down when they heard the doorbell.

Leonora frowned. "Now, who could that be? Carmela! Can you please get the door?"

Ben's jaw dropped as the housekeeper ushered the visitor into the dining room.

She leaned over Ben with air kisses. "Hi, sweetie!

As mother and son stared, the visitor strolled around the table to hug Leonora. "Mrs. Morgan, so good to see you!"

Ben stood up, almost toppling his chair. "Miranda, what on earth are you doing here?"

"Is that any way to greet your fiancée, darling?"

"Have you lost your senses?"

"Okay, fiancée in limbo."

She came around and hugged him, winking at Leonora, whose

mouth hung open wide enough to run a train through. "He's such a gadfly, isn't he?"

"Ms. Carlson, this is a surprise. Ben led us to believe you had broken up?"

"And yet here I am, prepared to do whatever I can to win him back!"

She smiled, gaze flitting from one to the other. Ben had forgotten how lovely his former lover was as her green-blue eyes batted coquettishly. Her ash-blond, shoulder-length hair was stylishly cut. Her silk blouse and black slacks were clearly expensive and chosen to flatter every inch of her too-thin, delicate frame.

"Miranda, we've been through all this."

"Oh, pooh, I'm kidding, sweetheart! I've got a boyfriend now. Just keeping you on your toes. No, I'm here because Chip and David sent me." She referred to his partners, and Ben knew what was coming next. "You are needed back in California, darling. The business cannot run without you."

For all her machinations about alternative matches for Ben, Leonora had never warmed to Miranda. Her sudden appearance had not altered her opinion of the woman. "Will you be staying in town?" she asked, her voice a bit icier than usual.

"No, probably not, unless your son and I suddenly reignite the flame."

"Well, I'll let you talk. I have work to do." Leonora excused herself with a tight smile and patted his shoulder on the way out.

Ben and Miranda chatted about the business for several hours. She had a number of documents for him to sign, and they maintained a focus on business-related subjects, leaving her farcical charade about rekindled romance buried where it belonged. He told her he was still thinking about the future and would communicate with his partners soon. When they had completed their discussion, she said, "Well, I guess I'll head back soon. Take me to lunch first, though, would you? I'd love to see Gracie."

As they drove into town, Miranda chattered away about her social life in Los Angeles and her latest travels. As Ben listened, he vividly recalled why he had decided to move on. They had absolutely nothing in common—not interests, values, or chemistry. As he parked the Rover in front of Gracie's, he prayed for fast service.

Forty-five minutes later they emerged. Miranda's incessant chatter over Greek salads had given him a headache, and he wanted nothing more than to send her on her way. As they stepped into the sunlight, he spied Maggie and Emma headed toward them, ice cream cones in hand.

"Ben, Ben," Emma cried, spying him. "We just got ice cream!"

Maggie's jaw dropped as she caught sight of the striking beauty draped on Ben's arm. The woman was talking nonstop, close to his ear, in the way of intimates. Even as Maggie's temper flared, she noted that Ben did not appear comfortable with their proximity.

"Hey, kiddo!"

He broke away from Miranda and swooped Emma from her chair, ice cream and all. Chocolate ice cream dribbled down his shirt front and over his shoulder.

Maggie stepped forward and extended her hand. "Maggie Williams. This is my daughter, Emma. I work at Morgan's Run."

"Miranda Carlson, Ben's fiancée. I'm an attorney. My firm does work for his company. Came down on behalf of his partners to try to lure him back." She circled around to the unsoiled side of Ben and rubbed his arm. "What an adorable child." As she spoke, she looked ready to bolt should the chocolate dribble in her direction.

Ben extracted himself and stepped away from his companion. "Former fiancée. Miranda brought some documents down for me to sign."

An awkward silence ensued as the three adults looked at one another. Ben sneaked licks of Emma's cone to prevent more damage to his already brown streaked shirt.

Finally Maggie said, "Well, nice to meet you. Emma and I have to get going." She motioned for him to set Emma down, not wanting to mar her tee shirt and shorts further. They were already streaked with sweat, grass, and dirt from their picnic in the park. *What a sight I must be compared to Miss Sophisticate!*

Ben settled Emma back in her chair and stole one more lick. The radiant smile he directed at the child was not lost on Miranda, nor was the longing in his eyes when he gazed at her voluptuous mother.

"Was a real pleasure!" she drawled as she leaned against him. "I always love meeting Ben's hometown friends. Bye, sweetie."

Through gritted teeth, Miranda smiled at Emma, who gave her a chocolaty smile.

Maggie seethed as she pushed Emma towards the clunker. *What a silly fool I've been, trusting him. Why did I ever tell him about Emma or get close enough to let the Morgans learn the truth? Fool, fool, fool!*

As soon as Maggie and Emma disappeared, Miranda withdrew her hand from his arm.

"Nice performance," he grumbled.

"Whatever do you mean, darling?"

He stopped, took a deep breath, and willed his voice to remain calm. She was a business associate, and her firm did good work for them.

"Look, Miranda, I'm not sure what you're playing at, but you and I settled things last month."

"I've missed you, Bennie."

"Well, I've moved on."

"With Elly May Clampett?"

"Be very careful, Miranda. I respect your work and appreciate all you've done for the company, but you and I are over. I've moved on and you should, too. What about your new boyfriend? Would he want you pretending to be my fiancée?"

"Oh, relax, will you, darling? I'm over you, too. Just testing the waters for when you return. Friends?"

"Friends. I'll communicate with Chip and David this week and work out a timeline. In the meantime, just email or fax anything you need a signature on."

As they shook hands, Miranda caught sight of a beat-up blue clunker coming up the street and saw Maggie behind the wheel. Leaning forward, she threw her arms around his neck and kissed him.

Too late, Ben pulled away just after the clunker passed by. "What part of friends don't you understand?"

Miranda smirked and winked, hopping into her car. "Gal's gotta be a little wicked, doesn't she? After all, you broke my heart, cowboy."

Ben turned and walked away, heart in his throat as he contemplated what Maggie had thought seeing Miranda's exhibition. He had a lot to explain and no time to do it. He and Harley were leaving for a five-day pack trip early the following morning. He tried to call her home and cell numbers all afternoon and into the evening, but she did not pick up. Finally, around eight, Ned Williams answered the home phone and said Maggie and Emma were out. Ben knew it was a lie. *Fine, but hell or high water, I will talk to you in the morning, Maggie Williams! I have to make this right. I will not lose you or our daughter.*

CHAPTER 40

Early Sunday morning, the crew was saddling the horses, loading up the pack mules, and running back and forth from the Lodge to the stables to collect guests and food for the trip. To Ben's irritation, Ben Senior had assigned him to group orientation, which meant he was stuck at the Lodge until just before their departure. When all the guests were shuttled away, he hopped in the Rover and raced down to arrive just as Jeb was leading a saddled horse from the barn. Scanning the crowd, he did not see Maggie.

"Hey, Jeb, where's your boss?"

"He's in the office."

"No, Maggie."

"Not working. She had a thing and it's such a small group, Harley told her not to come in."

Ben swore under his breath, heading into the barn to find Harley, who was on the phone. When he hung up, Ben said, "Look, man, I gotta run into town. Be back in half an hour."

"No can do, buddy."

"I'm not asking, I'm telling you."

"She's not home. And if she were, she wouldn't want to see you."

"So she told you?"

"No, but I know you and I know Maggie. We're not blind around here, you know. We've all noticed your cool behavior toward each other."

"What the hell are you talking about?"

"Cool it, buddy. You're as transparent as glass, the pair of you. You've been mooning around like a lovesick puppy, and every time I mention your name to her, she practically bites my head off. Now shake it off, and let's get cracking. The group's getting antsy out there. We've got some real beginners. I need to you be there with them and me. *Comprende?*"

Ben stormed out, grabbed his pack from the Rover, and headed to find Rowdy. *Lovesick puppy, indeed.*

AS THE GROUP made its way along the wide canyon trail, Ben's mind wandered from the two tenderfoots riding beside him to his home in Santa Barbara, the dream home that had represented his future. He had designed every inch of spectacular multilevel home that hugged the cliffs overlooking the ocean. It was assessed at over three million, and he was pretty sure it would sell for much more with its custom design and incredible location. *My home where I was going to live forever, until I met Maggie Williams and my daughter.*

He had to make a decision soon. It wasn't fair to ask Chip and David to keep on covering for him. Would Maggie and Emma want to move with him to California? That might be difficult when he and Maggie were barely speaking. The past weeks had been hell, but now, thanks to Miranda's little performance, Maggie wouldn't even take his phone calls.

A scream behind him brought Ben back to the present, and he turned in time to see a young executive in stiff new boots and stonewashed jeans slide off his horse and land in a bush. It appeared that Tara, his mount, had turned suddenly to nibble grass on the side of the trail and Mr. Oblivious, who was busy shooting photos, had let go of the reins.

Ben hopped down and grabbed hold of Tara.

"Lucky thing it wasn't a cactus."

He extended his hand to help the other man to his feet. Save for a bruised ego, the man was unharmed. Scowling, he brushed himself off and stiffly climbed back up in the saddle.

CHAPTER 41

Three days after Harley and Ben left on the pack trip, Maggie made her decision and phoned Dr. Heavers. Emma's surgery was scheduled for two weeks from Friday, with pre-op the week before. Ben would be returning in two days. She planned to tell him then, or over the weekend. He was Emma's father; he deserved to know, but clearly he was still involved with his California fiancée, even if he claimed she was an ex. Maggie intended to keep him at arm's length. Her heart ached with missing him and his strong, gentle presence, but she threw herself into work. Between lessons, pony camps, and the mustang program, she didn't have a minute of downtime to moon over Ben Morgan, who had broken her heart again.

"Hey, Maggie, nice morning."

Ben Senior stepped into the office and tipped his hat.

Startled, Maggie looked up from her paperwork. "Good morning, Mr. Morgan." She brushed the papers aside and stood up. "What brings you down here?"

"Slow day at the Lodge. Care to take a ride with an old man?"

Maggie hesitated, thinking of her campers, the new Border Patrol agent due that day, and all the private lessons in the afternoon. "Of course, sir, if you're sure you're up to it? It's been a while."

"I expect I can manage, and I know you guys are swamped. I'm too old to go far, so I won't keep you long. Can we also come up with another name for me? 'Sir' definitely doesn't fit, and 'Mr. Morgan' sounds way too stuffy. Could we try 'Ben'?"

Maggie nodded and stepped out to ask Jeb to saddle Royal. Ten minutes later, they headed out along the Red Rock Trail, a shady loop that would have them back in thirty or forty minutes. Maggie rode Tabasco, with Ben Senior at her side on a gentle chestnut morgan.

"I'd forgotten how pretty the valley is on horseback.," he said. "Haven't been in the saddle for over a year."

"Does Ben know about your heart attack?"

"Probably, but not from me, and I don't want to discuss it with him. At least, not yet. Don't want to spook him."

"Excuse me?"

"His mother prays every night that he'll stay around, and I do, too, but it's got to be his decision."

"I think his partners want him back. I met Ms. Carlson."

He chuckled. "Something, isn't she?"

"His fiancée, I understand."

"Only in her mind. Don't you believe a word of it! She's nothing to him, 'cept a member of the company's legal team. She's no more my son's type than those two flibbertigibbets we had for dinner last week."

Maggie laughed and checked Tabasco as he tried to veer off into the brush alongside them. "It's been my observation over the years that your son has a variety of types."

"Ah, darlin', now that's where you're wrong. No woman's ever been his type till you."

"I'm not sure Mrs. Morgan would agree."

"You kiddin'? She sees he's crazy about you, just like I do, and my Nora's scared to death. Not 'cause she doesn't like you, but because she's not in control of the situation. It's been this way his whole life. Probably why he ran outta town like a scared jackrabbit five years ago. He loves you, honey, and he's finally found his type—you."

"I'm not sure I can keep up."

"He loves you, honey. I can see it in his eyes whenever he looks at you. He's been mooning around the past few weeks, spreading gloom and misery wherever he goes."

Tears sprang to her eyes, and Maggie turned away, unsure what to say.

"Have you decided about Emma's medical situation?"

She nodded. "The surgery's scheduled for two weeks from tomorrow but please don't say anything to Ben. I'd like to tell him myself."

"That's the spirit! Now, let me confess the real reason I came down this morning. Saturday night is Ruthie's and my birthday party. Everyone thinks it's a secret, but I wriggled it out of Carmela. Just family, the whole gang, if I'm not mistaken. I know he's gonna ask you and Emma to come."

"But I'm not family, and it might be awkward."

"Ah, honey, but whether you like it or not, you are. It would mean a lot to an old man to have his granddaughter and her mom there. I may not be around forever, and I'd like all of us to be together. Please say you'll come. Ned, too, if he'd like."

"For you, Ruthie and Emma...if he asks, we will come."

As they came in sight of the east corral, they spied campers riding willy-nilly, horses loose and pawing the ground, and three of the college kids running from one side of the corral to the other.

"Oh, boy, I'll leave you to it, my dear. See you Saturday, if not before. I'll take care of Royal. Give two old friends a chance to visit."

As Ben Senior headed for the barn, Maggie jumped off Tabasco, her eyes scanning the yard for Jeb.

CHAPTER 42

Maggie stood in the shade of the barn talking with Steve Wheeler, the Border Patrol agent. Wheeler had arrived the day before and was staying in one of the ranch cabins that bordered the farm's strawberry fields. They each held a cold Dos Equis. Maggie rarely drank more than a glass of wine and never at work, but with the temperature still over 100 at five o'clock, it seemed like a good idea. They had pinched the beers from the coolers awaiting the return of the pack trip.

Wheeler caught sight of them about a mile out, a cloud of dust marking the group's passage, then turned to her. Bub, the palomino stallion they were training for him, had thrown the short, wiry agent four times over the last few days.

"I dunno, Maggie. I like a feisty mount as much as the next guy, but Bub's a handful." "Give him time."

She studied Wheeler more closely, mostly as a way to distract her attention from the approaching caravan. He was about her age, with skin the color of dark leather from years in the desert sun. His wavy black hair curled at his collar, and he sized her up with coal-black bedroom eyes, just as she did him.

"Bub hasn't been with us long. In fact, we told Nogales to hold off sending you for a week or two."

"And yet, here I am. You doing anything for dinner? Wanta grab something in town?"

"Thanks, but after this lot gets taken care of, I've got to head home to my daughter."

"Oh, you married?"

"No. Listen, I'd better get out there and help them."

Wheeler followed her around the barn, where they spied the first riders making their way along the edge of the west corral. An all-male group, they were five executives from a tech company based in Seattle. Except for one, this was their third time at the ranch, so they knew the ropes.

As Maggie and Wheeler strolled toward them, beers in hand, Ben caught sight of the handsome young stranger and frowned.

Let's see how he likes it. Maggie set down her beer and helped the first rider from his horse. As they unloaded, the crew led the horses into their stalls, and Harley and Ben distributed beers and sodas.

As Ben headed to the Rover to shuttle two of the riders to the Lodge, Maggie caught up with him.

"How was it?"

He shrugged. "Pretty good group. Glad to be back. How are you?"

"Fine. Busy."

"Who's the cowboy?"

"Steve Wheeler He's the agent training on Bub."

"Good luck with that one."

Ben couldn't remember when the sight of a woman had stopped him in his tracks like Maggie Williams. In faded, dusty jeans, scuffed boots, and an old Morgan's Run tee shirt, she literally took his breath away. The faded blue shirt hugged her breasts, and he found himself growing hard. *Whoa boy!*

"You better go up to the Lodge and get a baggier replacement for that tee shirt. Don't get me wrong, doesn't bother me in the slightest, but don't let Leonora see it or she'll throw a fit."

"Ben, are you coming back here tonight?"

"Wasn't planning on it. I need a shower bad. Why?"

"I wanted to talk to you, that's all."

"Oh, that reminds me. I have something to ask you, too. Lemme get these guys up to their Jacuzzis and I'll pop back in five minutes, okay?"

Maggie packed her things and locked up the office, then strolled through the stables and stopped at Tabasco's stall.

"Hey, boy."

She scratched the massive head and whispered, "Don't worry. Somehow, I'm going to find a way to keep you."

A thick layer of fresh hay ran the length of the barn, kicked out of stalls as the horses had been put up for the night. The hay muffled Ben's footsteps, and he startled her.

"Attached to him, huh?"

"He needs someone to love him."

"So why not you?"

"As you well know, I can't afford him. Your father's put a fortune into him, and he'll be headed south as soon as we find a rider who's not scared to death of him."

"You know that if Dad knew how you felt, he would—"

She raised her hand. "Stop right there."

"Well, you could at least find out what he's willing to take for the big lug. If the horse is so unpopular with the agents, he's probably worth shit."

"Maybe. We'll see. What did you want to talk to me about?"

"You first." He leaned against the stall door, studying her. She had changed into a clean shirt and her hair was down, falling over her shoulders to frame the delicate oval face.

Maggie swallowed hard. "I've decided to...well...Emma and I decided to go ahead with the surgery."

"When?"

"Two weeks from yesterday. Pre-op next Friday."

"Are you sure? No worries? Second thoughts?"

"I'm scared to death."

"How about Emma?"

"Can't wait. I mean, she's not too thrilled about being knocked out all day, but she wants to be like other kids." Her eyes filled with tears, and suddenly it didn't matter that they were barely speaking or that he seemed to have a woman around every corner. She needed his arms around her. She reached out, and Ben did not disappoint her.

"Oh, sweetheart." He swept her into his arms, and her nearness knocked the breath from his lungs. "I'll be with you and Emma every step of the way. We'll do this together, I promise."

Cupping her chin, he captured her mouth in a deep, lingering kiss, his tongue seeking hers, delving deeper and deeper as hers twined round, meeting him. Already hard, he reached down, drawing her legs up, wrapping them around his waist. "God, Maggie, I've missed you."

Her arms circled his neck, and she held on for dear life. She clung to him, not wanting to let go. They broke their kiss, and she buried her face in his neck and closed her eyes. *Home.* As kisses trailed down her neck, one hand cupping her breast, twirling and tweaking the nipple until it was hard, she felt herself cresting and cried out, "No! I can't do this. We can't do this."

She unlaced her legs and pushed away, easing herself to the stable floor.

"Why not? What's wrong?"

"Everything. You, your Ms. Carlson, California, your mom, the women who seem to follow you everywhere."

"I want to be with you. You and Emma mean everything to me."

"What about California? Are you going back?"

"I'm figuring all that out now. It'll be settled soon, I promise."

"Well, till then, I think it's best if we keep a little distance. You said you had something to tell me?"

"Oh, yeah, Dad and Ruthie's party. I meant to say something before we left on the trip, and could never reach you. It's tomorrow night. I'd really like you and Emma to be there."

"Okay, what time?"

"Okay? Just like that, okay?"

She shrugged. "What time?"

"I'll pick you up at six?"

"That would be fine. I've gotta get home. Emma'll be excited. See you tomorrow."

"Great."

He walked her to the car, still puzzled at her behavior. He'd been poised to activate all his powers of persuasion and hadn't needed a one of them. *What is Maggie Williams up to?*

CHAPTER 43

As Ben pulled the Rover into the drive at the big house, Maggie turned to him. "Am I dressed okay?"

"You look great." Understatement of the century. In a pale rose floral sarong that hugged every luscious curve, she took his breath away.

She had dressed Emma in a pink flippy skirt, frilly white blouse, and new white sandals, and the child looked adorable, as always.

"Here we go, kiddo. You ready?"

Ben lifted her out, and Maggie followed with the wheelchair and a bag holding their small gifts for Ruthie and her father. As they neared the door, it burst open and Robbie Morgan stepped out, grinning from ear to ear, the Morgan smile that made women go weak at the knees.

"Well, if it isn't the long lost brother, home to roost! Hey, Maggie, hey Emma, long time no see."

"Long lost brother, my you-know-what," Ben said, not wanting to swear in front of Emma. He grabbed Robbie in a bear hug.

"All here tonight, bro, so get ready for some serious razzing."

Not quite as tall as his brother, Robbie had the sandy hair and light complexion of his mother, but he certainly had the Morgan men's jaw and rugged good looks.

Remembering her huge high school crush on Robbie Morgan, Maggie blushed as he stepped forward to hug her.

"Hey, Maggie, great to see you."

"You, too, Robbie."

Ben regarded his brother turning on the charm, as usual. "Sara with you tonight?"

"Broke up, long story. Later, over beers when there aren't two gorgeous ladies present."

"Sorry to hear it. Thought Sara was a keeper."

"I'm stayin' around a couple of days. We'll catch up."

Leonora stepped onto the front porch and clapped her hands. "Let's go, you guys. Everyone's out on the back terrace. Hello, Maggie dear. You and Emma come with me!"

Still holding Emma, Ben headed toward the walkway that circled the house. "We'll go round back this way."

"Here, let me take that." Robbie grabbed Emma's chair from Maggie and motioned for her to go ahead.

Family to Maggie was the loving but taciturn Ned—who had had other plans tonight—and quiet, fleeting memories of a mother long gone. Thus, the crowd that awaited them on the terrace felt like millions.

"Hello!" Beth hugged Ben first, then her, pointing to Bill, her tall, lanky boyfriend. "He's manning the blender." She smiled at Maggie. "He makes a mean margarita. Would you like one?"

"Hey, brother. Hey, Maggie." Kyle, a shorter version of his older brother, same brown eyes, dark hair, strong sinewy build, gave each of them a bear hug before turning to Emma. "Hey, sweetheart. We need to get you a Shirley Temple."

Sam Morgan approached with a striking redhead draped on his arm. She wore a peasant blouse, a full skirt, and stiletto heels. "Good to see you, bro. You, too, Maggie. This is Rita."

Same dark features as Ben and Kyle, Sam was slender, with the body of the long-distance runner he was.

Rita wrapped her arms around Ben's neck, air kisses beside each cheek. "So good to finally meet you. Hi, Molly."

"It's Maggie," Ben said. "Nice to meet you."

He extracted himself from the other woman's arms to give his brother a bear hug. "Samuel, how goes the world of multimillion-dollar house design?"

Since grad school, a number of publications had pegged Sam Morgan as someone to watch. Several prestigious architectural journals had featured his spectacular home designs, and his creative, innovative work had really put his small firm on the map.

Before Sam could respond, Ruthie approached and flung her arms around her brother, winking at Maggie and Emma. "Hey, what about the birthday girl? You guys remember Chas?"

Her date stepped forward to shake their hands. Chas's dazed expression mirrored Maggie's own, and she smiled warmly at him. "Nice to see you again. Happy birthday, Ruthie! What fun to have your birthday the same day as your dad's."

Kyle poked his sister. "Some birthday present, huh? Maggie, what can I get you to drink?

She asked for a margarita and accepted a slice of quesadilla from Carmela, who passed an assorted tray of appetizers.

Across the terrace, Raoul manned the grill, while Ben Senior and Harley supervised. Each held a Dos Equis. Between suggestions to Raoul, the two men gazed out at the mountains, clearly enjoying each other's company and the beautiful, clear night.

"You're here, finally." Leonora air-kissed Maggie and hugged Ben. "Have you said happy birthday to your father?"

"You mean aside from at breakfast, and several times during the day?"

She swatted him playfully. "Don't be fresh. Maggie, how are you? Is someone getting you a drink?"

"Yes, thank you. What a lovely night for the party. Thank you for including Emma and me."

"Our pleasure." She leaned toward Maggie, eying Emma across the terrace, now chatting with Rita. "Ben tells us you've got a difficult road ahead with more surgery."

Maggie nodded, surprised at Leonora's cordial manner. She held up her bag. "Where would you like gifts?"

"Carmela will take them. Thank you, dear. Ben was supposed to specify no gifts!" Leonora grabbed Carmela's arm as she passed by and handed off the bag.

CHAPTER 44

Fueled by Bill's strong, delicious margaritas, the party livened up as they moved to the long rough-hewn table set up for the entire assembly on the grass below the terrace. Citronella torches surrounded them, more for light than to repel mosquitoes since Morgan's Run had invested heavily in mosquito traps. The traps plus a large population of brown bats kept the mosquitoes at bay. Platters of food covered the center of the long table. Raoul had grilled chicken, steak, corn on the cob, and an assortment of vegetables on the three-tiered brick stove. These were accompanied by his wife's rice, salads, polenta, and crusty breads.

Maggie had never seen so much food. Her daughter's eyes reflected her own amazement as dish after dish was passed. Emma sat between her mother and Ben, Kyle across from them making faces throughout the meal. Several times, Maggie caught Ben Senior gazing at them, a sad wistfulness in his eyes. Emma would like to have another grandfather, she mused, wondering if there would come a time when she could explain things to her.

"You're an angel, Carmela, thank you," Ben said as the cook placed a small platter of perfectly grilled portabella caps near his plate.

"Still a grass eater, I see," Kyle said as he forked a thick steak from the platter.

"Leave him be, son. Birthday boy's rules, even if he's snubbing Dillon's Certified Angus Beef." Ben Senior surveyed the table, eyes moving from one offspring to another. "This is the best kind of night with everyone here. Happy birthday to my baby girl." He raised his goblet of red wine and toasted Ruthie.

"Back at you, Daddy!" Ruthie blew her father a kiss and winked at Emma. Her pale blue eyes scanned the table and rested wistfully on Harley, who was listening to Bill Sampson's tale of a recent hiking trip.

As Carmela served fresh berry crumble, Rita turned to Maggie. "So, how did you and Ben meet? Sam never tells me any family gossip."

"Well, we both grew up here ,so we've known each other all our lives, or at least who the other was." *Or, I knew who he was.* "I was in Kyle's class, so a bit younger. We've just gotten reacquainted."

"Oh, I thought..." Rita leaned closer and whispered in her ear. "I mean, I thought you were Emma's parents. She bears an amazing resemblance to the Morgans, doesn't she?"

"What are you two whispering about?" Kyle said, comically cocking one ear as he leaned across the table.

"Kyle, for heaven's sake, be careful!" Leonora said. "You're about to set your shirt on fire with that lantern."

In tandem, Harley and Ben rose to get beers. "What in the hell does she see in Casper Milquetoast, do you think?" Harley said, eying Chas and Ruthie.

Ben shrugged. "No telling in matters of the heart. If you'd tell her how you feel, we wouldn't be talkin' about Chas or anyone else."

"Yeah, and your parents would be thrilled with that, wouldn't they?"

"My parents have nothing to do with it. Besides, she's here with a friggin' Internet date tonight, so I'd say they've lowered their standards a tad, wouldn't you?"

"Thanks a lot, buddy."

Ben watched as Maggie chatted with his father and Bill Sampson, thinking how natural it felt to have her here as part of the family. She was what he had been missing his entire life, especially the past five years. Their one-night stand had left an indelible impression he hadn't been able to shake even after starting two successful businesses, building a dream house, and courting a succession of beautiful, accomplished women. She not only was gorgeous and sexy but also had an inner beauty that shone through no matter what she wore, no matter whom she was with, no matter what she was doing.

"It's my dream to go back to U of A," she said to Bill. "I loved science and wanted to major in biology."

"Still can," he said. "Courses go day and night, and there are a ton of online courses now. For the sciences, you'd still need to come in for labs, but they make it pretty doable for working people."

"Maybe someday. Emma's still young. I wouldn't want to work all day, then drive into Tucson or have to study all night. I'd never see her."

Ben Senior watched, thinking how much he'd like to offer to pay for her schooling and living expenses, but knowing his son's proud, beautiful lady friend would never accept such an offer.

"You're one of the horse trainers, right?"

She nodded. "I also give lessons, run the pony camps, and help with whatever Harley needs around the stables."

"What's your dream? I mean, if you could do anything with or without a degree?"

Maggie stared at him, surprised at his question and unsure of what to say. "Well—"

"Come on, you must have a dream. Why did you want to study biology?"

"I was good at it, and I thought I might want to go on to vet school, but now I'm not so sure. My dream, if I had all the money in the world, would be to have a summer and vacation camp where disabled kids could come to learn to ride, take care of the horses, live in cabins or bunkrooms. A place where they could have a chance to be regular kids."

"You thinking about Emma?"

"Yes, and so many more children like her."

"What if her operation is successful?" Noticing her surprise, he added, "My dad told us about it before you arrived. We're all rooting for her."

"Thank you." She spoke softly, not that it mattered. Emma was paying no attention, she was so completely entranced by Kyle's antics. "Yes, even if her surgery is successful, there are still so many children out there with no hope of ever walking."

"Of course."

After dessert, Leonora herded everyone into the house to open presents. Ben carried Emma, Kyle brought her chair, and Ben Senior escorted Maggie.

"I'm so glad you and Emma could be with us tonight, my dear. It means the world to this old man."

She smiled, gazing up at the rugged, handsome man, his profile reflected in that of each of his offspring. "You are hardly old, Mr. Morgan. It's been a lovely party, and as you can see, Emma is thoroughly enjoying herself."

With her doting uncles, he thought. "She's a sweetheart. You've done such a marvelous job of raising her. Now, let's go in and see what newfangled gadgets and doodahs my family's gotten me this year."

WHEN THEY PARKED in front of her house, Maggie looked back to find Emma asleep in her car seat. Gently Ben unbuckled her and carried her in while Maggie unstrapped the car seat and unloaded her chair. "Just put her on the couch," she whispered, opening the door for him. "Dad's out, but I'll take care of her in a sec."

He set the still sleeping child on the couch, then turned to Maggie. "Thanks for coming tonight. It meant a lot to Dad."

"Thanks for asking us. It was fun. We're not used to large families. You have quite a crew."

"Overwhelming, huh?"

"No, you're lucky."

"Only when I'm holding you in my arms." He moved closer and lifted her so that her soft chest pressed against his. His loins stirred instantly at her nearness. "I don't know how this is gonna play out, Maggie, but I do know that I don't want to lose you or Emma. I have to go to Santa Barbara for a couple of days, but when I get back, I would really like it if we could get together and try to figure things out."

"There's nothing to figure out. Your life is out there; mine is here."

"It doesn't have to be."

Maggie shook her head. "Ben, I can't talk about this now. With everything that's ahead for Emma, I really can't think about us. I'm sorry, but she comes first right now."

"She will always come first." He set her down slowly, his arousal sending shivers through her body. "I would never expect to come before Emma. Ever. Can I at least have a good-bye kiss?"

She nodded and his hand cupped her chin, drawing her close for a searing, soul-stirring kiss. "I love you, Maggie," he whispered, then let her go.

I love you, too. But all she said was, "Good night," before closing the door behind him.

CHAPTER 45

Monday morning, Ben left for Santa Barbara. Maggie wondered if he would stop at the stables to say good-bye, so when Harley told her he was gone, her heart ached with loneliness and hurt. She shook herself and strode out of the office, calling to Jeb and the crew. *Maybe a few days apart is the best thing right now.*

The week passed quickly in a flurry of work. Friday morning came and Ben had not returned. *So much for being with us every step of the way.* A tear snaked down Maggie's cheek as she packed things up for the day in Tucson for Emma's pre-op appointments.

"Mom, what's wrong?" Emma pushed her wheelchair closer to stare at her mother, her dark brown eyes registering alarm.

"Nothing, sweetie. Just wishing I could do all this in your place."

"Will it hurt?"

"Remember what Rose and Dr. Heavers said? You'll just go to sleep and won't feel anything."

"But today? Will today hurt?"

"Well," she began, not wanting to lie to Emma. "They will take a little blood, but except for that, there shouldn't be anything that hurts. And you're so brave. It's gonna be fine."

"Where's Ben? I thought he was coming with us?"

She patted Emma's head. "He got tied up in California. He's thinking about you, though."

"Do you love him?"

"I love you."

She bent to kiss the top of Emma's head, breathing in the sweet scent of her baby's curls.

"I love Ben. I wish he was my daddy."

"He's a nice man."

"I wish he was here."

I do, too. "Well, Sweet Pea, I'm 'fraid you're stuck with me. You ready?"

Ned helped them into the car. "Not too late. I can come along if you like."

"Thanks, Dad. We'll be fine."

As she walked around the car, he patted her shoulder. "He'll be back, Mags. Just give it time."

She hugged him. "See you around three."

THE DRIVE to the Heavers Clinic took them into the heart of Tucson, but they arrived with plenty of time. Emma's pre-op appointments would take most of the day, with a short break for lunch. The most important one was with the anesthesiologist. During one of her previous surgeries, they had almost lost Emma to an adverse reaction to anesthesia. From then on, Maggie came armed with all her records so there would be no mistakes there, at least. As she pulled her backpack from the car, she suddenly regretted not bringing her dad. Her hands shook as she grabbed hold of Emma's chair.

"Okay, Sweet Pea, here we go!"

As they rounded the car, she was still adjusting her backpack and was startled by Emma's cry.

"Ben! Hi, Ben! I told Mom you were coming!"

Maggie paused, unsure of whether to laugh, cry, or dissolve into a puddle on the sizzling pavement. She had never been so happy to see anyone in her life. The sight of her beloved with a day-old beard, rumpled clothes, and a pack slung over his shoulder brought tears to her eyes. He gave her a soft, tired smile before turning his full attention to Emma.

"Hey, big girl, I missed you!" He swept her out of the chair for a bear hug, careful to bring her limp legs along with the rest of her. Maggie realized watching them that he had done this from the first time he'd picked her up.

Ben stepped around the chair and gave Maggie a quick hug. "How are you doing?"

"She's nervous," Emma said, always with wisdom and vocabulary beyond her years. "I've been trying to cheer her up."

Maggie leaned against him and drew strength and comfort from his solid presence. His warmth and his familiar scent of musk and the outdoors were like a balm to her frayed nerves.

"I'm glad you're here," she whispered as her arm circled his waist. For a short time, she rested her cheek on his chest.

"Me, too. Sorry about my appearance. Drove all night. Wanted to be here on time. I've been waiting till you arrived to go in. As soon as there's a free minute, I'll pop into a men's room and clean up."

She looked up and gave him a wan smile, then drew his face to hers for a soft, fleeting kiss. "Thank you for coming. And we couldn't care less how you're dressed."

His lips grazed her forehead, then the top of Emma's curls. "Ladies, shall we go in?"

CHAPTER 46

Maggie, Emma, and Ben emerged from the clinic late in the afternoon. After six hours in air conditioning, they were momentarily stunned by the intense heat. Ben carried Emma, and Maggie followed with the wheelchair. The child chattered away, waving her fourth lollipop of the day.

He strapped Emma into her car seat and gave her a kiss. "Good job today, Peanut. You were a brave girl."

Maggie closed the back hatch as he came to meet her. "Maggie, I didn't want to ask in Emma's hearing, but I wondered if you two would like to go on a picnic with me tonight? I can ask Carmela to make us up something."

"I don't know. It's been a long day."

"Then tomorrow? I could pick you up around four. I know a good spot." He took her hand, his touch sending warmth and electricity through her. "Please, Maggie. I've missed you both."

"Tomorrow would be fine. Thanks." Before she knew what was happening, his arms enfolded her, the scent of spicy aftershave and soap such a comfort as she returned the embrace. In the middle of a steaming hot parking lot in downtown Tucson, they shared a deep, unexpected kiss. Ben Morgan's arms around her always felt like home, even during their one-night stand years ago. Tears stung her eyes as she stepped back and turned away. "See you tomorrow."

"Maggie—"

"Hey, sweetie," she said, hopping into the car. "Ben's taking us on a picnic tomorrow. Would you like that?"

"Yeah!" Emma clapped her hands.

Ben opened the back door. "See you later, alligator."

"After while croc-dile!"

He watched the clunker pull out of the lot before heading to the Rover. It had been a long, difficult week, but he knew he had made the right decision.

He stopped at Gracie's for a quick dinner with Harley. No one was a better sounding board than his oldest friend. This evening was no exception. His buddy listened to all his plans with nary a word, except to say "'Bout time," when he finished. They said good night, with Harley sworn to secrecy, and Ben headed back to the ranch. As he stepped into the house, he was surprised to find all of his siblings in the living room with Leonora.

CHAPTER 47

Ben's eyes scanned the living room as he accepted the beer Kyle offered.

"What gives? The whole gang's here again so soon?"

"Your father's gone to bed," his mother said, waving him into a chair.

Kyle sat beside Sam and Ruthie on one of the room's three soft tanned leather sofas. "Yup, bro, the original seven, minus Dad, of course."

Ben looked from them to Beth and Robbie, seated opposite to the others on a matching sofa, and took a seat alone on the third. "So, is this a family conference?"

"Sort of," Beth said, quietly.

"We've been talking about your father, dear." Leonora's face, always youthful and smooth, tonight showed every one of her years, her eyes etched with sadness and fatigue. "He hasn't wanted any of you to know, but I think it's time. You all know about Dad's heart attack, but what we didn't tell you was his long-term diagnosis of congestive heart failure. His condition and the damage to his heart are not something they can repair with more stents, valve replacements, pacemakers, or any of the high-tech cardiac interventions they have now. His only option would be a heart transplant, and he refuses to consider it."

"Well, we'll have to convince him," Ben said, looking from one sibling to the other.

"Not that easy, brother," Sam said, looking at their mother.

"I was telling them before you came, dear. Dad's a poor candidate for a transplant for many reasons. It would be a very risky procedure with a poor long-term prognosis, which is one of the reasons he's so opposed to it."

"Have you gotten the top cardiologists involved? I can make some calls and we can take him back east, to New York, Boston, Baltimore?"

"We've been everywhere, Bennie. The answers are the same. Your dad's heart is dying, period, and his circulatory system with it. Right now he still feels good. In fact, great, most of the time. We just have to guard against his getting overtired."

"What can we do?" Sam asked. "How can we help?"

"Dad still has lots of life left in him, and we'd like to travel. Probably cruises and trips where he can rest when need be. We're already planning two river cruises through Europe."

"That's great, Mom. Go for it. We can manage here," Ruthie said, looking at Beth.

"We know you girls can manage the farm. Raoul and his men run the livestock operation now, and Harley and Maggie do a wonderful job running the stables. It's the rest, my darlings. The Lodge, the overall running of the ranch, the day-to-day coordination. Your father has not been able to let go. I've been after him for years, even before his heart attack, to hire a manager, but he's stubborn. Doesn't want to relinquish control to anyone. I've tried to help out quietly behind the scenes, but you can imagine how well that works. Your father always finds out."

"What about me?" Ben's asked, his tone grave.

Leonora gazed at her eldest for several minutes, her eyes sad. "That's a wonderful gesture, darling, but we couldn't ask that of you. I know, I know, I'm always begging you to stay home, but we're proud of you and happy that you've been so successful. Your place is in

California, running *your* company, living in your lovely new home, enjoying the life you've created for yourself. "

All of them knew the effort it had taken their mother to say those words. No one spoke as, mouths agape, they gazed at each other.

"I've sold my share of the company to David and Chip," Ben said. "I'm still an investor, but I'm no longer part of the day-to-day operations. And I put the house on the market last Tuesday. The realtor assures me it will sell quickly."

Rarely had any of them seen their mother so surprised. "But why?"

"My home is here. Dad and I already had a hypothetical discussion about this. It's what I want to do."

"It's because of the Williams girl, isn't it?"

"Emma and Maggie are part of the reason, yes. I love them both and want to be near them, but I'd be doing this even if they weren't in the picture. This is where I belong. Of course, if Sam, Robbie, or Kyle wants in, we can work together."

His brothers remained silent, their answers clear. All had established careers away from Morgan's Run. The ranch was not in their blood in the way it was in Beth's, Ruthie's, and Ben's.

"Are you sure, Bennie?"

He nodded. "I'd like to buy the old farmhouse from the ranch. I intend to renovate it and live there, if everyone agrees?" He referred to the homestead at the ranch's south end. It was practically falling down, but the location was spectacular, perched on a hillside overlooking a beautiful green valley, with a stream and a small pond nearby. The original rancher's home, it had been abandoned once their grandparents built the Lodge and Leonora and Ben Senior their house.

"It's in pretty bad shape," Beth said. "Have you been out there lately?"

"Took a quick peek before I left for Santa Barbara. The renovations don't scare me, especially since I'd like to hire my brother to draw up plans. That is, if everyone agrees to the sale?"

"Pish, tush, don't be ridiculous," Leonora said, rising to hug her eldest. "There will be no sale, or if there is, the price will be one dollar. Everyone agreed?"

They all nodded as one before clapping each other on the back and passing congratulations around the room.

Smiling broadly, Robbie rose to hug his mother. "Who's gonna tell Dad the good news?"

"You leave him to me," Leonora said. "He'll be pleased as punch. Now, I think I'll go up to bed." She turned to Ben. "You've made me— all of us—so happy, my darling."

"I hope so," he said. "Mother, can you wait one minute? There's something I'd like to tell you all. Please sit, just for a few more minutes."

Leonora sat beside him, her face stricken at his serious tone. Ben gazed at Ruthie, who seemed to know what he was going to say, even if their siblings gave him quizzical looks.

"I have to ask that you all keep this to yourselves, but I wanted you to know something that I hope will make you happy. It's about Emma, Maggie's daughter."

"I knew it!" Ruthie said.

Leonora looked at her youngest as if she'd sprouted horns. "Whatever are you sputtering about?"

Kyle nodded, while Robbie and Sam stared, waiting for Ben to speak.

"Emma's my daughter."

Leonora's face drained of color, and she leaned back into the sofa. "What!"

"She's my daughter, conceived before Maggie left for college. We were involved briefly, and Emma is the amazing result."

Kyle sat up, smiling broadly. "Of course she is. Too bad the poor kid looks just like you instead of her gorgeous mom."

Sam, Beth, and Robbie came forward to hug Ben with words of congratulations and joy.

"Who knew about this?" Leonora looked from one to the other of her children.

Ruthie waved her arm. "Dad and I guessed a few weeks ago."

"How?"

"We're not stupid. Kyle's right. Emma looks more like Ben than he does any of us."

"Why didn't you say something?"

"Not my place to tell." Ruthie winked at Ben, who was as surprised as his mother.

"I'll kill your father."

Beth sat up straighter at the edge of the sofa. "No, you won't, Mother. Dad was looking for the right moment to tell you, just as Ben was. Emma is your first grandchild, and you will welcome her into this family and love her as we do."

"Hear, hear," Sam said, rising to clap his brother's back. "I have a niece to spoil, and now I get to design my brother's dream house, which I predict he will not be living in alone."

Ben smiled. "Time will tell about who lives there. Are you staying the night?" Sam nodded. "If you have time, I'd really like to ride out there with you in the morning and look things over?"

"Sure thing," Sam said. "Isn't every day you get to design a dream house in a location like that one."

CHAPTER 48

At four on the dot, Ben pulled into Maggie's driveway, a huge picnic hamper stowed in the back, courtesy of Carmela. It was a gorgeous afternoon, the temperature cool and comfortable as they loaded up and headed out.

"Where are we going?" she asked as they drove out of town.

"You'll see. It's one of my favorite spots in the world."

"Is it a surprise?" Emma chirped from the backseat.

"Yup."

They drove by the main house, then the Lodge, before Ben turned down a dirt road that led south along a dry creek bed. In all her years working at the ranch, Maggie had never been down this road. When they rode, they always took trails running north or east to steer clear of the boundaries to neighboring ranches. She knew what lay south and west was mostly farm and pastureland that stretched to the Dillons' vineyards. The road became bumpier as the Rover hugged the creek. Finally, he veered right and the jeep began a slow climb away from the creek and over a rise to the fields, pastures, and mountains beyond. As they crested the hill, a beautiful, albeit dilapidated, farmhouse came into view.

"Oh, my goodness. Who lives way out here?"

"No one. It's part of the ranch, my favorite place on the ranch. My great grandparents built it and lived in it until they died. After my grandparents built the Lodge, and Mom and Dad built their house, no one seemed to remember this existed except me. When I wanted to get away from everyone, I'd ride up here. Harley and I used to spend nights here as teenagers. Could've been a great party house, but I never wanted to share it with anyone but my best buddy. Didn't want it wrecked, even though animals and the weather have done a number on it."

"Can we go in?" Emma asked as he lifted her out.

"Sure can. Just leave the food and the chair. We'll explore, and then I'll come back for it."

They stepped up onto the wide porch, careful to avoid loose boards and rotting wood. Ben reached above the doorframe and retrieved a key, then ushered them into a living room that spanned the length of the house. Tattered, dust-covered chairs, tables, and couches, braided rugs, and wrought iron lamps were scattered around the room. A massive stone fireplace dominated the center. Behind it, the kitchen featured white porcelain countertops, an old cookstove, and an ice chest. There was a small bedroom and bath to the right and a mud room that led to the back of the house.

Maggie sighed as she gazed out the kitchen window toward the mountains. "It's a magical place."

Ben set Emma down on the counter and took her mother's hand. "Except for Harley, you ladies are the only people I've ever brought up here."

Emma pointed out the opposite window that faced north. "Hey, you can see the ranch from here." Sure enough, the roofs of both the Lodge and the main house were just visible through the trees.

"It's not far as the crow flies. Only a five- or ten-minute walk if you take the path, not the road."

Emma looked wistful, and he realized his gaffe. Walking was one thing, pushing a wheelchair quite another.

"Hey, Peanut, what do you say that someday soon, I can give you a piggyback ride along the trail, and we can fight our way through the sagebrush together?"

Emma rewarded him with one of her beautiful, contented smiles.

"Okay ladies? Are you as hungry as I am? Let's go see what Carmela packed for us. Judging by the size of the basket, there should be enough food to feed an army."

He spread a large patchwork quilt in shades of autumn. Delicate embroidered diamonds and triangles alternated with bright squares of gaily-patterned fabric. He brought out plates, cups, napkins, sandwiches, salsa, chips, guacamole, a tin of cookies, a thermos of lemonade, another of iced tea, and a large fruit salad in a Tupperware container. "See, I told you she made enough to feed an army. We have portabella on a baguette with Carmela's special sauce, peanut butter and jelly, and turkey. What's your pleasure?"

Maggie and Emma decided to share the turkey and peanut butter and jelly, while Ben ate the mushroom baguette. As they loaded their plates, they chatted happily. From this ideal spot on the property, they had gorgeous views in all directions, north and south along the valley and east and west toward the mountains. After lunch, Ben lifted Emma to his shoulders, and they took a long walk on a path that followed the creek south to a small lake. Two thirds of it was dry, but the other third sparkled in the late afternoon sun, reflecting the green surrounding it. As they gazed across, they spied a small group of javelinas gathered at the water's edge. A coyote howled in the distance. Hawks circled beyond the ridge, and the hooting of an owl signaled the coming of evening.

As they headed back, Maggie took his arm. Ben hardly dared move for fear he'd spook her. His heart nearly burst with happiness as they neared the farmhouse. The woman he loved and his sweet, brave daughter were at his side.

When they reached the quilt, they discovered Emma had fallen asleep on his shoulder. Maggie reached up, took her gently from his arms, and placed her on the quilt, wrapping the edges round her.

He stowed the last of the food, then looked up at her. "Should we let her sleep or head back?"

"How about one glass of tea before we hit the road?"

They took their tea to the porch to sit side by side on the steps. "So, how was your week?"

"Same old, same old. Pony camp in full swing, lessons crazy. Your buddy has been AWOL for a couple of days, so that's added a bit of craziness for Jeb's and my schedules, but the college kids are great. Fully trained now. We'll hate to lose them."

"Sorry, that was my fault. Harley was doing a job for me that took him away."

"You're the boss. Were your partners glad to have you back?"

"Wasn't easy."

"Oh?"

"I've stepped out of the company. Still hold some shares, but I've sold my major interest to Chip and David."

"Why?"

"I'm needed here. Dad's not well, and I think I can help."

"I can't believe it. Wasn't it hard to say good-bye?"

He nodded. "I'm proud of what we built. We've made a lot of money using ethical business practices to market sustainable products. I'll also miss my partners. They're good friends."

"What about your fiancée?"

Ben gave her a wry look and decided that he did not have to describe Miranda's last-ditch effort to win him back. He cringed inwardly as he recalled the elaborate meal she had prepared at his house. On his last night in Santa Barbara, she had let herself into the house with the key she still had and greeted him at the door, wearing a pale pink diaphanous dress that left nothing to the imagination.

"As I've told you before, she is not my fiancée, except in her mind. Miranda and I broke up many months ago and should have split two years ago."

"Hmm..."

"What about you? Have you got some secret fiancé hidden away?"

She laughed. "Yeah, right."

"Seriously, we've never talked about it. You must date sometimes?"

Maggie smiled at him. *There has never been anyone since my night with you.* "Well, let's see, no one wants to date a pregnant teenager, and since Emma's birth, then her accident, there hasn't been much time for dating."

"No one?"

"I was fixed up once. Not sure if you remember Dara Littlefield? She was my best friend in high school?"

"Vaguely. Red hair and freckles?"

"That's Dara. Well, her brother, Ed, brought home two friends from U of A one weekend, and she and I went out with them. Nice guys. My date's name was Gary Something. I can't even remember." She did remember tall, gangly Gary Sinclair and his rough, urgent lips attempting to woo her with a good night kiss, but for some reason, she didn't want to admit it to Ben.

"One date?"

She nodded. "He called a few times, but Emma was a baby and I really wasn't interested."

"What about Jeb?"

"Are you insane?"

"I've seen the way he looks at you."

"Don't be ridiculous. Jeb's like my little brother."

"I'd be surprised if he views it that way."

"This is a silly conversation, and I see my little cherub moving around. It's unsettling for her when she wakes up lying down in a strange place. Maybe we should think about packing up?" She handed her empty glass to Ben and hurried down to help Emma sit up and orient herself.

Ben watched her go and smiled at her obvious discomfort. He knew there was nothing going on between Jeb and Maggie, but he also knew that, given the slightest hint of encouragement, Jeb and half the men in the county would be lined up at her door. He also knew that if he wasn't careful, he'd spook her again and perhaps lose her forever.

CHAPTER 49

"What the hell are we supposed to do while you're on a two-week vacation?" Harley asked as he went over the day's chores with Jeb and Maggie. It was only Tuesday, three days before Emma's surgery, and her boss could see the terror in her eyes. He and Jeb had been walking on eggshells for two days, and his attempts to lighten the mood did not seem to be working.

Maggie hopped up and began pacing. "I'll be home. You guys can call. I can come in if needed, and Dad can stay with Emma. Ben said he'd help, too. Or I can see if we can get some townies in, temps for the lessons and—"

"I was kidding, Mags. Kidding! You can relax. We've got it covered."

Jeb nodded in agreement. "We're cool, Boss. The crew is working like a well-oiled machine, and there won't be any new mustangs in till mid-September."

She gazed down at Harley, looking like a deer in the headlights. "What about when you're away?"

"The next pack trip isn't for a few weeks, and Ben says he can handle it alone, or he'll take Ruthie with him. She volunteered."

"Ruthie?"

"She's done it before. She'll be fine."

Maggie continued to pace, muttering to herself. "I'm so sorry. This is the worst time to be away. What'll we do about the fence repairs?"

"Okay, that's enough. I'm the boss, and if I say we'll be fine, we'll be fine."

"But, we've got Saturday lessons and no crew and—"

Harley stood, exchanged a look with Jeb, then reached out and grabbed her shoulders, bringing her closer for a hug. "She's gonna be fine, Mags. She's a trooper. She's gonna sail through this."

She collapsed against him as sobs wracked her thin frame, which Harley noticed had grown thinner these past few weeks.

"Okay, sweetie. Let it out." He held her until her sobs subsided. "Do you want to go home?"

"Absolutely not! There's a ton of work to do, and I'd like to get it done. Thank you both. Now let's get to work!"

At 3:30 a.m. Friday morning, Ben arrived to find Maggie and Emma waiting in the driveway. Gently he lifted his daughter from her chair. "You ready, Sweet Pea?"

Emma burrowed her face against his chest, and he looked up to study her mother, who was ashen-faced, dark circles under her beautiful eyes. "Neither of us got much sleep."

It was still dark as they pulled into the clinic.

"Ready or not, here we come," Ben said as he lifted Emma, holding her tight. "We don't need the chair, do we? I'll hold her, and they have chairs inside, right?"

Maggie nodded and walked beside him, her hand on Emma's thigh, as they headed into the steel-and-glass lobby. They were surprised to find Rose Dillon, dressed in street clothes—gray slacks and a soft pink sweater waiting for them.

Rose waved. "Hi, Emma." Emma smiled shyly, peeking from under Ben's arm. "I'm so glad to see you again. I'm going to be with you all day, sweetie." Rose smiled at Maggie and patted her arm as she led them into a small office, where a slim blonde in *Sesame*

Street scrubs sat at a desk, a basket of toys beside her. Cucumber-green eyes smiled at the child as she patted an empty chair for Maggie.

"Emma," Rose said, "this is my friend Lanie. She's going to talk to Mom and get you all checked in, okay? While you do that, I'll take Ben and show him where we'll be. Is that okay with you?" Emma nodded. Ben settled Emma on Maggie's lap, then disappeared with Rose.

"Are you ready for this?" Rose asked as they headed down a long hallway. "Emma is in good hands, but it's going to be a very long, rough day for Maggie. I'll be in the OR the entire time, but is there anything I can do before that?"

"Thanks, but you've been great, Rosie. I'll take care of Maggie."

She stared at him, a wistful expression on her lovely face. "I'm sure you will. She's very lucky, you know."

"I'm the lucky one."

"I hear you're moving back to Saguaro."

"News travels fast."

"I ran into Kyle this week. It'll be nice to have you back."

"Thanks. I hope so."

"Kyle says you're thinking of fixing up the farmhouse."

He nodded, remembering how close Rose's parents' ranch sat to the south end of Morgan's Run. As if reading his thoughts, she said, "We used to ride up there sometimes and play house on the porch, pretend we owned it. It's a beautiful spot."

"Yes, it is."

"I suspect you won't be living there alone for long."

He shrugged. "Are there things you wanted to show me?"

"Oh, yes, of course. The OR is on the third floor, but the parents' lounge is on the second floor. If you'd rather be alone, you are welcome to use my office. My assistant, Sadie, can let you in. I told her you might want to use it to rest or get away. Sadie can also get you food and drinks if you don't feel like braving the cafeteria."

"Thanks, but we may need a break from the lounge."

"Well, don't hesitate to call upon Sadie at any time. She's

expecting it. Waiting for a someone to come through an operation of this length is excruciating, especially a beloved child."

After Emma was prepped, they waited in Rose's office until the nurses and Rose appeared along with Dr. Heavers. After the IV was inserted, Heavers directed most of his conversation to Emma, who cowered against her mother and whimpered, refusing to look at him.

As soon as the entourage disappeared, Emma began to wail. "I don't want to, Mommy. I changed my mind! I wanta go home. Please, Mommy, I want to go home."

"There, there, baby, it's okay. It'll be over before you know it." She cradled her daughter, fighting to control her own tears that threatened to burst forth.

Ben's arms circled the two of them, their little family joined in a united front as if to ward off evil spirits.

"No, I don't want to. I want to go home! I want Grandpa!"

Ben leaned back and studied Maggie. He could see she was unraveling fast. "Okay, let's go. Let's forget the whole thing. I'll call the nurse and have her take that contraption out." He pointed to the IV.

Instantly, Emma stopped crying, her eyes big as saucers as she stared at him. Maggie's jaw dropped and she sat back, patting her daughter's back. "What are you talking about?"

"She doesn't want to have the operation. That's good enough for me. Let's get out of here."

"But..." Emma said, looking from one adult to the other.

"What's that, Sweet Pea?" Ben leaned close, taking her tiny hands in his rough, calloused ones.

"What about walking?"

"We can come back another time, when you're ready."

"But, I wanta walk now."

"Well, you know what that means." His kind eyes smiled, hoping the love he felt would come through and give his daughter courage. She took his hand and nodded. "Are you sure, baby?" She nodded again and leaned against her mother, a tear trickling down her cheek.

At that moment, Rose appeared. "Well, Emma, it's time. Are you ready?"

Chin out, Emma nodded.

"I'm going to put something in your IV bag that will make you sleepy. When you wake up, your mom and Ben will be here, holding your hands, okay?" Rose held the syringe and waited several moments, until Emma said, "Okay." Before she could count to five, Emma was asleep. Only then did Maggie stand, step away from the bed, and lean into Ben's arms.

"And, now we wait," he said softly. "Take good care of her, Rose."

"We will." As two nurses wheeled Emma out, Rose turned to Maggie. "My assistant, Sadie Thomas, will try to come out every hour or two and let you know how things are going. It's sometimes difficult for the team to break and give updates, so please don't worry if you don't see her, okay?"

They stood and watched as the group made their way down the hall, through double doors to the surgery elevators. When the doors closed behind them, Maggie broke down completely. He lifted her, carrying her to room 203. There they found a short, compact brunette with kind doe eyes and a lively gait.

"Hi, Maggie and Ben. I'm Sadie. Can I get you anything? Tea or coffee? Water? A soft drink?" As she spoke, she smoothed the front of her bright pink scrubs, patting her midsection.

He smiled at Rose's kind, very pregnant assistant.

"Just a quiet place would be great."

Sadie ushered them into Rose's office. "If you need anything at all, just ask."

She closed the door behind her, leaving Emma's parents clinging to one another on the office love seat.

CHAPTER 50

Ben said a silent thank you for the privacy of Rose's office as he held Maggie and she sobbed into a brightly colored pillow decorated with desert plants and animals. Finally she calmed, leaned against him, and closed her eyes. Shortly after, Sadie brought coffee and packets of cookies. Ben nodded, afraid to move a muscle.

Observing his dilemma, Sadie moved a small table within his reach and set a coffee mug and cookies down.

"Thank you," he whispered.

"Anything you need, just let me know."

She tiptoed from the room and closed the door.

It had been a lonely few weeks without his girls, and he had missed them terribly. How good it felt to hold Maggie with no expectation of anything but to give comfort and support to this woman he loved with all his heart. A short time later, he, too, nodded off.

Sadie's knock woke them, and Maggie sat upright and smoothed her rumpled shirt.

"Sorry to disturb, guys. I've just come from Dr. Dillon. She wanted you to know that all is going well. Emma's comfortable, and there have been no surprises so far. That's a good thing."

Her eyes teary and wild with fright, Maggie gazed from Ben to Sadie. "Surprises? What kind of surprises? They didn't say anything about surprises."

Sadie looked stricken. "I'm sorry. That might have been the wrong word. Everything is going well."

"Thank you," Ben said, smiling up at the kind young woman. "That's great news. Have you got any questions, sweetheart?"

"So it's going as they expected?"

"That's what Dr. Dillon said. They are progressing well. Can I get you anything?"

"I think we're set, thanks," Ben said, his arm around Maggie's shoulders.

After Sadie closed the door, he turned to her and cupped her chin for a soft kiss, noticing the fresh tears that snaked down her cheeks.

"Hey, hey, we've got nothing but good news here. Em's doing fine. That's what we want to hear."

He kissed her softly and Maggie nodded, resting against his chest.

"Want something to eat? I could run to the cafeteria or ask Sadie to go."

"No, but I could use a walk. Let's go down for a change of scene."

"That's the spirit."

They held hands and walked the second-floor halls as people scurried back and forth around them. Eventually they headed for the cafeteria, where they took a seat by the window and nibbled at their sandwiches.

Ben held up his veggie wrap. "I've had cardboard that tasted better than this. How's your chicken salad?"

Maggie had barely touched her sandwich, but his comment coaxed a smile. "I couldn't have gone through this without you."

"Well, I'm happy you don't have to." He reached across and took her hand. "There's nowhere I'd rather be, my darling. No matter what the outcome, I can't wait to kiss those rosy cheeks and rumple those curls."

"Did you have curls as a child?"

"Masses. Mother would be more than happy to spend hours showing you my little Lord Fauntleroy photos. I believe when I was a toddler, she was going through her 'get me off the ranch and over to merry old England' craze, so she dressed me in knickers and let my hair grow to shoulder-length curls."

"Oh, I'd love to see pictures of you. I have only a tiny handful of photos of me growing up. My mom left when I was so young, and Ned wasn't the picture-snapping type. He was always working, too. His sister, my Aunt Nina, might have taken a few."

"I bet you were adorable."

She shrugged. "Dad would say so, but he's a bit biased. And who are we kidding about your mom spending hours with me?"

"You wait. She'll soften up. She's letting go a bit. As you know, my dad's not well, and they'd like to travel while he still feels okay. She'll need to spend most of her time hovering over him, and she'll forget all about me."

"They must be thrilled that you'll be staying around."

"Understatement."

"Are you sure this is the right decision for you?"

"The rightest one I've ever made. I can't imagine being away from you and Emma. The pack trips are gonna be torture until they can find someone to help Harley and me take over the meet-and-greet game."

She smiled, thinking about Ben, dressed cowboy-gorgeous, schmoozing with guests at the Lodge.

"I'll get you for that smirk."

Suddenly, his expression serious, Ben reached across and took her hand. "Sweetheart, there's something I have to tell you. I hope you won't be angry. I haven't wanted to say anything the past few days with everything you had on your plate." Her eyes registered fear, so he hurriedly said, "I told my parents and siblings about Emma. Apparently Dad already knew."

She nodded.

"He spoke to you, didn't he?"

"Yes, while you were away."

"Ruthie, too, I guess." Another nod. "Family resemblance, I s'pose. I think Beth also suspected, but she keeps everything very close to the chest."

Before Maggie could reply, they were interrupted by Sadie. "Hi, guys. Thought I might find you here. All's well. They've had to give Emma some of her daddy's blood, but that's pretty typical for this kind of surgery. Dr. Dillon wanted you to know that the team is right on schedule. Things are going great."

Hand on her heart, Maggie said a silent prayer of thanks for Sadie's news and Ben's blood. *What would we have done without you?*

Heart in his throat and overcome with gratitude that a part of him was helping to heal his beloved daughter, Ben said, "Thank you, Sadie. Would you like to join us?"

"Oh, no, thanks. Got to get back. I'll keep you posted."

After Sadie disappeared, they gave up on lunch, tossed the remains in the trash, and stepped outside into a small shaded courtyard at the building's center. The heat felt good after the cafeteria's air-conditioned arctic temperature. They sat on a bench under a green-and-white-striped awning, and Ben took her hand.

"Do you think there will ever be a good or right time to tell Emma about me? That I'm her daddy?"

She ran her fingers over his rough, callused knuckles, loving the feel of his strong hand. "I've been thinking about that ever since we bumped fenders. I want to tell her, Ben. I really do, but I'm not sure if it would be confusing for her. I mean, believe me, she's crazy about you and wishes with all her heart that you were her daddy."

Sad, dark eyes gazed down at her. "I know."

"We'll find a way. I promise, for your sake and for Emma's. It's too important for her not to know."

He drew her close, drinking in the scent he loved so completely. "I love you, Maggie Williams. Words don't even begin to tell you how much."

"I love you, too, Ben Morgan."

Maggie's hand caressed his cheek, and he drew her nearer, taking her lips for a soft, gentle kiss, which she returned.

A moment later, she pulled away. "I'm not sure I trust myself with you right now. We'd better go in or risk putting on a spectacle for the cafeteria diners. "

CHAPTER 51

They walked the halls for a while, then returned to Rose's office. Sadie was away from her desk but had left a note taped to the door saying she would be right back. They dozed a little. Then Maggie called Ned and gave him an update. When she hung up and switched off her cell, she leaned back on the sofa and nestled in Ben's arms. When he gazed down at her, Ben saw that the tears had returned.

"Hey, hey, sweetheart. We've had good reports all day, remember?"

"I know, but it's been so long. I hate to think of her all alone in that cold, sterile place."

"She's not alone. She's got a whole team of caring experts with her."

"I wish I could have had the surgery in her place."

"Me, too, but she's in good hands, my darling."

Maggie's shoulders trembled, tears flowing in earnest now.

Ben checked his watch. It had been six hours. *How much longer can she hang on without going crazy? She's clearly at the end of her rope.*

A short time later, Sadie knocked and came in with her thumbs up, reporting that all was still going well. After she closed the door, Maggie reached for a tissue and was surprised to see Ben rise and kneel on the floor beside her. He reached forward and grasped both her hands in his.

"What in the world are you doing?"

"Well, I had hoped to do this at a more romantic time, with candlelight, soft music, and you in a sexy little dress, but here goes."

"Do what?"

"Maggie Williams, let me say this, please. I love you more than anything in the world, you and our daughter. I never knew love like this existed. I've come to the point where I realize that I cannot live without you any more than I could live without breathing. My darling, beautiful Maggie, will you marry me?"

From his pocket, Ben pulled a ring, which he set in his open palm. "Sorry, sweetheart, the box didn't fit in my jeans. It was my grandmother's. I had it reset when I was in California. If you don't like it, we can go shopping and find another."

Dark eyes peered up at hers, love and expectation in his gaze. Gently Maggie touched the ring with her finger. "It's so beautiful."

"Is that a yes?"

She withdrew her finger and rested it in her lap. "Ben, I'm overwhelmed and flattered. I think you know how much I love you, too, and how much I want to be with you. You and Emma are the center of my universe."

"Darling, please put me out of my misery. Are you saying yes?"

Her eyes sad, she shook her head. "This is all I can do right now, tell you I love you. Please don't be hurt. You honor me with your proposal. I just don't trust myself and my feelings right now. I can't give you the answer you want. These past few months have been joyful, but also incredibly tumultuous. Emma has such a long road ahead."

"A road we can travel together. We are together, aren't we?"

"Yes, we are, and for that I am extremely grateful." She reached out and folded his fingers closed, obscuring the sight of the stunning ring, with a deep-blue sapphire at its center, surrounded by tiny sparkling diamonds. "It's the loveliest ring I have ever seen. Please know that I want to give you the answer you desire, the one my heart cries out to give, but I can't, not today, not now. Not with the uncertainty of what's ahead."

Ben stood, pocketed the ring, and sat beside her. "Of course. I should never have asked. It was incredibly insensitive of me."

She reached forward to caress his strong jaw. "No, it wasn't, my darling. It was a loving gesture, and I'm deeply touched. I know it's not fair to ask you to be patient, but this is all I have to give right now, my love."

Ben forced a smile. "Hey, come here." His arms enveloped her, her face buried in the curve of his neck.

"Please don't be angry."

"Never. At least you didn't say no. That gives a guy hope, right?"

She cupped his chin with both hands and stretched up to kiss him. "Absolutely, and I promise, when this is all over, if you still want me, I will give you an answer from an unfettered heart."

"I'm holding you to that, Maggie Williams."

He drew her close, and Maggie felt his heart beating, his body tense. Her arm circled his waist. She was grateful for his warmth and strength. His body screamed anger and disappointment, but here he stayed, holding her. She closed her eyes and slept.

It was almost six when the door opened and Dr. Heavers and Rose stepped in. Maggie was still asleep. Ben nudged her gently. "Darling, wake up. It's over."

Maggie sat up with a start, terror in her gaze as she spied both doctors. As realization dawned, she smoothed her shirt and grabbed Ben's hand.

Dr. Heavers waited as she composed herself, a kind smile warming his eyes. "How you holding up, Mom?"

"It's been a long day."

"Yes, always hardest on the parents, I fear."

Nearly jumping out of his skin with the small talk, Ben said, "How is she?"

Countenance weary, eyes bright, Heavers gave them a long look before replying. "She came through surgery really well, and we were able to repair the damage to her spine. It was not as extensive as we anticipated, which is good. Her prognosis is excellent."

Maggie studied the doctor's eyes, sensing there was something he was not saying. She stood up. "I want to see her."

Realization dawned in Ben's eyes. "What aren't you telling us?"

"With surgeries of this length, there is sometimes a slower recovery. For the first few days, especially. Emma has had some fluid build up in her brain and along the spine."

Maggie paced, eyes wild with fright. "I want to see her. Take us to her right now!"

"She's not awake, my dear. We've induced a coma to allow her body to recover and to allow the fluid time to drain. This is the safest course with children of Emma's age."

Ben grasped Maggie's hand and drew her into his lap. "Coma or not, we want to see her."

"I'd like to get her settled in the ICU. Then Rose will come and get you. I promise it will only be an hour or two."

Rose stepped forward, stooped, and grasped Maggie's hand. "She's sleeping peacefully. She's comfortable and not in any pain."

Maggie shook her head.

Voice soft, almost a whisper, Rose asked, "Can I get you something?"

"Maybe a cup of tea?" he said. "If it's not too much trouble?"

"Of course. Be right back."

Rose disappeared, and Dr. Heavers took a seat in a plastic chair beside the sofa. "I know this sounds like a setback, folks, but it's very common in cases like Emma's, especially since she hasn't used her legs in several years. The coma allows her to rest and allows the spine to heal. Unless you have questions, I'd like to go back up and check on her now."

Maggie shook her head and Ben replied, "No, but please let us know the moment we can see her. We both plan to spend tonight with her, and Maggie will stay as long as Emma's here."

"Of course. I believe there is a cot already in the room, and I'll ask for a recliner to be brought in as well. Rose will be back very soon."

With those words, he stood. "You may not see me again today. After I check in on Emma, I'll go to one of the on-call rooms to sleep. I'm not much use to anyone if I don't. They know to call me if anything arises during the night. Here's my card with my cell number. If you need to reach me, do not hesitate."

Later, as they sipped cups of chamomile tea, Maggie's phone buzzed. When she looked up, she smiled. "We can go up now."

CHAPTER 52

Emma's tiny face was barely visible with all the tubes and machinery that surrounded her. Two chairs had been placed to the left of the bed and Maggie sat in one, reaching to take her daughter's tiny hand in hers. "I'm here, baby. Your daddy and I are here, and we love you very much."

Watching Maggie and hearing her say "Daddy" in reference to him brought tears to Ben's eyes. He sat and reached to cover their hands with his own. "That's right, brave girl. We're right beside you. We love you, sweetheart."

Except for a trip to the ladies' room, Maggie did not leave Emma's side all night. Before she went home, Sadie brought them soup and sandwiches. Ben persuaded Maggie to eat a few bites of sandwich and take a few sips of the warm soup. Rose stopped in at 10 p.m. to say that she, too, would be staying in one of the on-call rooms. She left her card with her cell number circled and urged them to call if they needed her.

Maggie fell asleep holding Emma's hand, Ben's arm around her. He woke with a start when a nurse came to check on Emma, but Maggie slept on. Stiff and exhausted, he stood and kissed Emma's forehead, then the top of Maggie's head, before going in search of the men's room.

When he returned a short time later with muffins and coffee purchased from a cart in the hallway, Maggie was awake, resting alongside Emma's bed. She gazed at him sleepily. "Will you stay with her while I go to the ladies room?"

Ben folded her in his arms, kissing her gently. "Of course, sweetheart. How you holding up?"

"I just want her back."

"Me, too. She'll be with us soon enough."

Just after 8 a.m., Dr. Heavers and Rose came in. They spent several minutes checking Emma's charts. Then Dr. Heavers turned to them. "She's comfortable. I'd like to keep her sleeping one more day so the spine has a chance to settle."

Maggie's face fell and tears rimmed her eyes. "If that's what's best for her, of course."

Ben and Maggie took turns throughout the day, sitting by Emma, holding her hand, while the other rested. When Rose came that evening, she explained that the medications inducing the coma would be slowly withdrawn in the morning, and the team expected Emma to be awake by noon. Once again, they slept at her bedside, Ben's arms enfolding Maggie as she held the tiny hand.

The next day, as noon passed and Emma slept on, Maggie grew frantic. Rose and Dr. Heavers assured her that it sometimes took a little longer for children to awaken. Ned had now joined them and made frequent trips to the cafeteria for food that no one touched. He brought fresh clothes for Maggie, and Ruthie brought a bag for Ben. The elder Morgans stopped by, but only long enough to embrace their son and Maggie and tell them to call if there was anything they could do.

As the afternoon stretched toward evening, Maggie finally broke down into uncontrollable sobbing. Watching her beloved, Ben, who was not in much better shape himself, went for a nurse and requested the sedative Dr. Heavers had prescribed in case Maggie needed it. He then ordered her to take the pill and lie down on the recliner near the window. Miraculously, she acquiesced and was asleep five minutes later. Ben watched as her beautiful face relaxed in slumber, and he breathed a sigh of relief.

He assumed Maggie's place at Emma's bedside and took the tiny hand in his. Gently he rubbed her arms, careful to keep them immobile under the tight strapping. "Hey, Peanut," he whispered, eyeing Maggie as he spoke. "You are the bravest girl I've ever known, and your mom and I are so proud of you. The day I found out I was your dad was the happiest day of my life. I love you and your mom more than anything in the world. We can't wait to have you home, my sweet, precious daughter."

Suddenly he felt pressure on his fingers. When he looked up, her eyes were open, and she was gazing steadily at him. She gave him a wan smile and whispered, "Hi, Daddy."

Her voice was hoarse from the breathing tube they had removed a few hours earlier, but he had heard her say "Daddy." In her groggy state, his darling girl had revealed how much she wished it were true. "Oh, sweetheart." He leaned forward to kiss her forehead, tears streaming down his face. "Hey, baby girl, you're back. Don't try to move. They want you to stay really, really still for a few days to let your back feel better. That's why they have these." He pointed to the straps. "Do you understand?"

She nodded, whispering, "Where's Mommy?"

"She's been holding your hand for two days, and she needed a nap. Let's wake her up, okay? "

Ben bent over the recliner and kissed Maggie's forehead. "Hey, darling, wake up. There's someone who wants to see you."

Startled eyes searched his. Then she looked toward the bed and spied Emma. "Oh, my baby!"

As Maggie stooped to kiss their tiny daughter, Ben went to find a nurse.

CHAPTER 53

For the next week, Maggie stayed with Emma as she recovered and began physical therapy. To their relief, her arms and upper body were stronger and more vital than ever. Dr. Heavers was optimistic about her legs and pleased with her progress. She now had slight sensation in both legs and was able to move them a little from side to side. "She's going to be very weak for a while," he told them. "Her legs show some atrophy after two years of immobility. We'll need to build her up slowly."

As one week stretched into two, they made the decision to move Emma to a rehab facility on the east end of Tucson. Ben and Maggie took turns staying with her. They were both exhausted, and Emma was cranky and begging to go home. One afternoon, Ned Williams came upon mother and daughter in a battle of wills in a therapy room.

"No, Mommy, it hurts! I'm not doing it. I want to go home. I hate it here."

Jane, one of Emma's regular physical therapists, stood next to her, coaxing and cajoling. A large woman in her midthirties, Jane had long straight black hair, and she wore stretch jeans, a pink floral top, and shiny black patent leather clogs.

"Come on, honey. Just a few more minutes. Wanta switch to the bars?"

Emma ignored Jane and scowled at her mother. "No! Take me home, Mommy."

"Baby, you have to stay, to get better, to get your legs stronger."

The three had not yet spied him as Ned watched his daughter from the back of the room. Maggie grew more gaunt and tired with each passing week, and dark circles ringed her eyes. Ned scratched his chin. *Clearly this cannot go on.*

"No, no, no! I want Ben! I want Ben!"

"Ben's working, sweetie. He'll be in tonight."

"I want him now!"

"Well, he cannot come now, Em,"

A hint of irritation had crept into Maggie's voice, and she looked as though she might burst into tears.

"I hate you! I want Ben! I want Ben! He's much nicer than you! I want him! Get him!"

Ned stepped further into the room. "Hey, there, Peanut. What's all the commotion?"

"Grandpa. Hi, Grandpa! You're here. Take me home, please."

Ned glanced at his daughter, who had turned away so Emma could not see her tears. Then he turned back to his granddaughter. "Let's give Mom a break. Jane and I can handle this, Mags. Why don't you head back to the room for a nap?"

She nodded and grabbed her sweater. "Thanks, Dad. Em, I'll see you in a bit." Without looking back, Maggie left the room.

Ned looked at Jane, and by tacit agreement they wheeled Emma to the parallel bars and started in. Battle with her mom forgotten, Emma tried her hardest. Ned watched sadly, noting how little progress she had made since his last visit.

Later, Ned pushed her wheelchair as they headed back to Emma's room. When they reached the elevator, he paused. "So, you were giving your mommy a pretty hard time back there."

She shrugged, suddenly interested in all the activity swirling around them in the hallway.

"Are you okay, Peanut?"

Another shrug.

"Let's go get ice cream and let Mommy have a little snooze, okay?"

Immediately, Emma's face lit up.

CHAPTER 54

Early Saturday morning, five weeks after Emma's surgery, Ned Williams drove his truck up to the big house and parked. He had called ahead and asked to stop by, so Ben and Leonora were waiting for him on the porch.

"Hi, Ned. Good to see you," Leonora called as he headed up the walk. "Let's go out to the back terrace. Much cooler, and Carmela has set out some coffee and scones."

Ned tipped his hat, then removed it. "Good to see you, too, Nora, Ben. Had a big breakfast, but wouldn't say no to a cup of coffee."

Ben patted him on the shoulder. "Come on back, then."

Once they were settled, mugs of coffee in hand, Ned sat up straight. "Thanks for seeing me."

"Anytime, Ned. Should've been sooner."

"I wanted to talk to you about Emma, and the kids."

"We've been so worried," Leonora said. "With Ben, it's best if we don't ask until he's ready to say something. We visited when she was at the clinic, but we didn't know the rules at rehab, and our son is not always the most forthcoming, especially with me. I keep checking, and all he tells us is that they've got things covered."

"Well, they clearly don't have things covered," Ned said. "I don't know the rules, either, but I know my daughter, and she's at the breaking point. Your son, too, I expect. Maggie's skeletal thin and so weak and exhausted, I'm 'fraid she's gonna have to be hospitalized herself if we don't do something. My granddaughter—our granddaughter—is giving her a very hard time, too. Em wants to come home."

"Can she?" Ben Senior asked.

"I don't know, but I do know that our kids cannot keep up this pace anymore. Whether they want it or not, they need help. I was at rehab yesterday, and I can tell you, things are definitely not covered. Emma's acting like a caged animal, and the active, defiant four-year-old she is. At the moment, her mama's bearing the brunt of her fury."

"Poor Maggie," the other man said.

"What can we do?" Leonora asked, standing to refill their mugs.

Ned set down his coffee and looked from one to the other of them. "I think it's time for an intervention. It's been five weeks since Emma's surgery, and there's been little progress. The doctors say the PT takes time, but I think we can guess the outcome here. She has some feeling in her legs, but they're limp as wet noodles, and she hasn't regained any more feeling since the day she woke up."

"Are you telling us you don't think there's a chance for Emmie?" Ben said.

Ned shrugged. "If I had to wager, I'd guess they're planning to release Emma in a month, maybe sooner, and order outpatient rehab for her. Won't be much easier on the parents time-wise, but it should improve Em's mood once she's home."

"But, there's hope, isn't there?" Leonora said.

Ned gazed from one to the other before speaking. "I think we have to prepare ourselves for the possibility that our granddaughter will never walk. I suspect her parents already know this but refuse to believe it, and they're getting more frayed around the edges every day."

Leonora stared at Ned, green eyes wide. "So, what do you propose?"

"My daughter, and your son, too, need to get back to some of their normal routines. Rest, yes, but Maggie, at least, needs the familiarity of routine and work. I was thinking that the rest of the family could get together and create a schedule so we can relieve Mom and Dad on alternate days. I'm retired, so I have lots of time. If we all pitched in a little, I could make my daughter rest, and maybe she could get back to work part-time. I heard from Ben that the pack trip next week is really shorthanded. If everyone pitches in, he can go with Harley. It's only five days."

Hands on hips, Leonora gazed towards the mountains. "Have you forgotten that both your daughter and our son are stubborn as mules and will never agree to this?"

"Yep, but that's why we need a united front. A real intervention, where we sit them down and lay down the rules."

Ben slapped his knee. "Count me in!"

Leonora sat down beside her husband. "Aren't you forgetting that they never leave Emma alone?"

"I thought of that, but I have an idea. Dara Littlefield, Maggie's high school friend, has been coming pretty regularly to visit Emma. If we asked her to come to the center and we got everyone together in the lobby, we could sit them down and present them with the schedule. Whether at the rehab center or home, they're going to have to accept help."

"Just tell us when and we'll be there," Ben said.

Leonora nodded her head in agreement. "I'll cancel everything and make myself available whenever I'm needed."

Ned laughed. "Whoa, now, we don't want the grandparents collapsing along with the parents. I know my limits, and we all should keep our own in mind. Any ideas how we can organize this?"

"Are you online?" Leonora asked.

"Not happily, but yes, I can find my way around."

"Perfect. I'll have Ruthie make up a table with times and dates for the next month or two, and then we'll circulate it among us, *all* of us. Ben's brothers and sisters will be happy to help."

"Think next Friday around five would be too soon to get that together? I saw Dara yesterday, and that's one of the days she gave me when she's free. I don't think it's necessary for all the players to be there, but as many as can make it. I'll make certain that Maggie is there, and maybe we can find a way to get Ben Junior there, too?"

"I'll handle that," Ben said. "I'll ask him to drive me down to see her."

Leonora clapped her hands. "I'll get right on the email this morning and ask everyone to get back to me by Wednesday. Ned, thank you so much for including us in this. It means so much to Ben and me." Tears rimmed her husband's eyes, and he nodded. "Emma's already precious to us, Ned."

"She's is pretty amazing kid, isn't she?"

CHAPTER 55

From the sidelines, Maggie and Ben watched their daughter and Jane. Emma lay on a mat, holding bright green stretchy bands that wound around the soles of her feet. The idea was to straighten her legs and swing them from side to side, a task that seemed elusive, at best, but at least they were talking and laughing.

"Do you know what tomorrow is about?" Maggie asked him.

"Not a clue." Ben cringed at the sight of his beloved, so pale, thin, and haunted. "Come here."

He attempted to draw her into an embrace, but she pulled away.

"No, I can't. Not here."

"I've missed you."

She shook her head. "Please, Ben, I can't talk about this right now."

He reached for her hand, but she placed it out of reach.

"What do you know about tomorrow?" she asked, deciding a change of subject was in order.

"Nothing."

"Well, I really don't want to leave Emma with Dara."

"We'll be right down the hall."

She shrugged.

"Maggie, she's gonna be fine."

"No, she's not," she said quietly, tears springing to her eyes. "We put her through that nightmare for nothing. She's never going to walk. "

"Hey, hey, sweetheart."

Ben could see that a meltdown was imminent, so he waved to Jane. "We're going to grab a coffee. Be back in five."

Jane nodded and waved. Emma was so engrossed in their game, she didn't notice.

Ben half lifted Maggie from her chair and led her out of the room. Once in the hallway, she collapsed against his chest.

"Okay, darling, okay. Let it out. It's okay."

He took her up in his arms and carried her down the hall and into the lobby, which was mercifully empty. He took her to a small room behind the vending machines and sat on one of the four couches, holding her in his lap. It was alarming to feel her spine and ribs, which stood out in sharp relief. Her soft curves had all but disappeared. Clearly this could not go on.

After a while, the trembling stopped and she wiped her eyes, resting her head in the crook of his neck. "What are we going to do?"

"Love her and love each other, sweetie. It's gonna be okay."

"I want to bring her home."

"Then let's do it."

"But what about the therapy?"

"We'll figure it out."

He cupped her chin and brought his lips to hers for a soft kiss.

"No! Please, Ben, I can't."

"Maggie, I'm sorry. I'm just trying to comfort you."

She jumped off his lap. "I just can't do this right now. Please, I've asked you to let me be and give me time."

"And I have given you time. Emma's my daughter, too. I need you, and I think you need me."

"Your daughter? Where were you when she was cutting teeth? Where were you when she had colic and cried all night? Where were you after the accident when we didn't know if she'd live or die?" She was screaming now, her voice shrill and almost unrecognizable.

"I'm here now." *And, I would have been there then, if I'd known.*

"Good. Fine. Look, I need to get back."

All the fight gone, Maggie turned with haunted eyes and left Ben sitting and wondering if their love had all been a dream.

CHAPTER 56

Friday afternoon, all the Morgan siblings as well as Ben Senior, Leonora, and Ned were assembled in the small room off the rehab center's lobby. Dara sat among them, catching up with Kyle as the others chatted and waited.

Leonora, Ben Senior, and Ned stood together. Finally Leonora clapped her hands. "Okay, everybody, we're all here. Thank you for coming. Ruthie has copies of the time schedule we created for the next six weeks. Once they agree, we'll churn one out for the next six weeks or longer. I imagine like your dad, Ned, and me, you're thrilled to be doing this for our family and our beloved granddaughter. Now I'm going to turn things over to Ned, as it was his inspired idea to do this. Ned?"

Ned smiled shyly and gazed out at the Morgans all staring expectantly in his direction. "Thanks, Nora. I guess we know who my daughter'll blame if they're not happy with this, too. Not to worry. I'm happy to take one for the team. In truth, folks, I don't think their sayin' no is an option. I refuse to watch my baby girl worry herself to death, and it sure isn't doin' Emmie any good, either.

"So I'll take Dara up and bring the parents back with me. Dara, you all set for the pushback?"

Dara laughed, holding up a canvas bag. "I've got toys, games, coloring books, you name it. Em and I'll be fine, and if past visits are any indication, she'll shoo her mom out so she'll have me all to herself."

Kyle watched his classmate and marveled at the transformation of Dara Littlefield from a slightly plain high-schooler to strawberry-blonde beauty. Her straight hair was tied back in a ponytail, and she wore little or no makeup, but her skin was flawless, lips a sweet cherry red. The light blue of her thin cotton sundress picked up the blue in her wide, smiling eyes. He made a mental note to ask for her number after the intervention.

Ned touched Dara's shoulder. "Okay, my girl, into the fire we go."

As they neared the room, they heard crying. Poking their heads in, they spied Maggie trying to coax Emma to eat some of her spaghetti and meatballs. It appeared that Ben had been reading a picture book to Emma, which lay open and forgotten in the commotion.

"I don't want it! I hate it! I want to go home! I want Grandpa's spaghetti."

"Hey, Peanut, what's all the fussin'?"

"Grandpa!" she cried, holding out her arms.

Ned did not disappoint. He crossed the room in three long strides and scooped her out of the wheelchair to twirl her in circles. "Givin' your mama a hard time again, are you?"

"I want to go home with you."

"I know, sweetie." He smoothed back chestnut curls from moist cheeks and brow. "Pretty soon, baby girl."

Emma rested her head against his chest and heaved a sigh as her mother stood and set the plate of pasta aside. The friends hugged, and Dara said hello to Ben, who came to give her a hug as well.

"So, what have they roped you into now?" Maggie asked her friend.

"That's for your dad to explain. I'm here to play with my princess."

Emma's face brightened. "What's in the bag?"

"Let's let Mom, Ben, and Grandpa leave. Then I'll show you, okay?"

Everyone else forgotten, Emma allowed her grandfather to return her to the wheelchair. With hasty good-byes and a wave from Dara, the three departed and closed the door. As they headed for the lobby, Maggie turned to her father. "Are you going to tell us what this is about?"

"Just a chat baby girl, just a chat."

CHAPTER 57

When they spied the group assembled, Ben and Maggie's jaws dropped, and for a minute, both were speechless. He found his tongue first.

"What the hell are you all doing here? The only one missing is Harley."

"Not, quite, buddy. Just late." Harley stepped into the room and moved to sit beside Ruthie on one of the couches.

Ben turned to his mother, eyes blazing. "This is your doing, isn't it? Can't let us live our lives. You always have to—"

"Hey, son, hold on now!" His father wrapped a protective arm around his wife.

"Whoa, Nellybelle," Ned said. "This was my idea, so if you want to fly off the handle and start yelling at someone, you can do it to me, later, after we're through. Now, sit. Both of you. This is not a suggestion."

Maggie and Ben walked to the two empty chairs, which he noticed were at the center of their cozy little circle, and Ned began laying out the idea of how the group planned to provide relief for them. He paused at one point and nodded at Ruthie, who handed out copies of the schedule. A man of few words, his speech lasted less than five minutes, at the end of which he said, "We are dead serious about this, you two. We want our kids back, and Emma needs her mom and dad to be healthy and rested. You both need to get back into life and work."

"With all due respect, Ned," Ben said, "this is what Maggie and I want. This is where we choose to be."

"Sorry, brother," Robbie said. "We're all agreed. You're gonna accept our help, and that's final. I wanta spend time with my niece. So do Beth, Ruthie, Sam, Kyle, and Harley. And you know how Mom and Dad feel. This is gonna happen. You guys have lost your perspective, and you're both driving Emma crazy."

"And, you're at each other's throats," Ruthie said quietly. "Sorry, guys, but I heard you from the hallway last time I came in."

Ben shook his head. "This is craziness. Sam is so busy he can't see straight, Kyle's studies don't leave him a spare minute, and we can't ask Beth or Ruthie to come off the farm at our busiest season. And what the hell do you think you're going to do?" he asked, turning to Harley. "Let the next group of tourists run their own pack trip?"

Beth put up her hand. "That's is why we have this." She waved a copy of the schedule in front of her. "We will *share* this responsibility, brother dear, so that everyone, including you, can continue to work, study, and do whatever they do."

Ben stared at his sister, amazed at her tone. "Listen, all of you, this is an amazing offer, but Maggie and I cannot possibly—"

Maggie placed a trembling hand on his arm. "They're right, Ben. I think we should try it."

Incredulous, he turned to her. "You can't be serious?"

"She is, bro," Kyle said, gesturing toward Maggie. "Look at her. Look at yourself. You're both exhausted. You cannot keep this up and we, your family, are not gonna let you."

"Besides," Robbie said, "Emma's probably so sick of you two right now. She needs some fun and a change of pace."

"Thank you all," Maggie said quietly.

Ben looked from his brother to Maggie and saw the tears had started. He put his arm around her thin, trembling shoulders. "Okay, okay, I give in. When do we start?"

Leonora rushed to embrace her son, and Ben Senior, tears in his eyes, hugged Maggie. "We won't let you down, darlin.' We'll all take good care of her, and her grandmother will be supervising me, so you don't have to worry about this ole man messing up."

Maggie returned Leonora's embrace, then made her way through the group to find her dad. "So this is your doing, huh?"

"Couldn't let my baby girl wither away to nothing, now, could I?"

CHAPTER 58

They moved Emma home three weeks after the intervention. The schedule they had devised was working beautifully, and Emma was being spoiled rotten by her grandparents, aunts, and uncles. Daily trips to Tucson for rehab continued, as well as lots of time at Morgan's Run, where her caregivers took Emma to roam the fields and corrals. Maggie returned to work three days a week, happy to have Emma close by on some of the days. As another pack trip loomed, Ben was busy preparing. This was a small, private trip for two movie stars, their children and several other family members. Harley had insisted that Ben accompany him, and Maggie had agreed. With Team Emma in place, they could easily spare him for the six days.

The day of the trip, the Lodge was hopping, the stars' entourage driving the staff crazy with the travelers' myriad requests for food, special bedding, and a host of other demands.

Ben found his father in the kitchen, red-faced and out of breath. "Hey, Dad, slow down."

"Son, you have no idea."

"Not like the group last year, huh?" he said, referring to another Hollywood power couple.

"Oh, to have Kyla, Keith, and their kids back. No, this group's gonna drive all of us crazy."

"Not on the trip, they won't."

"Long as you give 'em the right food and get them all tucked in."

"Yeah, right."

"Just try, son. Okay?"

"It's not me you have to worry about. Have you ever known Harley to coddle anyone?"

Ben Senior laughed. "If he offends 'em, we can always pretend we're gonna fire him when you get back. I'll send one of the guys down with the van in a bit. The guests say they want to walk down."

"Well, stay calm. Don't want you blowing a gasket. Besides, isn't this your and Mom's afternoon with Emma?"

"Yup, can't wait. Have a good trip, son."

With a hug, Ben headed out, hopping into the jeep just as the stars themselves stepped onto the Lodge's front porch. *Here we go*, he thought, waving as he drove past the group. When he reached the stables, Harley and Jeb were saddling the horses and organizing the pack mules in another corral. "Hey, guys, Maggie around?"

They pointed toward the office, so he headed in and spied her on the phone. She nodded, then continued talking, clearly speaking to their grain supplier. Ben sat and observed, pleased to see that she had regained some weight. Her rosy cheeks were no longer hollow, and her hair was pulled back in her usual careless ponytail. Her jeans no longer hung quite so loosely on her frame. He ached for her touch and would have swooped her up in his arms and kissed her silly if he hadn't known his actions would be met with an angry rebuff.

Aware of his presence even before he entered the room, Maggie yearned for his warmth, even as she was determined to keep her distance. She ended the call and wrote some notes to herself. Then, assuming her business face, she turned to him. "Hey, you ready for this crew?"

"No, I'd much rather stay here with you and Emma. You look great, by the way."

Ignoring the hunger in his gaze, she replied with a lightness she didn't feel. "I would give big money to see Harley when you set up camp tonight."

"He won't take any shit from them. Dad says I can fire him if they complain."

She laughed and flashed the beautiful smile he loved so much. "That's been known to happen before. Very effective, actually."

Ben closed the office door and pulled his chair close to hers. "Maggie, I'm dying here. I miss you so much it hurts. I love you and Emma. I want us to be a family, to be together."

He reached over and took her hand.

His heat took her breath away, and Maggie longed to throw herself into his arms, to bury her face in the crook of his neck, to feel his kisses everywhere. But her body felt numb, frozen, as if all feeling had been sucked out of her.

"Ben, I just need time. I told you. When Emma's better, we'll see."

Ben watched the ambivalence in her expression and believed that a part of her wanted him as much as he wanted her. Then the ice princess took over and froze him out.He stood and held out his hand to her. "One kiss before I go?"

Maggie took his hand and stood to gaze into his gorgeous chestnut eyes. Oh, how she had missed him these past months. Before she knew it, his lips found hers and captured her mouth fully, deeply, his tongue teasing hers as she kissed him back. His hands caressed her back and moved under her tee shirt to cup her breasts, his fingers gentling twirling her nipples to hardness. She moaned, helpless, and gave herself to him, wanting him with a desperate need.

Crazy with desire, she barely noticed as he magically divested her of her jeans and panties, his fingers between her legs, urging her to climax. Ben groaned, feeling how wet she was, how ready for him. His jeans dropped to release his erection, and he lifted her, wrapped her legs around him, and plunged in, a joint sigh passing between them as they became one.

"Oh, God, Maggie, I love you," he said, his voice husky. They moved as one, wild kisses of yearning and remembrance passing between them as they reached a crashing, simultaneous climax.

In the aftermath, Ben's legs wobbled. He held her, never wanting to release her, but he searched for a good place to rest. As he eyed their surroundings, they heard voices in the barn and realized Harley and Jeb were headed their way. Ben lunged for the door and pressed his back against it, their bodies still entwined. The door handle rattled and Harley called, "What the heck's going on with this door?"

"Hey, guys," Ben called. "Give us a minute, will you? Be right out."

Silence. Ben and Maggie stared into each other's eyes, waiting. Her arms circled his neck, holding on. They were afraid to breathe.

A moment later, they heard chuckles from the other side of the door. "Oh, okay. Come on, Jeb, let's go see if the van's here. They must be taking care of some urgent business in there." More laughing as they retreated.

Slowly, reluctantly, Ben withdrew and kissed her softly. Then, drawing her close again, he set her down. He was grinning, but his eyes were full of love, love Maggie had missed so desperately. Afraid to speak, she kissed him, her hand caressing his cheek. She hoped her eyes spoke the love she felt for him, even if she couldn't quite say it. Then she smiled and turned away to retrieve her clothes. "We're never going to live this down, you know."

"Don't care."

"Yes, but you don't have to work with those two every day, Mr. Hospitality."

"Well, I'm about to spend six days with one of 'em and he's not going to leave it alone, I guarantee."

Hastily she pulled on her jeans. "Oh, Lord, what were we thinking? Where's my hat? Where're my sunglasses? This is just too ridiculous!"

Ben watched her and smiled as he pulled himself together. Suddenly her frenzied rushing about ceased and she turned to him.

"Sweetheart, you okay?"

Tears in her eyes, she ran to him and jumped into his arms, burying her face against his shoulder. "Oh, Ben, I love you. I've missed you so much! I'm sorry, I'm sorry."

"Hey, hey, nothing to be sorry about, my sweet darling. I've missed you, too, but now we've found each other again, right?" She nodded against his chest, loving his hardness and strength. "The timing could be better, but I'll be back soon."

With another long, lingering kiss, she released him. "And, speaking of the trip, I hear voices. You better get out there."

"Sure can't hold you any longer or I'll have to wear my shirttail out." He laughed and kissed her forehead. "Are you ready to meet some genuine movie stars?"

CHAPTER 59

Ben and Harley had been gone four days, and the stables were quiet. Weeklong pony camps were over, college workers gone, and campers back to school. Jeb and Maggie ran Saturday pony camps during the off-season, but the first wasn't due to start up until the following month. 4-H had its own leaders and their activities mostly took place at the farm, where the kids raised rabbits, miniature goats, and pigs. Two girls kept minihorses at the stables, but they came and went under their leaders' direction. No mustangs had been delivered in over a month.

As Maggie and Jeb sat drinking beers at the end of the workday, he said, "What d'ya think, Boss? They discontinuing the mustang project or what?"

She shrugged. "Haven't a clue. Harley hasn't said anything to me."

"Guess we'll get to keep Tabasco, huh?"

"Hope so."

"Wonder how the trip's going."

"No emergency calls, no heckling from the entourage so far."

"They staying at the Lodge?"

"Yes, and driving everyone crazy, from what I hear."

"Guess you'll be glad when they're back?"

Maggie shrugged. "Gotta run. Picking up Emma from the big house. She'll be impossible tonight after being spoiled rotten all day."

Secretly, Maggie loved days Emma spent with the Morgans. Knowing she was nearby was comforting, and most days, she went up to have lunch with her.

"See you in the a.m., Boss. Have a good one."

Jeb watched her go and marveled as he always did at how gorgeous she was, even if she was off-limits. Besides, he'd been seeing a bit of Stacy Winchester, Gracie's best waitress, and she was pretty cute herself.

Maggie stopped in the barn to kiss Tabasco's nose, waved back over her shoulder, and headed for the big house.

Emma and her grandparents were on the back terrace, playing an animated game of horseshoes. Ruthie was there as well and seemed to be the retriever of all wildly tossed shoes. Emma's peals of laughter echoed through the house from the open terrace doors. "Just follow the noise, miss," Carmela said, smiling as she stood aside to allow Maggie to pass. "Can I bring you some iced tea or lemonade?"

Maggie declined. She and Jeb had spent most of the afternoon mucking out the stalls. She was filthy and eager to get home, shower, and change her clothes.

As she stepped out on the terrace, Emma spied her and cried, "Hi, Mom! Come play!"

"Hi, baby. Having fun?"

Leonora came to give her a tentative hug. "Hi, dear. Would you like a cool drink? Looks like you've had quite a day."

She laughed as Ben Senior pecked her on the cheek. "Yes, we've been up to our elbows in you-know-what all day, so I won't sit. Em, we probably should get going soon. A few more turns, okay?"

Ruthie had just deposited a fresh supply of horseshoes in Emma's lap, and her daughter nodded, turning back to the game. Leonora went to Emma's side, clapping as they started another round.

"Have you got a minute, Maggie?" Ben Senior indicated a wrought iron chair at the side of the terrace. "There's something I'd like to talk to you about."

Maggie sat, and he took the chair next to her.

"As you know, the mustang program has been important to the ranch. It's somewhat profitable, but that's not the major reason for its value to us. The collaboration with the feds has put us on the map and ensured that the land and the ranch will stay protected. We are also saving these beautiful animals that would otherwise be headed to the slaughterhouse for dog food."

She nodded. "Jeb and I were just talking about this and wondering why we haven't had any new horses."

"That's what I wanted to talk to you about. As you've no doubt been reading, the Border Patrol and all their facilities have been swamped with the thousands of unaccompanied minors comin' across the border. They can't release the agents long enough for them to come up and train, but they desperately need the mounts. There are a dozen or so of the mustangs down in Nogales now. Folks have been workin' with 'em, gettin' 'em used to the saddle and so forth, but they're not you, or Harley, or Jeb. They can't do what you do. Anyway, they called and asked if I'd send one of my people down to help out."

"I'm happy to drive down, but that's a long way for a day's work."

"They're askin' for someone to come for a couple of weeks, Maggie. To really get them where they need to be."

"That's impossible. What about Harley or Jeb?"

"I can't spare Harley, and Jeb isn't ready to do it alone. I'd like to send you both. Harley and Ben can hold down the fort, and I'll get a couple of local kids to help with the stalls."

"I'm sorry, Mr. Morgan."

"Ben."

"I'm sorry, Ben, but I can't be away from Emma for that long."

"I've already talked to your dad. He said he could handle it, Ben'll be back, and we have our well-oiled schedule working. Honey, please think about it. If you're willing, I'll pay you overtime, and I have another incentive I'm hoping will sway you. You go down and do this with Jeb, and Tabasco is yours."

Maggie's jaw dropped, and she stared at him. He was right, of course. Emma would be fine and happy as a clam. She was thriving with all the doting attention of aunts, uncles, and grandparents, and she would barely know Maggie was gone.

She smiled at him. "That's bribery. You know how much I love him."

"Who, the horse or my son?"

She laughed. "Both. When do they want me?"

"Next week."

"Can I think about it and let you know tomorrow?"

"Sure, darlin', course you can."

Sly old devil, Maggie thought. *You know darn well what my answer will be, even though I haven't any idea how I'll survive for two weeks without seeing my baby and her dad.*

CHAPTER 60

"Here they come," Jeb called as Maggie dragged a cooler of refreshments out to greet the returning riders. She had just hung up from speaking to Rose. Dr. Heavers wanted to see Emma Monday morning if they were free. Maggie had agreed and asked why, but Rose answered honestly that she was not sure. Her boss had not confided in her, but she told Maggie she thought it was probably just a routine checkup.

The first riders to appear were Julie Bliss and her daughter Ashley. An image of Julie from her recent film, a science fiction thriller, flashed into Maggie's head. She hadn't seen the film, but the trailers featured the gorgeous actress floating in space, her makeup intact, every hair in place. Today's visage was quite different. Julie Bliss's long auburn hair, stuffed under a designer Stetson, stuck out at odd angles, limp and snarled. Makeup-free, her pale face was smudged with mud, and her usually luminous brown eyes appeared haunted. Her freckle-faced, blonde daughter looked a bit better, but that wasn't saying much. Her face was twisted up in a scowl, and they could hear her whining voice from a half mile away.

"Uh-oh," Jeb said, leaning against the gate. "Somebody's not happy."

"Oh, Lord, spare us. The guys must be ready to kill themselves."

She craned her neck, trying to catch a glimpse of her beloved as Harley and Rowdy came into view. He was riding alongside Bliss's twelve-year-old son, who actually looked like he was enjoying himself. Two of the stars' assistants came next, looking better than the ladies.

Finally she spied Royal, who had not one but two riders. Boyd Rooney, star of dozens of action films, sat in front, his leg in a splint. Ben rode behind him, clearly ready to be rid of his fellow rider. When he spied Maggie, he waved his hat, grinning from ear to ear.

"Too bad about the privacy agreements we all signed," Jeb said. "We could make a small fortune with photos and a story documenting this."

"Perish the thought. Oh, Lord, better pull out the steps and call for the van. Looks like Mr. Dreamboat is going to be headed to the hospital."

Jeb called the Lodge, then pulled out the dismount steps just in time to greet Julie Bliss as she slid from her horse and missed the steps, flopping clumsily into his arms.

"Hey, Ms. Bliss, you okay?"

"Get me a drink. Now."

Jeb set her down on one of the lawn chairs. "What's your pleasure? We've got beer, water, and sodas. I'm a huge fan, by the way."

"I want a margarita, but a beer will have to do until we get up to that Godforsaken inn. Water, too!"

Jeb brought the bedraggled star a Dos Equis and two bottles of water as well as the soda Ashley had requested. Maggie tied up the horses and helped the assistants down, waiting for the others. Harley and the son took care of their own mounts, and each grabbed a drink. As Royal approached, Maggie came forward and patted his nose. "Hey, guys. Rough ride?"

Boyd Rooney said nothing. Ben rolled his eyes.

"Okay, let's get you down, Boyd," Harley said as he and Jeb reached up and grabbed the nearly comatose action star. "The van coming?"

"On its way." Maggie gazed up to find Rowdy's other rider grinning down at her. "Hey, you. Everything okay?"

"More than okay."

He dismounted and swept her into his arms. "Woman, you are a sight for sore eyes." Not caring who saw them, Ben kissed her long and deep. Maggie's knees buckled as she returned his embrace.

"Can we skip the Scarlett and Rhett routine and get some help over here?" one of the assistants whined, his face pinched and covered in trail grit. "In case you hadn't noticed, Mr. Rooney is gravely injured."

Reluctantly, the lovers broke apart and went to assist.

"What happened?" Maggie asked as Jeb and Harley loaded Boyd into the van.

"What didn't?" Ben said, arm circling her shoulder as they headed for the shade.

Once the guests had departed, Boyd to the hospital in north Tucson, the others to the Lodge, Ben sat and pulled her into his lap. "Oh, my darling, it is good to be home. Harley's fired, by the way."

Maggie nuzzled his neck, not caring about the thick layer of trail grit and sweat that covered his skin.

Later, all four of them sat in the shade and sipped cold beers, laughing as Ben and Harley recounted highlights of the week's trip. None of the group had ever ridden a horse. Apparently, matinee cowboy Boyd used a stunt double in all his Westerns, and Julie discovered on day one that she was allergic to horses. She hated practically everything about the trip, including most of the food. On day five, Boyd had fallen off his horse and twisted his ankle. He insisted his leg was broken, so they had splinted it, but Harley said he'd bet a month's wages it was nothing but a slight sprain. On the way back, Julie's horse had veered sharply, and she had slipped off into a minor stream. "Funniest damn thing you ever saw," Harley said, grabbing another beer. "Would've left her there if we could, she was screamin' so hard. That's when Mr. Morgan had to step in and fire my ass."

Later, after the horses had been cooled down, fed, and watered,

Harley and Jeb headed home. "I've gotta go, too," Maggie said as she and Ben walked arm in arm toward their vehicles. "Dad's got something tonight, so I've gotta get back and relieve him."

"I wish I could come take you to dinner, but I fear I'll be tied up with this lot today and tomorrow until we can get rid of them."

"No problem. I'm beat. Ben, are you free Monday morning?"

"Far as I know. Why?"

"Dr. Heavers wants to see Emma and us."

"For?"

"A checkup, I guess. If you're busy, that's okay, but I'd like it if you could—"

"Of course, sweetheart. I'll pick you up. What time?"

Maggie reached up, her arms circling his neck as she kissed him, loving his scent, trail sweat and all. "Nine, okay?"

He nodded.

"It's good to have you home."

CHAPTER 61

Monday morning, there was bumper-to-bumper traffic on their way into Tucson. They had lots of opportunity to talk about Maggie's upcoming trip. Ben assured her that between himself, Ned, and the team, Emma would be well taken care of. Maggie was sick with worry, but she had agreed to go, so she was going.

Dr. Heavers and Rose spent a great deal of time with Emma, talking with her, moving her legs, and testing reflexes and muscle tone. Ben and Maggie observed quietly as their brave little girl endured yet another round of poking, prodding, and sometimes painful manipulations. Afterward, they returned to Dr. Heavers's office and Sadie appeared, no longer pregnant but still plump with baby weight.

"Hi, Emma. How are you? Wanta go to the cafeteria for ice cream?" Emma nodded, and off they went.

Once the door closed, Dr. Heavers turned to Maggie and Ben, who sat side by side, holding hands on the love seat opposite him.

"Folks, thanks for coming on such short notice. I have to be back east for the next few months, maybe longer, so I wanted to check on Emma before I took off."

"No problem," Ben said. "How's she doing?"

"Everything looks good. Her spine has healed. The MRIs she had two weeks ago show no lesions, no breaks. The surgery was successful."

"But, she's not going to walk, is she?" Maggie asked quietly.

Dr. Heavers's eyes met hers, and he paused before replying. "I honestly don't know, my dear. All indications say she should be capable of walking, but she has not made the progress I would have hoped. One never knows what the future will hold, but it would be my recommendation to scale back her therapy to twice a week and let her return to school and her normal activities."

"Won't that hinder her progress?" Ben asked.

"No, at this point, I don't believe so. In fact, it will be good for Emma to rejoin her friends and get back into life away from the clinic."

They talked for a while longer. Then Ben and Maggie rose. They could hear Emma in the hallway, so Maggie went out to her and left Ben with Dr. Heavers and Rose, who had said little throughout their conversation.

He turned back to Dr. Heavers. "One question, Doctor. Emma really wants to ride. Months ago I had a special saddle made for her, but wanted to make sure it would be safe. Would it be dangerous for her spine?"

"At this point, the spine is healed. It's the nerves that need to get with the program, and they are not cooperating. So, no, it would not be dangerous—unless, of course, she falls off. The stimulation might actually be good for her recovery."

They said their good-byes, and Rose walked them out. As they stood in the parking lot, she looked sad. "Everything okay?" Ben asked as Maggie got Emma into her car seat.

"He's dying. He's going east for treatment, but there's not much hope. Pancreatic cancer, very advanced. I'm not sure he'll be back at all."

Ben embraced his friend. "So sorry, Rosie."

Maggie had heard Rose's words and came around to hug her, too. "If there's anything we can do, please let us know." Her words sounded hollow and useless, but she didn't know what else to say.

CHAPTER 62

Maggie's teary departure over, she was immersed in the work at Nogales, overwhelmed by the situation at the Children's Center. During the day, she and Jeb ran the mustang training, but every evening they headed to the center to assist with the kids' meals, baths, and bedtime. Some of the unaccompanied children were as young as four, alone or with an eight- or nine-year-old sibling to watch over them. One week stretched into two. Then, after much hand-wringing and many phone calls back and forth, they decided to stay on for a third week. Ben had given Emma a temporary cell phone, which the child kept in a tiny purse that was never far from her. Mother and daughter talked two or three times a day, Emma always full of chatter about her day's activities.

"If she wasn't so flippin' happy, I'd be out of here like a shot," Maggie told Jeb, but Emma *was* happy with the large extended family they had never had, so the decision to stay longer was easier.

Ben spent every evening with Emma and Ned, and many days, as well. The stables were quiet, and it was off-season at the Lodge. Two local teenagers were helping Harley with chores so Ben could spend time with his daughter. Every afternoon, he lifted Emma onto Sunny and strapped her into the special saddle. Like the slide months earlier, the first time she had been terrified, but then she took to riding like a duck to water.

One warm afternoon as Ben led her around the corral, she spied his best friend. "Look at me, Harley! Look at me!"

"You look pretty great up there, precious," he called, smiling at his friend, who gazed proudly at his beautiful child. When Emma was astride a horse, one could almost forget about her disability.

Ben turned and winked at his friend. "She does look great, doesn't she? Think her mom'll kill me when she gets back?"

"You haven't told her about this?"

Ben shook his head and gave Sunny freer rein as Emma circled them.

Harley whistled. "Good luck with that, buddy. Then again, once she sees Em so happy up there, she probably won't kill you."

"Hope so," Ben said, not wanting to risk Maggie pulling away from him again. He missed her so much and it had only been two weeks. Now they were stretching it to three, maybe even a fourth week.

"Gotta take off, guys. See you tomorrow." Harley waved and disappeared into the barn.

Emma circled a few more times as Ben marveled at how comfortable she was in the saddle. "What do you say, Peanut? Ready to call it a night? I was thinking pizza. Or we can call your grandpa and meet up at Gracie's."

"Okay, Daddy!"

The child's intense brown eyes stared at him, waiting for his reaction.

Dumbfounded, Ben stared at her. "You know?"

Sunny approached and Emma smiled shyly. "When I waked up, I heard you."

"You mean you've really known all this time?"

She nodded. "Are you mad at me?"

"Mad?" He unstrapped her and hugged her tiny body to his. "Not on your life, Sweet Pea. I've never been happier in my life to hear you say 'Daddy' and to be your daddy."

She nestled into his arms and sighed.

"Does your mom know?" She shook her head. "Only Grandpa. I told him, but we decided to keep it a secret."

"Why?"

She shrugged.

"You little stinker," he said, tickling her as she howled with laughter. "Won't Mom be surprised when she hears. Shall we wait and tell her together?" Emma nodded. "We'll have lots of surprises, won't we? Wait'll she sees you riding Sunny."

They had already agreed to surprise Maggie with the riding. Ned had gone along with it. Ben had another surprise, as well, but was keeping that one from both mother and daughter.

CHAPTER 63

Finally, the day came when Maggie and Jeb packed up to head home. It had been an exhausting stretch of round-the-clock work. Both were eager to get home, but they hated to leave the children. The center was so short-staffed, but the feds were sending social services personnel from all over the country within the week, so perhaps things would begin to ease.

Jeb had driven them down in his jeep. As he let Maggie off at home, they hugged.

"Take the day off tomorrow, Jeb. You've earned it."

"You, too, Boss. Take care."

As Maggie hoisted her bags on her shoulder, the door burst open and Ned, with Emma in his arms, headed down the steps to greet her. "Hey, stranger," he called as Maggie dropped her bags and scooped Emma into her arms.

Maggie looked past her dad toward the house. Ned followed her gaze. "He's not here, sweetheart. He wanted to be here but got called away."

Maggie shrugged. "Humph, don't know what you're talking about."

"Mommy, Ben's picking us up in the morning! We're going on an adventure!"

"Is that so?"

She gazed at her father, eyes questioning.

"Don't ask me. Those two have been thick as thieves the past week, planning something. Guess you'll find out tomorrow."

"Well, right now, I've got you two! What's for supper, anyway?"

They spent a lively evening, with Emma prattling on about her school and Maggie telling them about her time in Nogales. Finally, with Emma settled into bed sleeping, she emerged to find Ned reading in his favorite chair.

"How you holding up, Dad? You exhausted?"

"Naw, had lots of help."

"Any change?"

Knowing what she meant, Ned shook his head. "Not that I can see. Her teachers haven't seen anything, either. Happy at school, though. Some cute new kids and therapy goin' okay."

"Well, that's what's important," she said, bending to kiss his check. "Night, Dad."

As Maggie turned to head to bed, her cell phone rang. It was Ben.

"Hey, sweetheart, you home safe?"

"Yup."

"Sorry I couldn't be there. Had to go out of town. Am just coming over the pass now."

They had spoken several times a day while Maggie was in Nogales, and Ben had never mentioned having to go away. "Oh?"

"Business. Will tell you about it tomorrow. Did Em tell you about our adventure?"

"She did. Do I get to know what it is about?"

"Nope, it's a surprise. Pick you up around eleven. Is that okay?"

"What about work? I'm sure Harley's chomping at the bit to have us back on the job."

"He's fine. The local kids are still there. You are both ordered to take tomorrow off."

"Well, then, I guess I'd better follow orders. Ben, there's so much I want to say to you, to tell you. In between the long days and nights, I've done a lot of thinking."

"Me, too. Tomorrow, sweetheart. I love you. See you at eleven."

"Is this a fancy adventure?"

"No, jeans are fine. Have a good night."

He hung up before Maggie could tell him she loved him, tell him how foolish she had been and how much she didn't want to spend another day away from him, ever. How much she wanted them to be a family, how much she wanted to say yes and throw her arms around him and never let go.

CHAPTER 64

It was a beautiful fall day. The sun was out, the air crisp and cooler, the skies blue and cloudless. Ben appeared at eleven on the dot and strapped Emma into her car seat, a permanent one he had purchased for the Rover. "Ladies, are we ready?"

Emma giggled and returned his wink as he strapped her in.

"Whatever you two are up to, it'd better be good," Maggie said as she waved to her dad.

"Have a great time," Ned called, smiling at the little family as they drove away. Whatever Ben Morgan was up to, Ned Williams was pretty sure it would make both his precious girls happy. His respect for Ben had grown over the past few months as he observed the loving care he gave to Emma. He trusted the man and liked him. He was good for his daughter and granddaughter.

Maggie was in jeans and a light coral sweater. The white V-neck tank under it hugged her curves and the neckline plunged, revealing the swell of her breasts. Dara would call it a 'boob shirt,' and Maggie had chosen it because it made her feel wanton and sexy. Ben's expression and roving eyes when she had opened the door told her she had made the impression she wanted. He looked as if he wanted to devour her on the spot.

As she slid into the Rover, she spied a picnic basket, no doubt packed full of Carmela's delicious food. She smiled, looking ahead to a relaxed day with the two people she loved most in the world. Emma giggled in the backseat and Ben said little, aside from asking her about Nogales and her time there. It was small talk since he'd heard most of it before, just a way to pass the time until they reached their destination.

When he turned into the ranch, she assumed they were headed for the old farmhouse, a perfect spot for a picnic. As they started down the side road leading to the farmhouse, Maggie noticed that the road had been widened and graded, and the brush cut back. There appeared to be cleared land ahead that she did not remember from their last trip. As he turned the corner and pointed the Rover up hill, she gasped at the sight ahead of them.

There was the farmhouse, newly sided and painted. New windows now replaced the old, and additions on both sides stretched out, crab-like, to hug the hillside as if they had always been there. A brand-new barn stood to the left with a rustic-looking two-car garage beside it. White rockers lined the rebuilt front porch, and a russet front door stood ajar, inviting them in. Flowers bloomed in newly planted gardens on either side of the porch.

Speechless, Maggie stared straight ahead at the most beautiful house she had ever seen.

"So? What do you think?"

"Oh, Ben, it's beautiful. How did you? When did you?"

"Sam designed it. We began work right after Emma's surgery. Took some doing and lots of overtime, but the crew outdid themselves."

He carried Emma to the porch, where a wheelchair waited, and she scooted in, every floor surface ramped and wheelchair-accessible. Maggie followed. He took her hand and led her inside. Every room was beautifully furnished, the walls painted soft, muted colors of the desert and fields. The kitchen was state-of-the-art yet designed to look old, in keeping with the rustic farmhouse.

"Look, Mommy," Emma called from the end of the hall. "Come see. This is my room! Daddy says I can decorate it any way I want!"

"Daddy?" Maggie turned to him, tears in her eyes.

"She's known since after her operation. I was talking to her, thinking she was asleep, telling her how much I loved being her daddy, and she heard every word. She told me a couple of weeks ago."

"Oh, Ben, this is too much to take in."

"I left Emma's room and the master bedroom empty so you could decide what you wanted, but you can change the whole house if you want, get rid of this furniture, and we'll choose things together that you like. I brought a few things from Santa Barbara, too, but if you don't like 'em, they can disappear.

"But, my darling, I'm getting way ahead of myself. Em, can you give us a minute?"

Emma wheeled past them and headed for the front porch. Ben led Maggie to the back of the house and out the back door where a small stone terrace and garden area had been added. He pulled her to a stone bench, then knelt beside her. "I love you, Maggie Williams. I've tried to show you in every way I know just how much I love you. Please make me the happiest man alive and say you'll marry me. If you don't like it here, I'll go anywhere as long as I'm with you and Emma.

"I know I'm not always the easiest person. I'm not proud of all of my past exploits either, but I know that I cannot live my life without you. What can I do to convince you, my love?"

"You can stop talking, for one thing."

"Excuse me?"

"Yes."

"Yes, stop talking?"

"No, just yes. I'll marry you. I love you, Ben Morgan, and know I cannot live without you, either. That's what I wanted to tell you last night, but you made me wait. And yes to this house. It's absolutely perfect. What you've done so far is lovely, and I'll have fun choosing the rest with you."

"You said yes! Emma, she said yes!"

He picked her up and twirled her in his arms as Emma looked out from the back door.

"Told you she would, Daddy!"

The three of them twirled together through every room in their beautiful new home.

CHAPTER 65

Sated after one of Carmela's delicious picnic lunches, they lay, all three, on a quilt spread over the grass near the house, the valley and mountains stretched before them. Finally Maggie sat up and smiled at both of them, love shining in her deep azure eyes. "Thank you both for an absolutely perfect day."

"Not over yet, my love," Ben said, winking at Emma. "You ready, Sweet Pea?"

"Yup. You stay there, Mommy. We'll be right back!"

Emma reached up, and Ben swooped her up into his arms.

"Uh-oh, what're you two up to?"

"We'll be back in five minutes. You relax, sweetheart. Something else to drink?"

"No, thanks, I'm perfect." Maggie lay back and closed her eyes. "I'll take a little catnap while you two are off plotting." The sun warmed her face and the scent of honeysuckle surrounded her as Maggie drifted off, blissfully happy.

Enveloped in warm, peaceful slumber, Emma's voice startled her. "Mommy! Look at me, Mommy!"

Disoriented, she rubbed her eyes, expecting to see Ben returning with their child in his arms. Instead, he walked alone out of the barn, trailing a rope behind him. Sunny, the pony, came into view, and on his back, Emma sat proud and tall. Maggie stared in disbelief, then pride at her beautiful child so happy and confident in the saddle. Her daddy led them on, his whole body expressing his own pride and happiness at his daughter's accomplishment.

"Oh, Ben, is it safe?" she called, eyes never leaving Emma.

"Dr. Heavers himself gave me the go-ahead. Thought it might help with nerve stimulation. She can't fall off. Don't worry, sweetheart."

Maggie's shoulders relaxed, and her heart swelled with love as she watched father and child circle the corral. "Oh, sweetie, you're amazing! I'm so proud of you!" Ben Morgan had turned their lives upside down in so many ways. Emma might never walk again, but on horseback, she could feel whole again.

They made a few more circles. Then Ben led them back into the barn, and Maggie followed. Once they got Sunny brushed and fed, Ben carried Emma out into the sunshine. She yawned and rested her head against his chest. By the time they reached the picnic quilt, she was asleep. He set her down, and Maggie put fingers to her lips and whispered, "Let's let her sleep." She covered Emma with her sweater, then strolled toward the house.

Ben watched her closely. "Are you angry? About Emma on horseback, I mean."

In answer, she opened the front door and stepped into the cool of the living room. A wicked smile played across her face as she crooked a finger, beckoning him. "Leave the door open, Mr. Morgan, just in case she wakes."

"Does this mean you're not mad?"

"Do I look mad? Come here, cowboy."

As she backed up, she stepped out of her sandals, then slipped her sweater from her shoulders and let it fall to the floor. Slowly she unbuttoned her jeans.

As his eyes drank in the sight of her glorious body, Ben felt himself grow hard. "Why, Maggie Williams, what's come over you?"

"Can't I have at least one surprise, too? Remove your shirt and pants, please, or shall I help you out of them?"

He closed the distance between them and shed his clothes with lightning speed. "Oh, my God, Maggie, I love you so much."

Before he could make a move, her arms circled his neck. She drew him into a deep, luscious kiss, her tongue capturing his, teasing, probing, and driving him wild.

"What about Emma?" he asked, breathless and almost crazy with desire.

"She's fine. I can see her. I think it's okay for her parents to have a little fun, don't you?" She trailed kisses down his neck and chest. Her jeans and panties lay at her feet, and she brought one leg up, beckoning him.

Ben lifted her legs, wrapped them around him and plunged into her, deep and hard. "Is this—"

"No, no, deeper, take me. Please don't stop." She matched him thrust for thrust, her breasts rubbing and circling his chest until Ben thought he might pass out with needing her. He backed up to the wall and rammed into her over and over as Maggie cried, "More, more, don't stop. Love me more and more."

They climaxed in one explosive crescendo, their bodies sleek with sweat. Maggie rested her head on his shoulder and peered around the door to spy Emma still sleeping peacefully on the quilt. She kissed the scar on his shoulder from a bicycle accident in his youth, then made her way up his neck to find his lips waiting for hers. They shared a long, deep kiss, still locked together as one, leaned against the wall of their home. Finally she pulled back slightly and smiled sleepily. "How could I be mad when you've given my daughter such a precious gift? I've never seen her so confident and happy."

"Does this mean you'll still marry me?"

"You bet your sweet ass it does, Ben Morgan."

"Yours is pretty sweet, too, my beloved fiancée."

She felt him growing hard inside her and moaned. "Oh, how I wish we could do it again, my love, but our daughter is stirring."

Reluctantly, Ben lowered her, withdrawing from her wetness and warmth. They scurried to retrieve their clothes and dressed quickly. With one more kiss, they walked arm and arm to where Emma waited, eyes open, staring up at the vast blueness of the afternoon sky.

"Hey, Peanut. You ready to head home?"

"This is home, isn't it Daddy?"

As Maggie closed the picnic basket, Ben reached down to scoop Emma into his arms. "Yup, it sure is. Very soon, sweetheart. Very soon."

CHAPTER 66

The wedding date was set for the following month. Ben's parents had offered the big house for the occasion, and to Ben's surprise, Maggie had accepted gratefully. She had also accepted Leonora, Ruthie, and Beth's offer to make all the arrangements. When Ben asked her if she was sure, she answered truthfully. "I'm terrible at girlie things. 'Fraid you'll have to get used to that, my love."

"You're pretty terrific at some girlie things," he had responded, lust in his eyes.

The month before the wedding, the stables were hopping. Maggie, Jeb, and Harley were busy with fall camps, lessons, and winterizing projects. Ned was called out on a number of veterinary emergencies, and Ben was away for a week in California to settle the sale of his house, take care of closing accounts, and meet with his partners, Chip and David. During this period, Emma's care fell mostly to her aunts and uncles, who happily stepped in, Team Emma still going strong. Robbie and Kyle, in particular, cleared their schedules and spent days with her at the ranch and shuttling her back and forth to therapy. When her parents asked about her days, Emma gave somewhat vague monosyllabic answers, but she seemed happy.

A day at the ranch always included a ride, sometimes in the corral and sometimes on the trail. Kyle wasn't crazy about riding, but Robbie happily took her. Heart in her throat, Maggie watched them head off with Robbie chatting and laughing and Emma giggling beside him. "Be careful!" she would call, but they were usually so involved they barely had time to wave.

"Two peas in a pod," Harley said as he and Maggie watched them ride off.

Emma loved Robbie's company the most of all her aunts and uncles He seemed to possess the same capacity for joy that she did, and each day they spent together was filled with laughter and fun. Two peas in a pod was right.

CHAPTER 67

Mouth agape, Harley watched as Maggie drove up and parked the clunker. "What the hell are you doing here, woman? It's less than forty-eight hours until the wedding. Shouldn't you be getting a fitting or tasting wedding cake samples or something?"

"Ha, ha. Dress fits perfectly, and I trust that Gracie will make a delicious cake."

Maggie smiled, thinking of the cake controversy of several weeks earlier. She and Ben had promised Gracie that she could make the wedding cake, and Leonora, who was doing most of the arrangements, assumed Carmela would be making it. After a minor kerfuffle, they had compromised. Carmela was now making an armadillo cake for the barbecue the night before the wedding.

Ben and Maggie were hosting the barbecue at the farmhouse, with Raoul and Carmela cooking and serving. It was just family, the wedding party, and a few close friends from out of town.

The wedding party consisted of Emma as maid of honor, with Ruthie and Dara as bridesmaids. Beth had obtained a license that allowed her to officiate. Out of the blue, his sister had offered, and the bride and groom were thrilled. Since Ben refused to choose among his brothers, Harley was best man with Robbie, Sam, and Kyle his groomsmen. Chip, David, and their families were coming in and would stay at the Lodge. The wedding itself was small. A few of the Morgans' friends and neighboring ranchers, the Dillon family, Jeb Barnes and his date, and about a dozen townspeople rounded out the guest list.

"Seriously, Mags, what the hell are you doing here?"

"Working, of course."

"Oh, no, you're not. There's nothing to do, and we've got it covered."

Her cell phone rang, and Maggie saw her dad's number. She raised a finger and mouthed "hold on" as she turned away from Harley. "What's that, Dad? You're breaking up. Who called?"

"Your mother."

Stunned, Maggie sat down hard on a stump. "What?"

"Honey, I love you, but why didn't you say? You could've given a guy a little warning? I'm surprised you'd want it."

"I didn't. Dad, let me check on this, and I'll get back to you. Do you have a number?"

She fished around in her purse and found a pen and scrap of paper. "Go ahead. Okay, got it. Don't worry. I'll take care of it."

Maggie snapped her phone shut and turned back to her boss. "Did you know about this?"

"What're you talking about?" he asked, knowing full well to what she referred. When Ben had told him he was tracking down Julianna Williams as a surprise for Maggie, Harley had counseled against it. Based on what little he knew of the story of the wife and mother's abandonment of her family, he felt pretty certain that Julianna's appearance would not be a happy surprise for her ex-husband or her daughter.

"You know damn well what I'm talking about. When has your friend ever not told you what he's up to? Where is he?"

"Last I heard, he was going into town, picking up the liquor. Listen, Mags, he doesn't know any better. He thought it'd make you happy."

"Do I look happy? This is absolutely *not* happening. I would never put my father through the pain of seeing her, and Emma's never heard of her. That woman is absolutely not coming. Where is she, do you know?"

"I think there was talk of her staying in town, maybe at one of the B and B's? The boss lady made the reservations, I think."

"This is unbelievable!" Maggie stormed past him into the barn, shoving open the office door and slamming it behind her. Her hands trembled as she opened the crumpled scrap of paper and dialed the number.

"Hello?" The voice, vaguely familiar, was huskier now.

"Is this Julianna?"

"Yes? Who's calling?"

"It's Maggie."

Silence.

"Oh, hello, darling! I'm so excited to see you again and meet Emily and your future husband."

"My daughter's name is Emma."

"Oh, sorry, sweetheart."

"It's fine, and expected. You've been no part of our lives—mine, Emma's, or Dad's."

"I'd like to change that, sweetie. It's been a long time. I was thrilled when your fiancée contacted me."

"Well, he was wrong to do that. I knew nothing about it and now that I do, I'm going to have to ask you not to come."

"But I wanted to see you, baby."

"I'm sorry, but this is not a good time for us to get reacquainted. I won't do that to Dad, Emma, or me."

"I'm all packed."

"That's too bad, but I cannot have you come and upset the day for us, especially Dad."

"Well, how about I come and stay? Maybe you and I can have breakfast, and I can meet the handsome groom? His folks have been kind enough to put me up at a B and B. I haven't been to Saguaro in ages. I'd love to catch up with old friends, and you, too, of course."

"No."

"Excuse me?"

"I said no, and I will be telling my fiancé and his parents no as well. As soon as I hang up, I'm cancelling the B and B. I can't stop you from making your own reservations, but I won't have my family subsidizing this trip at this time."

"Well, if that's the way you feel."

"That's the way I feel."

"Maybe someday?"

"Maybe someday. Good-bye, Julianna."

Maggie hung up and slipped the phone into her bag with trembling hands. Then she doubled over, head between her knees, and sobbed, which was how Harley found her several minutes later.

He sat beside her, patting her shoulder, and Maggie leaned against him. "Hey, hey, Mags. You okay?"

A short time later, she sat up, wiped her eyes, and stiffened her back.

"Better?"

She snapped her fingers at him. "B and B, which one?"

"How the hell should I know?"

She stood and grabbed her bag. "I'll be back."

"No, you won't. Go home! Do your bride stuff. We're all set here."

Maggie drove up to the big house and found her future mother-in-law in the kitchen chatting with Carmela. The two women were consulting over what looked like a large lump of clay.

Leonora spied her and smiled. She was dressed in denim capris and white tee shirt, an apron adorned with giant chili peppers tied round her waist. "Hi, darlin', how're you doing?"

"Hello. I'm fine, thanks."

"You don't look fine. Here, come sit. Carm and I can leave the armadillo for a minute. Frosting's not ready yet, anyway. Want something cool to drink? Iced tea, lemonade, water?"

"No, thank you. I'll only stay a minute. Mrs. Morgan, I—"

"Leonora, please, honey. In two days we'll be family."

"Leonora, it's about Julianna Williams, my mother."

"Oh, darn, Ben will be so disappointed. It was supposed to be a surprise. Who spilled the beans?"

"She called my dad."

"Oh?"

"I do not want her at the wedding. I've told her that, and I need to cancel the B and B. Which one did you or Ben book?"

"Shadowbrook. It's lovely, right on the creek. Jeanie and Norm Stevens run it."

"Do you have the number handy?"

"Darlin', don't give it another thought. I'll call and cancel myself right now. You run along and do whatever you have to do, and we'll get back to work on the armadillo."

As Maggie pulled the clunker beside the barn, her heart no longer raced. She was still angry that Ben had not asked her, but she decided to put her feelings aside and work for a few hours until Emma and Robbie returned from their ride. Her dress was hanging in her room, Raoul and Carmela had the barbecue preparations well in hand, and the Morgans had made all the arrangements for the reception at the Lodge. They were to be married in the small Saguaro Chapel, a nondenominational sanctuary shared by many of the local churches.

She found Harley in the barn.

He glanced up at her and shook his head. "Thought I told you to go home. Everything straightened out?"

"Let's not talk about it, okay? Any sign of the riders? I thought I'd work until Emma's back. Then we'll take off."

"They're planning to be out most of the day, and they're eating lunch with Beth and Ruthie over at the farm. Planning a picnic, I think."

"No one told me."

"We're trying to free you up. You're the bride, remember?"

Anger rose again, and Maggie grabbed her bag. "Fine, I'm free. Since no one seems to want me around, I'm taking off."

"Good idea. If you see your fiancé, tell him I have some questions for him."

"I better not see him!"

"Hey, give the guy a break, Mags. He was tryin' to please you."

"Well, he didn't."

Harley followed her out of the barn, grinning as he watched her stalk to her car. "See you at the barbecue."

"We'll see!"

She slammed the door of the clunker and took off in a cloud of dust.

CHAPTER 68

After Harley related Maggie's reaction to the news of her mother, Ben called her cell and apologized profusely.

"It's fine. It's over. Can we just not talk about it?"

"Want me to come over?"

"No, thanks. I need some time alone."

"How about tomorrow? Want to have breakfast, go over last-minute prep for the barbecue?"

"It's all set. Carmela and Raoul are pros."

"Maggie, please."

"I'm fine, Ben, really I am. I just wish you'd told me. I feel like with the wedding plans, the past few weeks my life has been spinning out of control. I've barely laid eyes on Emma."

"She's having a ball. Ruthie just called to tell me about the picnic today."

"That's my point! They've been doing all these things with my daughter."

"Our daughter."

"Fine, our daughter, and no one thinks to ask me if I'm okay with it."

"Are you?"

Silence.

"Sweetheart, they're only trying to help to give you time to prepare for the big day. They are crazy about Em, and they love spending time with her."

"I know, and she's having a wonderful time. I just wish people would tell me what's going on. I don't like surprises, especially ones like Julianna Williams."

"No more surprises, I promise."

"Listen, I've got to run. Dad's just pulling up, and we need to talk. See you tomorrow at around four, at the house?"

"I'll see you when I bring Em home."

They rang off, and Maggie told Ned about her conversation with her mother.

"You sure about this, sweetie?"

"Absolutely."

"'Cause I can suck it up for the day if it's what you want. I was just surprised."

Maggie went into his outstretched arms, her beloved parent, the only mother and father she had known. "Never. No one's sucking it up, least of all you, or me, or Emma. This is what I want—you, me, and Emma, together as a family."

"Don't forget your fiancé."

"Humph. I guess we can include him."

Beers in hand, they went out on the back porch to relax, which is where Ben and Emma found them an hour later.

While Emma regaled Ned with stories about her day, Maggie walked Ben out to the Rover. "Thanks for bringing her home."

"Still mad?"

She shook her head. "No, just ready for life to calm down."

"You and me both." He pulled her into his arms and kissed her forehead. "Two days, my love."

Maggie leaned against him and absorbed his warmth and strength. "Do you promise?"

"I do."

"I don't suppose you'll tell me where we're going after? There's another thing I know nothing about, one more surprise."

He leaned back, cupped her cheek, and gave her a tender kiss. "If the surprises are putting you over the brink, I'll tell you, sweetheart."

Unbidden tears sprang to Maggie's eyes, and she shook her head. He read her so well, and his generosity never ceased to astound her. "No, I'll be brave and let you have the fun of this one last surprise, if you promise it has nothing to do with Julianna Williams or other unbidden ghosts from the past."

"Not a chance."

He kissed her deeply and felt himself grow hard.

Mischief twinkled in her eyes as she gazed up at him. "Missed me, huh?"

"I'm in agony. Don't s'pose you'd like to go for a ride and put this cowboy out of his misery?"

Maggie's hand traveled south from his chest until she caressed his erection, which now strained at his jeans. "No can do, cowboy. I've gotta get in to see our daughter. Hear about all the things she's been doing without me."

"You're a wicked one, Maggie Williams."

Reluctantly he let her go. She pecked his check, then headed up the walk, waving over her shoulder. "Call it revenge for all the ups and downs of my day."

"I'll get you for this!"

"I'm counting on it."

CHAPTER 69

It was a perfect night for a barbecue. Carmela and Raoul outdid themselves with everything from the incredible appetizers to the huge armadillo cake. To Emma's delight, they ceded the honor of cutting into it to her, and Ben held her aloft as she wielded the enormous knife Carmela handed to her, revealing the moist red velvet cake inside.

Ned, Maggie, and Emma went to Gracie's for breakfast on the wedding morning, then returned home for a few hours of quiet time. After a small lunch, Maggie insisted Emma nap, and she, too, shut her eyes. Then, before they knew it, it was time to change and prepare. Maggie had refused the services of a professional stylist, so Dara came to help with her hair and a touch of makeup. Ruthie had volunteered to dress the maid of honor so that the bride could focus on her own preparations. She picked up Emma at two. "See you at the chapel, ladies."

"See?" Maggie said to her friend, pointing as Ruthie loaded Emma into the Rover. "My life is no longer my own."

Dara patted her shoulder. "Lucky you with all this help."

Maggie had elected to wear her hair long and flowing, no veil, a few desert flowers her only adornment. When she was finally ready, she gazed into the mirror with tear-rimmed eyes.

"Hey, sweetie, what's this? You'll wreck all my beautiful makeup work!"

"I just can't believe how lucky I am, Emma and me. I'm afraid it will all disappear. Like I've been in a dream the past year."

"No chance. You've landed the most eligible bachelor in the valley, and he is crazy about you. He's a lucky man."

Maggie hugged her dear friend. Dara was dressed in the pale blue sheath that all the bridesmaids would wear. The color flattered her. Her long red hair was swept up in a chignon at the base of her neck. Ben had bought all the bridesmaids and Emma simple pearl necklaces. This would be their only adornment save pearl earrings for the women. Carmela had sewn tiny pearls into Emma's flowered headband to match the other jewelry, and Emma and Ruthie had decorated her wheelchair with blue ribbons and desert flowers in pinks, blues, and white.

Ned whistled as his daughter stepped into the living room. "Wow, sweetie. You look like a million bucks. Ben Morgan's gonna have a really tough time concentrating on his vows."

Maggie smiled at her dad in his dark navy suit. "You look pretty spectacular yourself, cowboy."

He extended his arm. "Limo's here. Ready?"

As Maggie and Ned came in to many compliments and accolades, Leonora and Ben Senior waited in the vestibule. Her soon-to-be father-in-law wore the same suit as Ned, as did all the ushers and Ben. Maggie and Ned stepped into the anteroom and waited as guests filed in. At Leonora's suggestion, Maggie and Ned would walk down the aisle first, followed by the ushers and bridesmaids. Robbie would push Emma's chair, and they would come at the end, with Harley, the best man, behind them.

Finally, strains of "Here Comes the Sun" sounded, and Ned offered his arm. "Okay, sweetie, I believe this is our cue."

She nodded. "I wish I could see Emma before I go. Where is she?"

"Over across the hall. She wants to surprise you with how pretty she looks."

They proceeded slowly, the soft music lilting as they neared the tiny altar where Ben waited.

Spying her beloved took her breath away, so handsome in his dark suit, tanned face smiling at her, his eyes telling her everything she needed to know. This man loved her, cherished her, and was clearly pleased by her dress. The simple lines of the off-white sheath hugged her curvaceous body in all the right places. The dress tapered and fell into a silky bell at the bottom. A plunging collar of silk revealed glorious cleavage, and Ben could not take his eyes from her as he reached to take her hand.

Beth leaned forward and smiled. "You look gorgeous. Both of you."

The music changed, and the bridesmaid and ushers came down the aisle arm in arm, the women in blue, the men in dark suits and blue ties that matched the bridesmaids' dresses. Maggie craned her neck, trying to catch a glimpse of Emma. Out of the corner of her eye, something distracted her, and she spied Emma's wheelchair parked at the side of the altar, just behind Ruthie.

"What's happening?" she whispered to Ben. "Is he going to carry her?"

Ben shrugged as the side door opened. Robbie stepped into the aisle, another handsome Morgan in his dark suit and blue tie. Beside him walked a lovely child in white crinoline and lace with a garland of flowers in her hair. She leaned heavily on her uncle as they slowly made their way down the aisle. With each step, Emma's smile widened as her parents, mouths agape, watched with tears streaming down their cheeks.

"She's—" Ben said, squeezing Maggie's hand.

"Yes." Maggie nodded, vision blurry as Emma neared the altar.

Ruthie rolled the wheelchair nearer and whispered, "One last surprise."

As uncle and niece reached them, Ben caught Emma up in his arms, and they both hugged and kissed her. Then he set her in the chair and gazed from his daughter to each of his siblings, not a dry eye among them. "I'll settle up with you all later."

"If I forget to tell you," Maggie whispered, "this is the happiest day of my life."

CHAPTER 70

The Lodge was festooned with flowers and brightly colored ribbons. Tiny lights twinkled as the sun set beyond the mountains. The reception was held on the back terraces. Ben and Maggie had not wanted a sit-down dinner. Instead, tables groaned with cheese plates, fruits, vegetables, and all manner of appetizers. Wait staff passed small plates of tapas. Guests sat or stood casually in the glowing light of early evening. The Farleys, a wonderful local band, played whatever was requested, and Maggie and Ben danced and danced, often with Emma in their arms.

As Rose Dillon watched the newlyweds with misty eyes, Sam came to stand beside her. "You've loved him a long time, haven't you, Rosie?"

She nodded. "But she makes him happy, doesn't she? Look at him. Look at them. They're perfect together, aren't they? I'm happy for them."

"We all are. There's someone out there for you, Rosie."

"Where's Rita today?"

"We broke it off a few months ago. Timing was perfect, as it gave me more opportunity to help with Emma."

"Emma's progress is remarkable. A miracle, really. I'm only sorry Dr. Heavers isn't here to see."

"How's he doing, anyway? Ben said he wasn't well."

"Poorly, I'm 'fraid. The treatments aren't working as hoped. They're talking about hospice. He's home in Baltimore with his son and family."

"What a shame."

"Yes, he is a wonderful person, and he's been such a supportive teacher, mentor, and friend. I miss him terribly."

"I know you don't feel much like dancing," Sam said, extending his hand as a slow dance began. "But dance with me, Rosie. One dance?"

She smiled shyly and let gentle, drop-dead gorgeous Sam Morgan lead her to the dance floor. They made a handsome couple as they glided across the floor, Rose in a pink linen sheath and glittering silver jewelry, her hair soft and loose, and Sam in his dark suit, his handsome features so like his older brother's. As they chatted, they passed another couple, Harley and Ruthie. He had asked her to dance and immediately swooped her into his strong arms. Ruthie's eyes as they waltzed by left no doubt of her feelings for the tall, gorgeous cowboy. Harley, usually so guarded, gazed down at her, his eyes soft for a few seconds, allowing her to see the love he had felt for her for over a decade.

"Hmm," Maggie said as she and Ben stood arm in arm, watching the dancers. "There seem to be some interesting matches brewing out there."

"The Harley and Ruthie match has been brewing for years, but Sam and Rose? That's a new one on me."

Beth and Bill passed by the newlyweds, calling congratulations.

"We should have everyone out to the farm for dinner soon," she said. "I barely know Bill, and he seems like a great guy."

"He is, and he's good for my sister."

Emma danced with Kyle, her feet six inches from the floor as he swung her around. Her parents watched her proudly, and Ben shook his head. "Pretty amazing, huh? They've been at it right under our noses."

Maggie laughed. "Even Dad didn't suspect. Kyle told me they've been working most of every day to get her this far. I'm so proud of her."

He nuzzled her neck. "I'm the luckiest man in the world."

His touch warmed her, and Maggie leaned into him, rubbing her body against his. "Can we sneak off and make passionate love somewhere soon? I need you inside me in the worst way."

"Don't you dare start this now, my beloved wife. I can't walk around with a hard-on."

She laughed, pointing to waiters circulating. "Uh-oh, it looks as if it's toast time."

The wait staff passed trays of champagne in fluted glass etched with the Morgan's Run logo. When everyone had their drink of choice, Ben Senior and Leonora ascended the steps leading to the house and called the party together with a clink of glasses. They invited Harley as best man and Emma as maid of honor to give the first toasts. Harley came forward, Emma in his arms.

"Ladies first," he said, setting her down, his arm round her waist for support.

Her grandfather had explained toasting, and Emma was prepared. She stood proudly, holding her Shirley Temple in a fluted glass. "To my mommy and daddy, happy wedding! I love you!"

After the group's applause died down, Harley toasted his friend and coworker, his speech amusing and touching. He ended with, "Buddy, if you don't take good care of her, you'll have to answer to Ned and me. Love you guys."

Finally Ben Senior stepped forward, arm around his wife. He cleared his throat and smiled at the group. "On behalf of my girlfriend and me, I want to thank everyone for coming. We couldn't be happier for our son and his beautiful bride, nor prouder of our darling, beloved granddaughter. Maggie, Emma, and Ned, welcome to our family. We are blessed indeed. Ben's momma and I want to give the couple a gift, something that reflects our pride in them and our hopes for their future."

He reached behind him to grab a long rolled-up sheaf of papers. "As you know, Ben's home for good and is slowly taking over running the ranch and the Lodge so Nora and I can travel. I know he'll do a great job. He already is, as a matter of fact. Even so, we think he needs a little something more to sink his teeth into, to keep him from being bored. And our talented daughter-in-law has a dream that we want to help make a reality. So, if the newlyweds could come forward, we have a gift for you both."

As Ben and Maggie climbed the steps to join the elder Morgans, Ben Senior handed his son the rolled-up papers tied with brightly colored ribbons. They moved to a nearby table and unrolled the gift —blueprints for bunkhouses, a new barn, a recreation and dining hall, and corrals for a children's camp.

Maggie gasped. "It's too much."

"It's your future," Leonora said softly. "Please accept this gift we want to give to you. We love you both so much."

"Sam and I have scouted around the entire property, and there are several sites that would work," Ben Senior said. "You two can decide when you're ready."

They embraced both parents, Maggie now in tears. Ben hugged his dad, then turned to Leonora. "Thank you," he said softly. "I love you both so much."

CHAPTER 71

Later that evening, settled into their suite at a luxurious hotel in Phoenix, their honeymoon luggage set by the door with one shared overnight bag all they needed for the night, Ben reached for her. "Champagne, darling?"

"Thanks, but I think I've had enough." She ran gentle fingers along his jaw.

"You looked incredibly beautiful today, my beloved wife. I mean, you are gorgeous every day, but today you literally took my breath away."

"Ditto," she whispered huskily, kissing his neck. "When I saw you standing there, looking so incredibly handsome, I was afraid I might faint. I fear I've broken many women's hearts today."

"Baloney." He smoothed back her hair and removed the few clips that held remnants of desert flowers.

Maggie turned. "Can you give a girl a hand getting out of her dress?"

"Is there a surprise underneath?"

"Hmm, maybe. I bought a lacy little thing for tonight, but—"

"Let's save it for the honeymoon, okay? I want you too much to wait."

As her dress fell round her ankles, she turned back to him,

unhooking her bra and dropping it. "Speaking of the honeymoon, it's time to 'fess up. I know you had Dara pack for me and I wasn't supposed to look, but I did peek. Mostly warm-weather clothes and not many of them."

"I predict that we will spend very little time in clothes," he whispered, and he captured her full lips in deep kiss. He cupped her breasts and teased her nipples.

"Oh? Won't that shock the neighbors?"

"We won't have any neighbors. We'll be on an island, my love, in the Seychelles, only us and very discreet cook who will be dropping off food and provisions each day. There's housekeeping if we want it, but my vote would be no, since I want you all to myself every minute of every day."

"Oh, Ben Morgan, I want you so badly it hurts."

"You have me, my love, now and for the rest of our lives." As his hand traveled down her stomach, fingers slipping between her legs, he looked down. "Why Maggie Williams, are those lace panties? On a cowgirl, no less?"

"You bet your gorgeous ass," she said, allowing him to slip them off as she dived into a sea of sensation, his lips and fingers setting her on fire. "And it's Maggie Morgan to you, cowboy, and don't you forget it."

Ben stilled. His hands held her motionless and his eyes stared down at her. "Are you serious? I thought you wanted to keep the name Williams?"

She smiled up at him, eyes full of love. "Emma and I talked it over and we agreed. We want to be Morgans, for now and forever."

"In that case, come here, Ms. Morgan, and let me get acquainted."

Suddenly shy, Maggie looked up at him, then wrapped her fingers around his erection, stroking and caressing.

"Oh, no, you don't, my darling. The first time, we're doing this together."

Tears rimmed her eyes and Maggie's arms circled his neck as Ben lifted her, wrapping her legs around him. His tongue was everywhere, drinking her, devouring her until she was delirious with wanting him.

"Please, Ben, I need you now, inside me," she moaned.

He shifted slightly and, hands under her, plunged into her depths, holding tight as he pumped and withdrew with wild abandon.

Maggie climaxed more quickly than she ever had, and she clung to him, every fiber of her being begging for more. She buried her fingers in his hair, keeping him close. Ben groaned as his climax matched her own, the two of them crying out in a thundering release as they fell to the bed, wrapped around one another, wanting to stay as one forever.

Breathless, he nuzzled her neck, kissing her sweetly. "I thought we'd made love before, but that was beyond amazing. If this is what happens when you get married, let's repeat the ceremony every day."

"Hmm," she murmured. "It was pretty amazing, wasn't it? Want to see if we can top it?" Her voice was teasing as she stroked his side and buttocks.

Laughing, he withdrew and sat up, gazing down at his beloved, her thick chestnut tresses spread out on the silk coverlet. "You want to kill me before the honeymoon begins?"

"Not a chance. Have I mentioned how much I love your chest?" She stroked him, hands moving lower.

"I didn't think I could love you any more than I have this past year, but you've made me happier than any man deserves, Maggie Morgan."

"And you deserve to be happy, my love."

"*We* deserve to be happy," he said, bending to kiss the tip of her nose. "And so does our incredible daughter."

"So, what do you say, cowboy? Wanta to see if married sex is still great the second time?"

"Can I recover for a few minutes first?"

"Well, okay," she whispered, snuggling into his arms. "But don't wait too long. I don't feel the same with you over there and me over here." She smiled up at him, eyes mischievous. "You know, disconnected and all."

"I love you, sweetheart."

"I love you, too, my darling husband. And I was only kidding. Take all the time in the world to recover. We have the rest of our lives."

"I like the sound of that, but my dearest wife, I can't wait that long. Come here, Ms. Morgan, and let me see what this cowboy can do for an encore."

Click this *link* for the opening chapters of *Lang's Return,* book two in the Morgan's Run series.

AUTHOR WEBPAGE AND NEWSLETTER SIGN-UP
FOLLOW ME ON BOOKBUB!
FOLLOW ME ON TIKTOK
FOLLOW ME ON INSTAGRAM
FOLLOW ME ON FACEBOOK

If you have five minutes, please <u>review this book!</u>

ALSO BY M. LEE PRESCOTT

Mystery

The Ricky Steele Mysteries

Prepped to Kill

Gadfly

Lost in Spindle City

Poof!

Lady Love: A Cautionary Tale

Stalking Evil

Also, featuring Ricky Steele:

Jigsaw

Roger and Bess Mysteries

Book 1: *A Friend of Silence*

Book 2: *In the Name of Silence*

Book 3: *The Silence of Memory*

Book 4: *Silencing the Pen*

Mapletree Club Murder Mysteries

Book 1: *The Labyrinth Walk*

Contemporary Romances

Well-Loved Romances

Widow's Island

Hestor's Way

Book 9: *Cottage at Barnum's Ledge*

Young Adult Historical Romance

Song of the Spirit

www.ingramcontent.com/pod-product-compliance
Lightning Source LLC
Chambersburg PA
CBHW061027120726
47910CB00006B/2128